MAN FEAST

KRISTA SANDOR

CANDY CASTLE BOOKS

For David, the love of my life.

CHAPTER 1

ELLE

"Eleanor Jayne Reynolds. That's you, right?"

"Yes."

"You're twenty-nine years old."

"That's right."

"That's weird."

"What's weird about being twenty-nine?"

"No, not your age. Your name. Jayne is spelled with a *Y. J, A, Y, N, E.*"

Eleanor, Elle Reynolds—nobody called her Eleanor aside from her parents—cradled her head in her hands. "I don't want to seem rude, but I think the spelling of my middle name is the least of my problems."

"It's kind of strange, though, don't you think?"

Sweet. Baby. Jesus.

For eight hundred dollars an hour, Allen Parker, the man dubbed as Denver's top civil litigation attorney, specializing in financial fraud, was not inspiring much confidence. He did look the part. Salt-and-pepper colored hair. Check. Tortoiseshell glasses. Check. A seasoned, questioning crinkle to his brow. Check.

Elle lifted her head and attempted to smile. After what had

happened, however, she really wasn't in a position to judge anyone's credibility.

She straightened in her chair. "Would you mind if we skipped over the oddities of my middle name and dove into my case?"

Allen glanced down at the stack of papers on his desk. "That's easy. You're pretty much broke."

Elle's jaw dropped. "That can't be right!"

The man folded his hands on the desk, the crease in his brow deepening. "Did the FBI investigators explain the pump and dump scheme to you?"

"The what?"

"Pump and dump. It's a common type of fraud perpetrated on wealthy individuals like yourself. Well, like you used to be."

This couldn't be happening. She was a successful writer. She'd penned over a dozen travel guides, three novels, and several hundred articles, and Oprah had recommended her book. A studio had purchased the rights to her last book and made it into a movie.

Last she checked, her bank statement was seven figures.

Last she checked.

She should have close to eight million dollars in the bank, but now she was broke thanks to her former money manager, Monty-freaking-Morris. She should have known, any guy with a lounge lizard name like Monty Morris would be up to no good.

But she barely had time to breathe these days, let alone keep up the daily grind of bills and bookkeeping.

Her travel and work schedule over the past five years had been insane. Monty Morris seemed like a godsend when he'd come along and offered to manage her finances. An accountant and money manager for several prominent authors and celebrities, she'd figured, if he was trusted by half of the New York Times Bestseller's List, he should be a good fit for her.

Boy, was she an idiot! A Monty-fucking-Morris level idiot!

FBI agents had knocked on her door a little over a week ago to break the news. Monty had stolen millions, urging his clients—

including her—to invest in a hot stock which turned out to be a shell company secretly controlled by the fraudster himself.

Pump and dump made sense. Pump your investors for all you can get then dump them and run off with the goods.

And all the money he'd stolen? It was currently rusting away at the bottom of the Baltic Sea.

Monty had used the ill-gotten funds to buy a super-yacht under the table from a Russian oligarch in need of some fast cash. The FBI explained that Monty planned to live out his life in international waters in the lap of luxury, until members of a Latvian organized crime family, who had a beef with the former owner, sank the boat, not knowing it had been sold to an asshole American accountant.

Karma is a bitch.

Unfortunately, karma wasn't at all good at procuring millions of dollars from shady oligarchs and Eastern European mafias.

And that's why she was sitting across from Allen Parker. After the FBI left, she'd called her agent in a panic. He'd worked his magic, found Allen Parker, and made her an appointment.

The Monty Morris scandal had hit a few of his clients. But only she had gone all in and allowed Monty to invest the majority of her holdings.

So damn stupid!

She'd sent all her paperwork to Allen's office, hoping that his legal team could help her reclaim some of her earnings.

Elle stared at the deepening crease in the attorney's forehead. That crease pretty much said it all. She wasn't going to get squat.

She lifted her chin. "What can I do? Can I sue Monty?"

The man leaned back in his chair. "Mr. Morris declared bankruptcy. He owes a lot of people a lot of money. Federal prosecutors have already charged him on several counts. We can proceed with legal action, but—"

"But you can't get blood from a stone," Elle finished on a defeated sigh.

"It certainly would be difficult, and the legal fees you'd incur would most likely exceed anything you'd get out of Mr. Morris," Allen added.

She shook her head. A tight, frustrated movement. She'd barely listened when Monty called her with the investment proposal. She'd taken the damn call just as she'd boarded a ship headed for Antarctica—her mind focused on observing Emperor penguins not the bank account she thought was in safe hands.

Elle cringed. She hadn't even batted an eyelash when Monty had suggested she invest ninety percent of her assets.

Allen's brow crease softened. "How about we discuss what you still have."

Elle gasped. "My Denver apartment and the house I just bought in Vermont, are they…"

The man pulled a sheet of paper from the stack. "Those assets are all still safely yours. You paid in full for each up front."

Elle released a tight breath and swallowed back tears of relief.

She was not going to cry.

She was Elle Reynolds. Tough as nails, Elle Reynolds.

While most women would shy away from a month at sea, sailing the dangerous waters off the coast of Africa with a crew of sun-battered, crusty sailors, she'd drank them under the table and kicked their asses in poker every night.

It was going to take a hell of a lot more than this to knock her down.

But had she lost that house in Vermont, that would have come close to wrecking her because that house belonged to—

"Your mother," Allen said, holding up another document.

Elle blinked. "Excuse me?"

"The house in Vermont is in your name and your mother's name."

"Yes, I purchased the home for my mom."

"I see she recently filed for divorce from your father."

Elle sucked her teeth and nodded. She wasn't about to get started on Gavin Reynolds. "Yes, my mom filed for divorce a couple of months ago."

The attorney nodded and didn't press.

Maybe he was worth the money—and he seemed to know her finances inside and out.

Elle swallowed hard. "There should also be a trust for my mother. Did Monty dip into that, too?"

She tensed and waited for Allen to answer. She hadn't mentioned this financial fiasco to anyone. Not to her mother. Not even to her cousin, Abby, who had recently moved to Denver. Elle loved Abby fiercely, but she was the older of the two, and Abby was like a little sister to her. It just didn't feel right to dump all this on her.

And her mother?

Lila Reynolds had been through enough, and Elle was hellbent on making sure her mom didn't learn of this financial disaster. She'd sell a kidney on the black market to help her mother, if that's what it took.

Allen slid a piece of paper across the desk. "No, he didn't touch the trust. I suspect that's because it would have raised too many red flags. He would have needed your and your mother's direct permission."

Elle stared at the numbers. There was nearly two hundred thousand dollars in the account. Plenty for her mother to live on—for now. The house in Vermont was paid for, and the woman lived simply. Her mom would be all right—for the time being—and it could give her some time to save up some cash. Her mom would never have to know her daughter was broke. She could spare her that heartache.

"What do I do now?" she asked. A childish question, but she couldn't hold it back.

Allen shuffled the papers and pulled out a few sheets. "You keep doing what you do, Miss Reynolds. I see you've signed a contract to work on a project with Bergen Enterprises."

Bergen Enterprises.

Her gut twisted.

Allen's eyebrows nearly met his hairline as he paged through the document. "Quite a lucrative contract. This could significantly rebuild your finances."

She nodded begrudgingly. The man wasn't wrong. At first, the Bergen offer seemed like the opportunity of a lifetime. Who wouldn't want to spend five weeks traveling around the world, visiting five-star resorts? They wanted her to immerse herself into the brand and share her experiences, making sure to highlight the fresher, edgier aspects of the company to help captivate the modern traveler.

She'd met with the company's founders, Harriet and Raymond Bergen. They were lovely people. Happily married for over fifty years, they'd left New York City as newlyweds back in the sixties and headed west for the Mile-High City. With hard work, grit, and determination, they'd turned one small mountain sports shop into a billion-dollar mountain sports empire with properties all over the globe and retail stores across the country.

But what sold Elle on the deal wasn't just the money. Sure, it was flattering to be offered such a generous sum, but it didn't come down to that. It was her rarely seen sentimental side that tipped the scales in saying yes. When she saw the way Ray and Harriet gazed at each other, she couldn't help but smile. Ray looked ready to give Harriet the moon, and Harriet blushed every time her husband paid her a compliment.

Elle didn't believe in Prince Charming. Not anymore. But the Bergens' admiration for each other was all-encompassing. It sparked something small and forgotten deep inside her. It made her hopeful. For what, she didn't know, but it compelled her to grab the pen and sign on the contract's dotted line on the spot.

Unfortunately, the love bubble she'd created around Harriet and Ray popped when she found out she wouldn't be working directly with the inspiring couple on the project.

Nope! Instead, she'd be working hand in hand with Ray and Harriet's oldest grandson, Bergen Enterprises CEO and all-around master curmudgeon, Jasper Bergen.

She didn't use the term *curmudgeon* lightly. She saved that word for the crabbiest, crankiest of killjoys. In all her travels, to every continent and remote corner of the world, she'd never encountered anyone more inflexible or more infuriating. She'd known brick walls with better personalities.

She'd only met with him once, but that was enough to know what she was up against. With his starched collars, dour expression, and that minute twist of a smirk, just the thought of the man made her want to smash something. She glanced around Allen's office looking for something to chuck against the wall when the attorney broke into her thoughts and halted her near-homicidal urge.

"Pardon me for asking, Miss Reynolds, but isn't your cousin engaged to one of the Bergen grandsons?"

Christ on a cracker! Allen Parker, Esquire, did his homework.

Elle nodded. "Yes, my cousin, Abby Quinn, and Brennen Bergen are engaged."

She held herself back from groaning out loud.

The fucking Bergen brothers!

Now there was no escaping them!

There were three brothers in all, and not only did she have to work with the oldest brother, just a few days ago, her cousin had agreed to marry the middle brother. The youngest Bergen brother was overseas living the life of a hermit in Europe—thank God—because she wasn't sure she could handle another.

Granted, Abby's fiancé, formerly one of Denver's biggest playboys, had fallen ass over elbow in love with her cousin and seemed to have changed his womanizing ways. She had to give him that. And his laid-back persona, oozing with Colorado mountain charm was almost—*almost*—starting to grow on her. Still, her skeptical heart wasn't ready to let its guard down yet.

The attorney's features softened as he relaxed into his high-back chair. "That's wonderful news! I'll have to congratulate Ray and Harriet the next time I see them. You're quite lucky to be connected with the Bergens, Miss Reynolds. They're good people, and it looks like they're your best hope in getting back on your feet."

She forced a smile. "That certainly seems to be the case."

Allen narrowed his gaze. "Do you like honey?"

She cocked her head to the side. "Excuse me?"

The man chuckled. "My wife and I do a little amateur beekeeping on our ranch outside the city."

Elle bit back a grin. That was one thing she loved about Denver. Between the surgeons who moonlighted as bathtub craft beer brewers and the tech entrepreneurs by weekday and urban farmers cleaning out backyard chicken coops on the weekends, there was nothing odd about her high-powered Colorado attorney dabbling in beekeeping.

She released a resigned breath. What the hell else was there to do? "I love honey. When I was a girl, we used to get some from a little stand near where I grew up in Maine."

The man's face lit up. "You'll have to let me know what you think of our Colorado honey."

"Honey's sort of my thing. I like to try to find it when I travel."

She'd sampled honey from India, Turkey, Ukraine, New Zealand, and Mexico. Food was an integral part of her work. She might not always speak the language of the places she visited, but the language of taste was universal and partaking in a country's sweet treats was one of the best parts of her job.

"What's your favorite?" Allen asked.

"Still the honey from that little booth in Maine."

The attorney watched her closely. "Good memories?"

She thought of her parents, before she learned the truth. "A few."

The man went over to a cabinet near the door and removed a glass jar filled with the dark amber-colored nectar.

Elle came to her feet. "You keep the honey in your office?"

"I only give them to my favorite clients," he said with a fatherly nod.

She took the jar, remembering simpler days when there were no money managers and no signed contracts.

Allen patted her shoulder. "I wish I could have done more to help you, Miss Reynolds. I'll have my people take another look at all your financial statements, but my advice to you is to move forward. You're young. You're talented. Don't let the past hold you back."

She froze.

Don't let the past hold you back.

That was a hell of a lot easier said than done.

She regained her bearings and slipped the honey into her travel-worn leather backpack—a purse didn't fit into life on the go.

"Thank you for the honey and for your time," she said as it hit her.

Time!

Shit! She was due up at Bergen Mountain today. Harriet and Ray were throwing Abby and Brennen a little engagement party at their sprawling mountain mansion.

She left the lawyer's downtown office and headed back to her apartment on foot. Early spring in Colorado could mean a lot of things. It wasn't at all uncommon for a blizzard to blanket the budding flowers starting to poke up through the dormant soil.

But today wasn't one of those days.

Elle stepped onto the sidewalk and turned her face toward the sun, allowing the warmth to seep into her bones. With the blue sky and the buzz of the city around her, she steadied herself. She may be broke, but she still had a home and didn't have to worry about this setback affecting her mother.

She pulled out her phone and checked the time.

Damn! It was nearly ten.

She'd walked to Allen Parker's office. She should have driven. She'd be cutting it close.

The plan was to arrive at Bergen Mountain today and spend the next few days at the ski resort property with Abby and Brennen, Ray and Harriet Bergen, and Abby's new friend and teaching colleague, Cadence Lowry and her young son, Bodhi.

Oh, and the king curmudgeon himself, Jasper Bergen, was supposed to be there, too.

Whoopty-doo!

She went to pocket her phone when the screen lit up.

Jovy Jones. Her agent extraordinaire.

She accepted the call, but before she could get a word in edgewise, her longtime friend was already going a mile a minute.

"Are you broke, lovely? Do you need me to overnight you some Dom or Godiva? Wait, no! You function better on carbs. I'll have my assistant find the best cupcake place in Denver and have two dozen sent to your apartment. You still have your apartment, right? Oh, that awful little Monty Morris!"

The breath caught in her throat. For her mother's sake, she didn't want anyone to know about the state of her finances. "I'm going to be all right, but don't breathe a word of this to anyone. Most of the money is gone, but I still have my apartment, and everything I've put in place to help my mom is safe."

"Thank the stars! And I'd never breathe a word to anyone about your plundered bank account. We need everyone thinking Elle Reynolds is still the rich, fabulous adventurer we both know you are. Now, you need a night out in New York City! Jump on the next flight—you'll be flying coach, but you'll survive—and I'll take you to all the best gay bars Manhattan can offer."

It was tempting. Clubbing with her agent meant all the dancing and all the champagne without the bother of straight men.

She kicked a pebble across the sidewalk, and it plopped into a puddle. "I can't, Jov. I'm expected up at Bergen Mountain."

"Right, right! Your cousin and that handsome manwhore just got engaged. I saw it on social media. It's everywhere!"

Her agent was right. Social media was blowing up. Brennen had proposed to Abby during a televised charity event a few days ago, and the internet was still buzzing with the sweet story of the former bad boy billionaire falling under the spell of the pretty first-grade teacher with a heart of gold.

Good girl tames bad boy.

Elle weaved her way through downtown Denver, dodging the pools of water left from the melting snow from last week's storm and headed toward her apartment. "I hate to break it to you, but he's not a manwhore anymore."

"And you sure he's straight?"

She barked out a laugh. "As straight as they come."

Her agent sighed. "Too bad. I guess, good for her. Blah, blah, blah. Tell them they have my blessing."

"Yes, I'm sure they've been dying to receive the go-ahead from you, Jov." Elle smirked.

"You are one sassy, broke bitch," he shot back, but she heard the smile in his voice.

"You know you love me."

Jovy grew quiet.

She frowned. "What is it?"

"Are you emotionally stable enough to talk a little business?" he asked, his playful tone gone.

"I've lost most everything, and I'm still standing. Think of me as the twenty-nine-year-old version of Pat Benatar and hit me with your best shot."

Papers rustled in the background.

"So, that issue you wanted me to look into with the Bergen Enterprises contract."

She knew where this was going. "I'll stop you right there, Jov. I need the money. I have no choice but to comply with the contract."

"Good! Because I had a quick convo with their legal team and that contract is ironclad."

Elle blew out a tight breath. She wouldn't expect anything less from a company with Jasper Bergen at the helm.

"The Bergen gig is my best shot to get back on my feet and build up my savings again."

Jovy snapped his fingers, and the sharp click popped through the line. "Working for the man. But that Jasper Bergen is quite yummy. All cheekbones and dead eyes. I'm staring at his bio on the Bergen Enterprises website right now."

"Gag!" Elle said, switching from a stroll to a brisk walk as she passed a group of tourists. "Have you ever actually spoken with him?"

"No, just their legal team."

Elle glanced into a candy shop and grinned. "You know those chocolate bunnies that look delicious, but then you bite into it and it's brittle and hollow, and the chocolate crumbles all over the damn place?"

"Yes, total fucking gyp!"

"That's Jasper Bergen. All yummy looking on the outside. Hollow and empty on the inside."

Jovy lowered his voice. "Maybe you should take a bite out of that man candy and test your theory."

Elle sidestepped another puddle. "Not if he was the last hollow chocolate bunny on the planet."

"I'm just saying you don't know what's under the hood until you take a look," Jovy shot back.

"I won't be taking any looks. Zero looks."

Jasper's face flashed before her eyes. Strong jaw. Piercing eyes. And that body. The man clearly took care of himself. She'd never seen him in anything other than a suit. But holy hell, he could stop traffic.

She shook off that thought. What the hell was wrong with her? That man was the devil.

A couple holding hands passed her going the opposite direction. "Jovy, how long has it been since I've dated?"

A pause.

"That guy in Iceland?" he offered

Her jaw dropped. "That was three years ago! And I didn't even date him. We had dinner."

"You didn't sleep with him?"

"No! We shared a triple chocolate torte. But no sex."

"My lovely girl, it's been a minute. That's for damn sure."

He was right! She hadn't had anything serious since Tate.

Fucking Tate.

"You'll need to start dusting off your lady parts pretty soon," Jovy added.

She was ready to tell him what he could do with his man parts when her phone beeped. "Hold on. I've got another call."

She glanced at the screen.

The Dalton.

Why would her apartment building be calling her?

Unless…

"I'm going to need to call you back, Jovy. I think my doorman is on the other line."

"Is he hot?"

"If you think hot is a jowly man in his seventies who hasn't smiled since 1962, then sure, he's a dreamboat." The phone beeped again. "Sorry, Jov. I need to take this."

"No worries! Do consider jumping the hollow bunny. You need to get laid, my dear."

Elle sighed, shook her head, and tapped the screen to switch to the incoming call. Before she had the phone to her ear, Harvey barked her name.

"Eleanor Reynolds!"

She groaned. Besides her parents, only Harvey the doorman called her Eleanor.

"Hello, Harvey! Did I forget to close the recycling bin again?"

The line went quiet.

"Harvey, are you there?"

The man cleared his throat. "You know your car?"

She smiled. She loved her candy apple red Porsche Cayenne SUV.

"Yep."

"Did you forget to pay a bill or something?"

Her stomach dropped.

"Why?"

The man huffed, and she could almost see the disapproving set of his jaw. "It's getting repossessed. Two men with a tow truck are here."

She blinked once then twice as the city went blurry. "Harvey, tell them to stop! Please, tell them it's a misunderstanding! I can explain everything. I'm five minutes away."

He said something, but she wasn't listening and ended the call.

"You're tough as nails. You can get through anything," she whispered.

She stepped off the curb then reared back as a bus thundered by, striking a giant puddle and spraying her with an icy cold, gray, watery slush.

A woman walking by stopped and gave her a sympathetic smile. "Looks like it's not your day."

Elle wiped a piece of wet sludge from her cheek. "You have no idea."

CHAPTER 2

JASPER

"Collin, I don't see the earnings forecasts on this spreadsheet, and the retail numbers are coded in yellow. I specifically asked for them to be marigold."

Jasper Bergen stood, pressed his palms to his massive desk inside the corner office of the Bergen Enterprises building and surveyed the chaos. Somebody put a goddamn book on his desk.

Her book.

Nobody touched his desk. Nobody rearranged his desk. Nobody was to add to or take away from his desk. The cleaning crew were under strict orders not to lay a finger on any part of it.

His assistant Collin Chavez knew this. After running through a slew of incompetent idiots, Collin finally made the cut and had been with him for three years now. Collin knew better than anyone, he didn't need this hassle.

Not today.

"Sorry, sir," Collin said, entering the office.

Jasper's jaw tightened. This book was messing with his mojo. He thrived on order, structure, and routine. This business trifecta ensured that the billion-dollar Bergen Enterprises remained profitable.

And the thought of straying from his prescribed course set him on edge.

That damn book set him on edge.

It was an anomaly. A fly in the ointment. A kink in the line.

Collin set a coffee—black, the way any respectable adult should drink their coffee—on the sideboard.

"Rough night?" the man asked.

"Rough night. Rough morning. And now I'm looking at yellow when I asked for—"

"Marigold," Collin offered with a grin.

How the hell was this guy always so happy?

Oh yeah. He wasn't responsible for the welfare of a Fortune 500 company, and that took complete focus and dedication.

When the hell did Jasper Bergen have time to smile?

Never.

His every minute of every hour of every day was precisely scheduled. He woke at four thirty in the morning for an intense ninety-minute cardio and weights session. After a quick shower and his sixteen-minute hygiene regimen, he dressed. Pressed and starched, all his suits were precisely cut and tailored to his body. Then he'd have a slice of toast spread with peanut butter and a cup of unsweetened vanilla yogurt. The same breakfast he'd eaten every morning for the last…since the day after…

He cleared his throat. "My brother didn't have the right bread," he huffed, scanning the spreadsheet.

Collin frowned. "I thought you were going to stay at the Ritz while your place was being renovated. I made all the arrangements."

Jasper's jaw clenched a fraction tighter. "It's no longer a simple renovation."

What was supposed to have been a week-long construction project putting in new hardwood floors had exploded into a full-blown asbestos abatement situation. His swank home in Denver's high-end Cherry Creek neighborhood sat tented while men dressed head to toe in white coveralls and blue gloves duct-taped to their wrists wore protective headgear and respirators to remove the toxic substance.

"I'm sorry to hear that, sir. I must say I'm a little surprised that you're staying in The Dalton's penthouse. Doesn't your brother still live there?"

"My brother's not in town at the moment, and he's indicated that he and his fiancée will be living in her bungalow. It doesn't make sense for me to stay in a hotel while the Bergen penthouse sits empty. It would be a waste of money."

Collin took out his phone and started typing. "I'll message the market and have everything you need delivered."

"Don't bother. I won't be there tonight."

"That's right," Collin said, gaze glued to the phone's screen. "You're scheduled to be up at Bergen Mountain for the next three nights for your brother and Miss Quinn's engagement celebration." Collin looked up, eyes brimming with wonder. "Will *Elle Reynolds* be there, too?"

Elle fucking Reynolds.

Jasper glanced down at the book on his desk and scowled. "Why do you say her name like that?"

The entire building seemed to be losing its mind over her. And who was she? Just some writer.

Collin's brow knit together. "How do I say her name?"

"All dreamy."

He nearly gagged. Did he just say dreamy?

A wide grin stretched across his assistant's face. "Well, because she's Elle Reynolds. She's been around the world. Her travel guides make you feel like she's right there with you, introducing you to the local culture and leading you away from the tourist traps so you can experience the true essence of a place. And then there are her novels."

"What about her novels?" Jasper grumbled.

He hadn't read anything she'd written. He knew one of her books had been made into a movie, and that was as much effort as he'd put into researching the woman.

Serious decisions had to be made regarding Bergen Mountain Sports rebranding and retooling of their image. Decisions that needed to be based on numbers and facts and concrete data. Not travel tips on how to avoid diarrhea abroad.

But the writing was on the wall, and while Bergen Enterprises continued to be profitable, their overall revenue had flattened out. Whichever way he ran the numbers—and he ran them every day —he had to admit that the company needed a course correction.

But the one thing he knew for damn sure was that it wasn't Elle Reynolds.

They'd met only a few days ago. His grandmother had set up the meeting for just the two of them. A get to know you say hello thing. The kind of easy breezy, waste of time, forced encounter he loathed.

And she was four minutes late.

Four fucking minutes late.

He could complete thirty-seven tasks in four minutes. He could check in with his VPs in Europe, Asia, and Australia in four minutes. He could review the safety protocols at all the Bergen ski resorts in four minutes.

What did he do instead?

He waited. He stood there like the last kid to get picked for dodgeball and fucking waited.

Then, once she sauntered in and graced him with her presence, she had the audacity to tell him the schedule he'd mapped out for her contribution to the rebranding project was too rigid and lacked imagination.

He pressed his lips into a hard line as his blood boiled. The nerve of that woman!

He never lost his cool.

Never.

But by the end of their brief tête-à-tête, they were nose to nose and red-cheeked from yelling at each other. Soft, chestnut tendrils framed her stubborn face as she jabbed her phone into his chest and told him off. Had his brother, Brennen, not walked in on them at that moment, he wasn't sure what would have happened. She'd looked ready to claw his eyes out, and all he wanted to do was…

Fuck!

He'd never been so riled up. Her damn lapis blue eyes blazing. That petite, toned body mere inches from his. The air between them charged and crackling. He'd left the office and laced up his Nikes the minute he got home. It took him eleven miles of hard trail running before he was able to work Elle Reynolds out of his system.

But had he actually purged her from his thoughts?

Had he forgotten those flashing blue eyes?

Double fuck!

He'd be a liar if he said yes. She was everywhere. The sky at dusk. The awning of his favorite restaurant. Even on this morning's trail run, the crocuses emerging from the hard ground burst with the deep blue hue.

Jasper glanced around his office. Jesus, it was warm in here! He had the urge to unbutton the top button on his dress shirt and loosen his collar. An urge he fought. He needed a plan. Even if his grandparents thought Elle Reynolds was the best thing since sliced bread, he was not about to put the reputation of his family's company in an outsider's hands.

"Have you read it?" Collin asked, gesturing toward the book.

Jasper shook his head then glanced at it. Face down on his desk, the back cover greeted him with a profile shot of a pensive Elle Reynolds standing on a beach, chestnut hair blowing in the wind. His fingers twitched, wanting to tangle themselves in the flowing locks.

Triple fuck.

He did not need this kind of distraction. Not when the company required his full attention now more than ever. The sweeping rebranding effort focused on highlighting Bergen Enterprises' philanthropic and environmental work as well as targeting segments of the population they'd lost traction with. Not a small task.

Collin shifted his stance. "She's a good writer. I've read all her stuff. It's no wonder she's a bestseller. This is the book that was made into the movie. I listened to her interview about it on NPR. She says it's a work of fiction. But when you read it, it's so compelling and so visceral. There's got to be a connection to her real life."

"What's it about?" Jasper asked, reaching for the book but stopping short of touching it.

"A woman who takes a solo trip around the world after learning the man she thought she was in a relationship with had a wife he'd never told her about. It has an *Eat, Pray, Love* and *The Pilot's Wife* vibe to it."

Jasper stared at Elle's image. "I don't know what that means, Collin."

Jesus! What did the man think? He sat around reading chick lit in his free time?

Collin chuckled. "It's an empowering, *find your own path and make your own destiny,* kind of story."

Jasper inwardly cringed. Fucking perfect! They had an angsty, *follow the rainbow to your pot of gold* type guiding the rebranding charge.

Collin tapped the book with his fingertips reverently. "There's a quality to her and her writing that feels accessible. Like she could be your best friend. Like each day is a new opportunity for adventure. Like she's always on the cusp of surprising you. It's magical."

Who had time for magical?

Jasper pulled his gaze from her picture. He didn't like surprises. He liked predictability.

Collin went over to the large worktable on the other side of the room—the table Jasper allowed others to touch—and arranged a series of folders. "She's only recently made Denver her home, and I was surprised to hear she's single."

Had Jasper been a retriever, his ears would have perked up. He mentally chastised himself. It didn't matter if Elle Reynolds was single, married, or screwing the whole of Denver. She wasn't the right fit for the company.

"There was a bit of controversy about her back when the movie came out, but nothing really came of it."

He frowned. The last thing Bergen Enterprises needed was negative press.

"What was the controversy?"

"Just tabloid fodder. You know, what happens to a lot of successful women. People like to throw around that she might have slept her way to getting a book deal or the movie deal. But nothing came out of it, and now she's more popular than ever in the travel and literary communities."

"What's this about the travel community?"

Jasper glanced up to see his grandmother and grandfather enter his office.

"Hello, Mr. and Mrs. Bergen. We were just discussing Elle Reynolds," Collin replied.

"Isn't she something!" his grandmother gushed, settling herself into one of the chairs at the table.

His grandfather took the seat next to her and crossed his legs, getting comfortable, and Jasper wasn't sure what level of fucks he'd reached now—quadruple, quintuple? Was that even a word?

He huffed out a breath. Having Gram and Grandad park themselves in his office usually meant *a chat*. He nodded to them and opened his laptop, waiting for one of them to start in on him.

Grandad turned to Collin. "We are so impressed with Elle. She's quite a remarkable young woman."

Jasper stared at his laptop screen, unable to focus on the string of emails. "I wished you would have discussed it with me before hiring her."

Gram leaned back in her chair. "Darling, my book club had just read her novel, and your grandfather has read all her travel books. She exemplifies the exact energy our company needs. We had to strike while the iron was hot. When our people reached out to her agent and learned she was between projects, I knew it was meant to be. Elle Reynolds appeals to women and the younger generation's sense of adventure, and that's the demographic we need to target with our rebranding."

Jasper went to the window and stared at the Rocky Mountains to the west, still covered in spring snow. He hated to admit it, but she was right. He'd gone over all the survey results. He'd watched the focus groups meet with the marketing team. He'd seen the sales reports.

Bergen Mountain Sports was a trusted brand. They had loyal customers, but in the age of social media and the twenty-four-hour news cycle, companies had to entice and engage customers at all times and from different angles. According to the information gathered in-house, they'd lost their edge with the eighteen to twenty-four age group, and there was a trending decline in twenty-four to thirty-two-year-olds—especially with women.

Yes, they needed to respond.

Absolutely, rebranding was a powerful tool to address their issues.

But Elle Reynolds wasn't the answer.

Gram gave an excited clap. "And the best part is that she's going to be part of the family soon."

A muscle ticked in Jasper's jaw. He took a breath and checked his reflection in the window. He didn't need his grandparents thinking Elle Reynolds could get a rise out of him.

He joined them at the table but didn't sit. "Abby is going to be family. Sweet, kind, dragged Brennen's ass into line, Abby, is going to be a part of our family. Elle Reynolds will not be a part of the Bergens."

"She is Abby's cousin, Jas," his grandfather said, sharing a look with his gram.

Jasper stiffened. "I could marry Elle Reynolds if I wanted to. That definitely makes her *not family*."

Collin, his grandmother, and his granddad stared at him.

Gram narrowed her gaze. "Now that's an odd thing to say, darling."

Jasper shifted his stance. "You know what I mean. She's not…
It's not like…"

Sweet Christ! He was stammering, and he didn't stammer.
Jasper Ryan Bergen was cool under pressure. He thrived on
competition. He loved complex negotiations.

He didn't get tongue-tied over a woman.

He changed tack. He needed to steer the conversation away
from his ludicrous comment.

Marry Elle Reynolds? He couldn't even stand being in a room
with her.

He kept his expression muted. "Did you need something? I
have quite a bit to do before I head up to the cottage for Bren and
Abby's engagement thing."

Even after all these years, he still thought it was comical that
they referred to the mountain mansion as a cottage. The cottage
was about the furthest thing from a cottage you could get. With
eleven bedrooms, a movie room, a sauna, and an outdoor pool
heated year round, Bergen Cottage was the family's palatial
retreat and residence when they were up at Bergen Mountain.

But it was more than that.

It was the setting of many of his happiest childhood memories.
Playing Battleship with his father late into the night as winter
storms rolled in. Listening to their mother sing them to sleep after
a day tearing down the slopes, chasing his brothers as they
weaved in and out of the trees.

Tree bashing, that's what they'd called it. Brennen, the middle
Bergen brother and younger than him by two years, led the pack
as Camden, the youngest, tried to keep up. But Jasper always
stayed back. Sure, he could have caught up to Bren. Hell, he could
have pulled ahead. But he never did. He was the oldest Bergen
brother, and although nobody had charged him with this, he
knew it was his duty to make sure his siblings made it down the
mountain in one piece—more or less.

There was that one time when Cam caught a rough edge and
wiped out, skis flying and poles sailing through the air. By the

time he'd gotten to his little brother, the snow was dotted crimson red. He'd imagined the worst until he realized that the five-year-old had only lost a loose baby tooth.

Jasper was only nine at the time. But during the whole ordeal, he'd remained calm and measured. He'd pulled off his glove, fished out the liner, and pressed it into the vacant space in his little brother's mouth. They never found the tooth, but Jasper had found his calling.

At least, he'd thought he did.

From that day forward, he focused on becoming a strong enough skier to make the ski patrol. By sixteen he'd earned a coveted spot. By nineteen, he'd completed EMT training. Everything was falling into place. He wanted to study medicine. He'd splinted and boarded patients on the mountain, but his dream was to become a surgeon and help those people he'd loaded into ambulances or—if it was a life-threatening injury—onto medivac helicopters. He'd started down that track, earned his bachelor's in biology, and had been accepted into medical school.

Then everything changed.

His parents died.

And even with all his training, he couldn't save them.

All he could do was ensure the family legacy, and that didn't include a doctorate in medicine. It required an MBA—Master of Business Administration.

His grandmother rose to her feet and walked the length of the room, stopping at his desk. She glanced at the book. "I'm glad Nina got this to you."

He nodded. Nina. The receptionist. She must have breezed in when his assistant was away from his desk. He made a mental note to have Collin refresh the woman's memory regarding his no touching the desk policy.

His grandad leaned forward. "Your grandmother and I wanted to have a little chat before we left the city."

There it was—the little chat.

As if on cue, Collin picked up a file and headed for the door. "I'll leave you to it."

His grandmother turned to the man. "Oh, Collin, before you go, could you call and make sure Klaus has everything ready for our family gathering up at the cottage? I told him to plan a feast to celebrate my first grandson's engagement."

"Confirm with Bergen Mountain's executive chef. Got it," Collin said aloud as he typed the note on his phone then closed the door behind him.

His gram joined his grandad back at the table and gestured to the chair across from them. "Sit with us, darling."

Jasper glanced at his watch.

"This won't take long, Jas," his grandfather added.

He sat down as his grandparents leaned forward and clasped their hands.

Shit! They were going into Brooklyn mode.

Harriet and Raymond Bergen weren't native Coloradans. Born and bred in Brooklyn, New York, they left the subways and cement the day after they married and headed toward the Rocky Mountains to open a small mountain sports shop in Denver. A shop that had grown into a billion-dollar mountain sports empire.

But they never lost that city edge ingrained in every New Yorker. They could drop the relaxed Rocky Mountain high attitude in a heartbeat and pin you with a gaze that said *do not bullshit a bullshitter* at the drop of a hat.

His grandfather cleared his throat. "We know how your meeting with Elle Reynolds went the other day. Her agent called legal and asked about terminating the contract."

Excellent!

Jasper bit back a grin. "If she wants out, let her out."

Gram and Grandad shared a look, and he knew he was screwed.

Gram gave him her best *get with the program* grin. "We're not releasing her from the contract, darling. Luckily, we just received word from her agent that she had a change of heart and wants to remain part of the rebranding effort."

Dammit! That figures! Even when the woman wasn't here, she made him crazy.

"We want Elle because she's the push this company needs. She's the fresh perspective we're looking for," his grandad added.

Jasper stiffened and crossed his arms. "We don't need her. This is your company. Our company. I've dedicated my life to ensuring its legacy. Mom and Dad deserve that."

His grandad's gaze softened. "Do you know what your father would say?"

Jasper remained silent, hating himself for bringing up his parents.

"Great things can only happen when you push past your comfort zone," his grandad answered.

Jasper didn't respond. He could almost hear his dad, nudging him to press harder. It was his father who'd helped him prepare for the ski patrol tryouts. His father, who made sure he could navigate the steep terrain and treacherous backcountry of Bergen Mountain like a pro. His father, who, when he wasn't sure he was good enough, told him he could be if he trusted in himself and didn't let that nagging voice inside his head hold him back.

Gram smiled, her eyes growing glassy. "Darling, Elle Reynolds is the PR boost we need. I believe your father and your mother would agree with this decision."

Grandad nodded. "And you know that we've already made the bulk of the rebranding decisions. That's been in the works for several months. Think of Elle Reynolds as the bow on top, tying it all together."

Jasper released a tight breath. "I want to be involved with every aspect of Elle Reynolds's contribution to the rebranding. I don't want any surprises."

And he wanted to make damned sure she didn't write or say anything that could negatively affect the company.

"Darling, she believes in this company. Your grandfather and I met with her for several hours. She grew up skiing in Bergen gear. Her first mountain bike came from a Bergen Sporting Goods Store. She's visited our resorts in the US and Europe. She's a good fit. She's the right age. She's got the right experience, and she can use her celebrity status with women and the travel world to highlight all the key points of our rebranding plan."

He crossed his arms, ready to list all the ways they could accomplish that aspect of the rebranding without Eleanor Reynolds, when the door opened and Nina, the executive floor receptionist, poked her head into the room.

"I'm sorry to intrude. Mr. and Mrs. Bergen, your car is here to take you to the reception."

"Reception?" Jas asked.

"A reception for the Down Syndrome Association. We'll head up to the cottage after it finishes," his grandfather said, helping his gram out of her chair.

"Um, Mr. Bergen, did you see the book I put on your desk?" Nina asked meekly.

Jas glanced at the receptionist, said nothing, and held the woman's gaze.

The receptionist's bottom lip quivered. He seemed to do that to people around here.

His gram glanced over at his desk. "Yes, he certainly did see it, my dear."

The fear he'd sparked in the woman diminished, and she pressed her hand to her heart. "Do you think you could ask her to sign it for me?"

"You think Bergen Enterprise's CEO has time to get a book signed for you?" he shot back.

This Elle Reynolds fanfare was too damned much.

She stared at the floor. "Well, I was just hoping…"

Gram went to his desk and picked up the book. "Nina, do you mind if I ask how old you are?"

"Of course not. I'm twenty-five."

"Have you been to Bergen Mountain recently?" she pressed.

The receptionist blushed. "No, ma'am. My girlfriends and I like to do spa days and brunch. Isn't Bergen Mountain just geared for families and skiing?"

Gram eyed him then smiled at Nina. "Did you know we have an award-winning spa and three five-star restaurants at Bergen Mountain?"

The woman's eyes went wide. "We do?"

"We do."

She cocked her head to the side. "Huh."

Gram took Elle's book and pressed it into his chest. "I'm sure Jasper would be happy to ask Miss Reynolds to sign your book. We'll be seeing her today."

"Wow! Thank you!" Nina said, edging out of the room with a smile plastered across her face.

"We'll see you at the cottage, darling," Gram said, a slight lift to the corner of her mouth. A clear indication she knew she'd made her point.

Grandad put a hand on his shoulder. "Nina works for us, and she doesn't know all the things our resorts have to offer women in her age bracket. Imagine what one article or thirty-second spot by Elle could do. Your gram and I know asking you to work with her is out of your comfort zone, Jas. But we need you onboard. We need your expertise, too. Nobody knows the financial ins and outs of this company like you do."

Jasper knew what he had to do. He'd be on Eleanor Reynolds twenty-four seven to ensure she didn't damage the company's reputation. He swallowed hard. "I'll always put the company first. You know that, Grandad."

His grandfather nodded and held his gaze with the same steel-blue eyes as his father. The same steel-blue eyes he and his brothers shared. The Bergen men's unifying trait. A similarity he'd tried to block out for the last ten years with hundred-hour work-weeks and weekends spent crunching numbers. Anything to distract him from the pain.

His grandad squeezed his shoulder. "I know you will, Jas."

Jasper saw his grandparents out then surveyed his office.

Fuck!

He wasn't going to get anything done here. Not today. He glanced at the book in his hand, grimaced, then shoved it inside his briefcase along with several files and his laptop. He left Collin with a list of tasks, then rode the elevator down to the parking garage, and got into his Audi.

He released a long breath then glanced into the back seat.

Goddammit!

He'd forgot his suitcase. He slammed his palms against the steering wheel. All this damned commotion around Eleanor Reynolds was making him sloppy, forgetful, and tongue-tied.

That ended now.

He started the car, exited the parking garage, and sped down the boulevard toward The Dalton. It wasn't a long drive, and soon, the building was in sight. But he wasn't able to turn into the side street to get into the building's parking garage.

A woman stood in the middle of the road blocking traffic. Jasper parked his car on the side of the road and got out to see what was going on. Arms waving wildly, this crazy lady blocked a tow truck from leaving the garage.

He took a step forward. "What's going on here?"

The woman whirled around, red-cheeked and lapis blue eyes flashing.

CHAPTER 3

ELLE

Elle spun around.

This day couldn't get any worse.

Striding toward her like he owned the road, Jasper Bergen whipped off his Aviators and pinned her with his steel-blue gaze.

She pressed her hands to her hips. "What the hell are you doing here?"

"I was trying to park my car in the garage. But you're in my way." He glanced past her toward the tow truck. "Are you having car trouble, Eleanor?"

Eleanor! Jesus! What was it with this guy?

She glanced at her beautiful car hooked up to the towing mechanism and currently blocking the entrance to the underground parking garage. "Yeah, you could say that."

"Lady, get out of the way! We're taking the car! That's the end of it!" the driver called, craning his head out the window.

Jasper's gaze darted between her and the truck. "Are they repossessing your Porsche?"

Dear Universe, you suck!

Clothes spattered with gray flecks of wet sludge. Her hair twisted into a damp bun and mascara running down her cheeks.

Of course, she'd run into Jasper Bergen at this exact craptastic moment.

"You should be more diligent with your finances," he said with a frown.

That frown.

That trademark, judgmental, curmudgeon curl of his lips.

She held up her index finger, signaling for the tow truck driver to wait while she turned her attention to the jackass in front of her. "You know what, hollow bunny? In the last hour, I've been pumped and dumped. I've been slushed by a bus, and now there's a misunderstanding with the lease on my car. I don't have time for your buttoned-up bullshit."

He took a step closer, nostrils flaring. "Buttoned-up bullshit? Is that how you speak to your employer?"

Oh, hell no!

"Employer?" she bit back.

"Yes. That's when an entity, me, pays an employee, you, for services rendered."

The nerve of this man!

"I'm under contract to consult with Bergen Enterprises, the company your grandparents founded. Can you say nepotism?"

"Nepotism or not, I'm still the CEO of Bergen Enterprises. That means you work for me. I'm not sure what we're supposed to get out of this collaboration, but I know what you're getting out of this. I'm still floored my grandparents offered you such an outrageous sum of money."

She felt the heat rise to her cheeks. "What I get out of it? Remember this, Mr. CEO. Your people came to me. Your very lovely grandparents want me."

Her chest heaved inches from his. She stared into his eyes and hated that he could evoke this kind of response. She watched him. The frown was gone, and he clenched his jaw. He seemed to be doing everything in his power to maintain that icy, untouchable Jasper Bergen demeanor. He held her gaze, and she'd be damned if he was going to make her blink.

"Really? We're doing this?" he asked.

"Doing what?" she hissed, gaze locked with his.

"A staring contest. A little juvenile."

She opened her eyes wider. "Then blink."

He lowered his voice. "You blink."

"I'm not going to blink."

"This is insane, Eleanor."

"Then end it and blink, Jasper."

Her eyes watered, but there was no way in hell she was backing down.

Yes, this was childish.

Yes, she was a twenty-nine-year-old woman engaging in a staring contest with a billionaire. The way her day was going, she wouldn't be surprised if the sky opened up and hail started falling.

"Enough, Eleanor," he said through gritted teeth, the gravelly hint in his voice settling beneath her belly.

She matched his tone. "Stop calling me Eleanor."

"Why? It's your name," he answered, that low rumble fanning the flame inside her.

She opened her eyes wider. "I go by Elle."

He leaned in, unblinking. "Eleanor suits you better."

The warmth of his breath tickled her lips. It sent a rush of heat through her body.

She doubled her resolve. "How do you know what suits me? You barely know me. I bet you haven't even read any of my books."

"Nope, not one chapter. Not one page. Not one word," he said, gaze widening.

"Then I guess you wouldn't know that a shaman in Tibet taught me how to go into a deep staring trance. I could do this all day, Bergen."

"Did you put that in one of your travel guides?"

"I guess you'll never know."

The corner of his mouth turned up. "I call bullshit."

Jasper's almost-smile was not helping her ignore the electricity coursing through her body. Fighting with Jasper Bergen elicited a buzz akin to skydiving.

"You might as well blink. You're not going to win. I have mystical powers."

"I always win," he bit back.

Now it was her turn to almost smile. What was it about this idiot that made her act like a deranged beauty pageant contestant?

"Lady! I don't know what the hell kind of weird mind shit you and your boyfriend have got going on out there. But I need both of you to get out of the street. We've got other repos to get to!"

She gasped, blinked wildly, and spun toward the truck. "He is not my boyfriend. This man is the furthest thing from my boyfriend. He is a hollow bunny, and I will not be taking a bite out of him!"

Oh shit! What the hell was wrong with her? She was a master of words until Jasper Bergen appeared.

The driver looked at Jasper. "Does she need medication or something? I can always call the cops, and we can do this the hard way."

Jasper glanced at her. "I'm going to speak with the driver. Stay here."

"I'm not letting you talk to the driver. And I'm certainly not staying put!"

"Eleanor, that guy looks ready to call the police and report an unhinged woman who is impeding his ability to do his job. Would you like to spend the day in a holding cell?"

She chewed her lip. Her cousin would be heartbroken if she got herself arrested and missed her engagement party.

She crossed her arms. "Fine."

"Don't do anything crazy."

She raised her hands in mock surrender. "I'll be sure to keep these where everyone can see them."

"Good call."

She sighed. "I was kidding."

"I'm not. No sudden movements. Do you understand?" he said, the gravelly tone coating his words.

Jesus! Why was his take-charge, tin man routine getting her so amped up?

"Eleanor?"

She pushed the thought out of her mind. "Yes, I've got it."

Jasper turned and walked to the driver's side of the tow truck. He shook the man's hand and leaned in. Elle closed her eyes and pressed her fingertips to her eyelids. She'd met a shaman in Tibet. That part was true. But the staring trance malarkey? The hollow bunny was right—total bullshit.

She dropped her hands, opened her eyes, and caught a glimpse of herself in the reflection of the mirrored building across from The Dalton. Hair falling out of a half-bun. Lipstick and eyeliner smeared as if she'd allowed a toddler to give her a makeover. A slash of dishwater gray across her white jacket where she'd taken the brunt of the splash. She was surprised the repo guys even believed this shiny Porsche belonged to her.

Jasper tapped the hood of the tow truck, and the vehicle crept forward. He walked to her and lightly gripped her elbow. "We have to get out of the street now."

His touch was gentler than she'd imagined. Steady. Reassuring.

She released a shaky breath. "I'm not letting them take my car."

He fished an item from his pocket. "Here's the towing company's business card. Once you get everything sorted out with your lease, the guy says they'll be happy to return the vehicle."

She plucked the piece of paper from his hand and stared at a smudge across the logo. "Oh, for fuck's sake!"

"Jesus! What?" he asked.

"Look, it says, for all *you're* towing needs. *Y, O, U, apostrophe, R, E.*"

"Yeah?"

"They used the wrong *your.*"

A muscle in Jasper's jaw ticked. "Eleanor, we need to get out of their way. The guy really does have nine-one-one ready to go. As we speak, his greasy thumb is hovering over the call icon."

She sighed. "Okay, already! I'm moving! I'm moving!"

She clenched the card in her hand and allowed Jasper to guide her to the sidewalk. The roar of the truck's diesel engine cut through the crisp air, sending a puff of black smoke toward the sky. Chains rattled as the vehicle dragged her beautiful SUV down the road like a prisoner.

Frustration coursed through her in angry waves. Her money. Her car. And all for what? For that smarmy man to buy a boat. Every word she'd written. Every place she'd visited. All the work she'd done. He'd stolen the fruits of her labor. She was back to square one. She glanced at the tow truck driver's card, and anger edged out frustration, and she exploded.

"You have a spelling error on your business card! That's a major grammar violation, you car towing cretin!" she called out as the truck rumbled by.

The driver extended his hand and flashed her the bird, and her vision went red.

"You piece of..."

She started to chase the truck. Arms flailing as her backpack slipped off one shoulder and dangled at her side. She pitched forward, stumbled, and nearly ate it on the pavement. But before she hit the ground, hands gripped her waist and pulled her back.

"Jesus Christ, Eleanor!" Jasper said, surprise lacing his words.

She leaned against him, gasping, and watched the truck sail around the corner with her beautiful car and disappear into the city.

"It's just a car," he whispered against the shell of her ear.

Just a car? It should come as no surprise that someone who'd grown up wiping his ass with hundred-dollar bills would say that.

She'd worked hard, damned hard, and earned every penny that moron shyster Monty stole. She swallowed back the shame of her situation just as Jasper's hands tightened, and in the space of a breath, she was fully aware of his body, strong and solid behind her. And those hands. They spanned her waist. Fit her curves. And was he…

Before she could decide if Mr. Billionaire CEO was getting hard at her misfortune, he stepped away from her and cleared his throat. Universal man code for I don't know what the hell to do, so I'm going to stand here and make guttural sounds.

Elle slipped the fallen leather strap over her shoulder and stared at the man standing in front of her. Why the hell *was* he here?

"Did you come to see your brother or something? You know he and my cousin are already up at Bergen Mountain."

"No, I didn't come to see Brennen. I'm staying in The Dalton's penthouse."

"You're staying here? Since when?"

"Since yesterday."

"Why? Don't you own like three hundred other houses you could go to?"

"Seven."

"Seven, what?"

"Seven houses. My family owns seven houses. Four in Colorado and three in other parts of the world. There are several condos as well."

She stared him down.

He cleared his throat again. "I'm having some work done on my place in Cherry Creek. It's taking longer than I'd expected, so I've decided to stay in the penthouse."

She cocked her head to the side. "I live in this building."

Now it was his turn to stare at her like she was an idiot.

"I know you live here, Eleanor."

She nodded. "Right! Whatever! I'm going inside. I need to change and grab my bag so I can head up to—"

"Bergen Mountain," he supplied.

"Oh, shitballs!" She groaned, running her hands through her hair and demolishing what was left of her bun.

"Shitballs?" he repeated.

"Yes, shitballs!" She pulled out her phone. "I have to call a car service."

He cleared his throat—a-freaking-gain.

"Stop doing that throat thing and just say whatever you want to say, Jasper."

He held her gaze. "You can ride with me."

"All the way to Bergen Mountain?"

"No, I'm going to kick you out of the car and make you walk the last mile."

Her jaw dropped.

"Yes, all the way to Bergen Mountain. What the hell kind of person do you think I am? We're going to the same damn place, Eleanor. Your cousin is going to be marrying my brother. And for better or for worse, you're a part of the Bergen rebranding. How about we call a truce?"

She weighed his words, remembered her very lightweight bank account, then thought of her mom. She couldn't screw up this job.

"Fine, truce."

She put out her hand, and he took it. His palm pressed to hers, and again, she was surprised by the ease in which they fit together. He brushed his thumb across the back of her hand, and the contact sent a buzz through her body. She pulled back, but that brief touch was enough to leave her missing his warmth.

Sweet Baby J, she needed to get laid! Her vibrator wasn't cutting it anymore. That had to be it. Between the stress of her financial situation and her prolonged sexual drought, she wasn't in her right mind.

Jasper started to clear his throat, then stopped. "Here's the plan. I need to head up to the penthouse and get my bag, and you need to..." He waved his hands as if he was Cinderella's fairy godmother, trying to transform her from her current troll state to something more pleasing to the eye.

She pointed to her face. "Do you have an issue with this?"

"No, I just thought you'd like to freshen up."

She stood there.

He shifted his weight. "Can we just go inside, get our shit, and head up to the mountain, Eleanor? We're already going to be arriving later than I'd wanted."

She sighed, the adrenaline rush wearing off as fatigue set in. "That works for me."

They entered The Dalton and rode the elevator in silence. The doors opened onto the eleventh floor, and she stepped out.

"I'll come down and knock on your door."

She nodded. "Give me ten minutes. I'm in 11B."

She watched the doors close and listened to the mechanical hum as the elevator ascended one floor up to the penthouse level.

She walked down the hall, mulling over her situation. Abby was engaged to Jasper's brother. She was under a contractual obligation with Jasper's company, and now the man was living on the floor above her.

She unlocked her door and threw her keys on the table. She'd only just returned from a trip a few days ago. And in those few days, life had gone topsy-turvy. She'd had her first blow-out meeting with Jasper Bergen, had Brennen Bergen ask her to help plan a surprise marriage proposal for Abby, and she'd learned her finances were in shambles.

She didn't bother turning on any lights in the main room and nearly tripped over a shoe or something on the floor before heading to the bathroom. She flicked on the light switch then reared back.

Holy Mary!

She looked like a bag lady who'd walked through a car wash then rolled in the gutter just for kicks. She grabbed a brush and worked it through the tangled mess of thick chestnut hair, which only made things worse. Frizzy pieces stood out between hardened slush-encrusted clumps. Glancing around, she spotted her beloved Fell's Peak ball cap and pulled it on. Then she wet a washcloth and tried to do damage control on her face when she heard the door to her apartment creak open.

"Eleanor, are you ready?"

Oh, crap! Was he here already? At least she was packed.

She checked her reflection—hideous but passable for a human being thanks to the hat—and darted out of the bathroom and into the darkened living room.

"That wasn't ten minutes!" she said, taking off her white slush-splattered coat and grabbing another jacket hanging off the back of a chair.

He glanced at his watch. "It was six minutes."

"Right! When a woman tells you ten minutes, you give her the full ten. A real gentleman would tack on a few more."

Confusion marred his features. "Like twelve minutes?"

She blew out a frustrated breath. "Fourteen seems reasonable to me."

He turned on a light and met her gaze. "So, when you tell me you need ten minutes, I should give you fourteen?"

She crossed her arms. "You don't spend much time with women, do you?"

"Well, there's my grandmother."

"She doesn't count."

"She's a woman."

Good God! This man!

"She's your grandmother. I mean, women your own age. Don't you date?"

He shifted his stance. "Do you date?"

"Let's just go," she said then stopped and stared at the giant pink vibrator in the middle of the room.

"Is that a…?" Jasper began.

This damned day!

"It's a neck massager," she answered reflexively.

"Why is it laying in the middle of the floor?"

What was she supposed to say? *Because I decided after God knows how long that I needed a little relief and found thirty seconds of battery-powered bliss on my living room floor?* She glanced at Jasper, who was biting back a smile. The bastard thought this was funny.

She waved her hands in frustration. "Because it is. Can we go?"

She glared at the pink plastic, hoping she'd spontaneously acquire laser eye superpowers and be able to fry the damn thing to a crisp. After five long seconds spent staring, she gave up and met his gaze.

"Are you sure you don't want to pack it and bring it up to Bergen Mountain? What if your *neck* starts hurting?"

"My *neck* is none of your concern."

She bent over, swiped the faux cock off the ground, and tossed it into her bedroom where it hit the floor with a thud and started vibrating, the soft buzz rattling against the hardwood.

"Looks like the batteries are all charged up," Jasper remarked without even the hint of a smile.

Jackass!

He feigned concern. "Don't you think you should go turn it off? We'll be gone a couple of days."

"It's fine," she shot back.

"What if your neck hurts when you get home? You won't be able to use it if it's out of batteries."

She pointed to the door. "I'll buy more! We're leaving!"

———

In one day—no, in one hour—Jasper Bergen had witnessed her car being repossessed and got to see her vibrator. Even more mortifying, it wasn't even lunchtime yet.

Neither of them spoke during the elevator ride down to the lobby. They left the building and headed toward Jasper's Audi. She could still smell the tow truck's diesel exhaust in the air and cringed, remembering the tow truck fiasco. And her car! Her beautiful car! She'd never driven a luxury car before. That Porsche was her *you made it girl* present which was now probably sitting in some dirty lot under lock and key.

Jasper cleared his throat and she shook her head, pushing her car blues away, and turned to him. "What are you doing?"

"Opening the door," he replied as if he was trying to figure out if she was asking him a trick question.

She didn't move. "That's the passenger's door."

He stiffened. "I'm sure as hell not letting you drive my car."

"I wasn't insinuating that I'd drive your car, but you don't have to open my car door."

He nodded and looked away. "Force of habit."

"Ah, right! You must do it for your grandmother."

"Yeah, I do. What's wrong with that?"

She slid into the seat. "I'm not your grandmother."

"I'm well aware of that, Eleanor."

She held his gaze and hated herself for the butterflies that erupted in her belly when he said her name.

Eleanor.

The moniker didn't exactly conjure up sex kitten. Not to mention, she was named after some pruny aunt who died eons before she was born. But when he said it, each syllable came out wrapped in a layer of filthy naughtiness that made her press her thighs together.

Stop!

It didn't matter if angels wept at the sound of Jasper Bergen saying her name. The guy was a complete bottom-line focused, Brooks Brothers-wearing bastard who was sort of her boss.

"Is this all you've got?" he called from outside as he loaded their suitcases.

"Yeah, Abby took all my ski gear with her when she and Brennen went up."

"It's a small bag."

"I've learned to travel light."

Jasper closed the back hatch and got into the driver's seat, and she pulled out her phone.

"What are you doing?"

"Calling Abby to let her know we're on the way, and then I was going to pick a playlist."

Jasper started the car and guided it into traffic. "A playlist for what?"

"Music for the drive. You didn't think we were going to talk, did you?"

"I don't listen to music."

Her jaw dropped. "Ever?"

"There are some places where it's unavoidable. Coffee shops. Elevators."

"Elevators?"

"Yeah, elevator music."

"When was the last time you danced?"

His grip tightened on the steering wheel as evergreens replaced skyscrapers, and they left the city.

"I don't know."

She turned in her seat and stared at him. "Okay, even dancing by yourself in your bedroom counts."

"What kind of grown man dances alone in his bedroom?"

"The kind who enjoys a good beat and likes to have fun."

"Is that all life is to you, Eleanor? Always looking for fun?"

So much for the truce.

"Music and fun are good for the soul. Good for creativity. Good for freaking longevity. One would assume the CEO of a mountain sports empire basically built on people having fun would understand that."

"People like exercise," he replied robotically.

"Is that what you think people are doing right now at all your resorts? They're there because they want some exercise? No wonder your grandparents sought me out with you at the helm."

He barked out a laugh. "That's rich coming from an irresponsible woman who can't even make a car payment on time."

Her knee bounced as her heart rate kicked up. A rush of heat overtook her body, and she needed to get out of that car. She needed air. She needed to put more than six inches between herself and Jasper Bergen.

"Pull over!" she belted.

"Onto the side of the road?"

"No, drive up the side of the mountain! Yes, pull over on the side of the road!"

"Why?"

She tugged at the collar of her jacket. "Because I need some air, and you and I need to get a few things straight."

He shook his head, eased the car onto the shoulder, then jerked the gearshift into park.

Elle threw open the door and stomped over to the guardrail. She took a few deep breaths with her gaze trained on the snow-covered sea of trees with tall mountain peaks in the distance. The rumble and grind of semis spitting dirt and pebbles weaved with the whoosh of cars zooming up the mountain, not ten feet from where she stood.

She took another deep breath, then froze, as a tingle worked its way down her spine, and she knew he was there. All restrained emotions and button-up intensity, every cell in her body registered his presence.

She turned, lifted her chin, and held his seething gaze. "Despite what you may think, I'm good at what I do. It seems easy and breezy and fun because I work my ass off to make it look that way. And here's what I've learned. Life is not some start at point A to get to point B. It's not all dollar signs and bottom lines. It's about the journey. It's about the surprises. It's about being open to adventure."

He took a step toward her. "I disagree. People crave stability and continuity. Why do you think they keep coming back to Bergen resorts and continue shopping at our stores?"

She threw up her hands. "Because they want to connect and experience life in a way that makes them happy."

"Happy is subjective."

She shook her head. This man could give the Grinch a run for the money. "It's not! Happy is doing something that brings you joy."

His expression turned as hard as stone. "Would you like to know what brings me joy?"

She crossed her arms and looked away. "Let me guess. Staring at spreadsheets and scowling at puppies?"

He closed the distance between them. "Keeping Bergen Enterprises solvent and competitive. And if you think for one damned second that I'm trusting someone like you with my family's legacy, then you've got a lot to learn about me. I've given everything to this company, and I will not see it diminished."

She grabbed his coat and pulled his face down close to hers. "Oh no! I've done my research. I know your company. I've been skiing at your resorts and buying your gear since I was a little girl. And I know where you're losing customers. I know your sales have flattened out. If anything, you and your smug, curmudgeon ways are what's *diminishing* Bergen Enterprises."

He gathered her hair in his hand and twisted the locks, knocking off her hat, and bringing her lips millimeters from his. The stoic facade disappeared, and his eyes blazed. "You've got a lot of nerve, Eleanor."

Her breaths came fast, and it wasn't the crisp mountain air that had her body thrumming. It was him. It was the dysfunctional push and pull between them that made her want to throttle him one second and jump him the next.

The tip of his nose brushed over hers, and she tightened her grip on his coat.

"Here's the thing. I'm your best shot at getting Bergen Enterprises back on track. Your grandparents understand that."

He lowered his voice as his lips grazed her cheek. "Do not lecture me on Bergen Enterprises. I eat, breathe, and sleep it every day."

"But you don't enjoy it. You don't love it," she whispered.

His fingers tangled in her hair, and he leaned into her, his forehead resting against hers. He reached around and gripped the back of her coat with his other hand like he was holding on for dear life. And she let him, not because she felt sorry for him, but because at that moment, his touch was the only thing keeping her from falling apart.

He pulled back and met her gaze. "Eleanor."

She couldn't respond. She could only stare into those steel-blue eyes swimming with pain and anger and regret. She brushed her fingertips over his cheek. Was this him? Was this the real Jasper Bergen? Did the hollow bunny have a heart? Was there more to the tin man than just his pragmatic shell?

She swallowed hard, lost and found at the same time, when a loud crack pulled them apart, and a rock the size of a football fell off a truck hauling gravel. It ricocheted off the highway, and with marksman precision, completely took out the Audi's driver's side mirror.

"Holy fuck!" Jasper yelled as the tenderness drained from his face. "Look at what you did! Look at what happened because of this insanely stupid side-of-the-road escapade. Somebody could have gotten hurt. That rock could have hit you, Eleanor! That rock could have killed you, and I wouldn't have been able to do a damn thing!"

She reached out to him, but he stepped away. "We're fine, Jasper! Nothing happened!"

He ran his hands through his hair. "Nothing happened? You saw the size of that rock! Now get in the car!"

"Do not speak to me like that. You are not my father."

"No, I'm your boss. Now get in the car, or I'm going to pick you up and throw you in there myself."

She raised her hands in surrender. "Just let me get my hat. It fell off somewhere."

She turned to look when two large hands gripped her from behind and plucked her off the ground.

"Put me down, Jasper! I need my hat. It's important to me."

"I'll get you another damn hat. It's just a Fell's Peak Ski Resort ball cap. I own the damn resort!" he growled, thrusting her into the passenger's seat.

She looked past him. Her hat was right there until a gust of wind carried it over the guardrail.

"No!" she cried and tried to push past him.

He held her in place. "Stop being reckless, Eleanor! It's not safe! It's just a stupid hat."

His gaze burned into her. Anger fused so tightly with gut-wrenching pain, it was hard to tell where one began and the other ended.

She brushed an angry tear from her cheek. "You're an asshole."

A muscle twitched in his jaw. "What made you think I was anything different?" he shot back and slammed the door.

CHAPTER 4

JASPER

Jasper clenched his jaw as he steered the Audi—now missing its damn driver's side mirror—off the highway and onto Bergen Mountain Drive.

He glanced at Elle. Arms crossed and body angled toward the car door, she looked ready to bolt the minute the vehicle stopped.

They'd driven in an angry silence for the last ninety minutes. That meant he'd spent the previous five thousand four hundred seconds trying to figure out what the fuck had happened on the side of the road.

He'd become a master of maintaining a cool, stoic demeanor over the past decade. That was how he coped. Without the safety net of constant work and a punishing routine, he'd be lost. Anytime his mind would wander to thoughts of his parents, he'd double his commitment to the grind. Another hour running the trail. Another night combing through sales reports.

And then Eleanor Reynolds crashed into his life like that damn rock that toppled off the truck and obliterated the Audi's side mirror. Bold and unfiltered, her words cut straight to his core.

He flexed his fingers, aching to touch her again, then gripped the steering wheel until his knuckles turned white. Damn this woman! Damn her for making him question every decision he'd made over the last decade.

He loved Bergen Enterprises, didn't he?

He'd crafted a life where all he did was devote himself to the company. Wasn't that love, or had he mistaken the emotion with obligation?

It didn't matter. He knew his place in the world, and it was at the helm of the company his parents and grandparents had built.

He sucked in a tight breath and released it slowly as they passed the Bergen Ski Resort's east village. Settled at the base of Bergen Mountain, Bergen Village was divided into three interconnected parts: the east village, the center village, and the west village. This drive used to bring him a sense of peace. But not today. Not after Elle Reynolds ripped off the bandage he'd used to cover his wounds and exposed him to the reality that had been gnawing beneath the surface.

Was he happy?

Did he love his work?

Questions once easily dismissed now sat like stones in his belly, weighing him down, forcing acknowledgment.

He turned on the windshield wipers as a gentle spring snow added a fine layer of feathery-white powder to the road. To a ski resort owner, seeing snow was like watching dollars fall from the sky. But was Elle right? Was that all he saw?

He swallowed hard. So what if it was? One of the Bergen grandsons had to step up and put this company first. After their parents' death, Brennen chose the route of capricious playboy while Cam jumped ship and left Colorado to live a life of solitude and work as a ski lift operator at a resort—not one of theirs—in Switzerland.

He glanced at Elle as a wave of resentment and desire rushed through him. Who was she to judge him? Who was she to lecture him on love? He had responsibilities that went beyond himself— that superseded something as silly as love. He ran a company that employed thousands of people, and while his grandparents still played a major role, they were phasing out the day-to-day tasks, leaving them to him as CEO.

"What's all that?"

Elle's words caught him off guard, the sweetest and most wretched sound he'd ever heard.

She straightened in her seat and pointed toward the road where a few news trucks sat parked next to a Bergen Mountain Security SUV. It looked as if the security team had set up a roadblock. He pulled up to where the men were standing, rolled down the window, and waved the guards over.

"Sorry about all this, Mr. Bergen. The press is here for your brother and Miss Quinn. But your brother asked not to be disturbed, so we set up a makeshift roadblock."

The engagement seen around the world. Of course, the press would be staked out here.

Jasper nodded. "Thank you. I appreciate you taking on this extra duty."

The man gave him a wide grin. "It's no trouble at all, sir. Every time your brother and Miss Quinn order in, they always make sure to send a feast for us. Please thank them. Those crème brûlée crepes are the best."

Fucking perfect! He and Elle were going to be surrounded by a couple who were crazy in love, while things between himself and Eleanor Reynolds were just fucking crazy.

What was he thinking when he tangled his fingers into her hair and pulled her close?

That was the problem. He hadn't been thinking. He'd been reacting, responding to the need to touch her, the need to bask in whatever the hell it was that made her so damned hard to resist. That brutal honesty that had his lips a breath away from hers. Christ, it made him hard just thinking about it.

He shifted in his seat, nodded to the guard, then rolled up his window as Bergen Mountain security cleared a path for them.

"You know what we're walking into, don't you?" she said, gaze trained on the road. "They took that man fast seriously the last couple weeks. Those two probably had enough sexual tension built up to power the mountain for a year."

He knew damned well what they were walking into. Abby had recently moved to Denver after a bad breakup and put herself on what she'd called a man fast. She'd decided to focus completely on her new job as a first-grade teacher and not date or give any man the time of day—something that had given her an A-plus in his book—until his brother got stuck volunteering in her class and the two fell madly in love.

But he owed Abby. His brother was on a collision course to being kicked out of the family business because of his reckless skirt-chasing antics. Thanks to Abby not taking any of Bren's shit, his brother found the motivation to clean up his bad boy ways and take his position as president of the philanthropic arm of the company seriously.

Jasper schooled his features. "I know what we're walking into, Eleanor. I'm not completely void of emotions."

"I'd beg to differ," she shot back.

He remained silent. What the hell was there to say?

"I swear to God, Jasper, the last thing I need is to walk in on Abby and Brennen screwing each other's brains out."

"We'll knock on the door," he said. At least they agreed on one thing. He was just as opposed to walking into a PDA blitz as she was.

She glanced down at her phone. "Dammit!"

"What?"

"My cell's out of juice."

"You didn't charge it before we left?"

She pinned him with that lapis blue gaze. "I was a little busy."

He pulled up to the cottage and parked the car. "That's right. Busy having your car repossessed."

"Busy trying to sort an issue with the lease on my car," she corrected.

"Yeah, you don't pay it, they don't let you keep it. That's Finance 101."

She gave him one of the best *go fuck yourself* grins he'd ever seen. "Thanks for that super helpful tip."

"Anytime," he added with his own *go fuck yourself* grin.

She pressed her palms to her face and groaned.

"I'll take that as you're ready to go inside," he replied.

She huffed out a breath and got out of the car. He followed a step behind, then knocked on the front door.

He waited as Elle paced the length of the porch.

He knocked again. "Do you think they went skiing?"

Elle stopped and cocked her head to the side. "If you were finally alone with the woman you loved after a period of prolonged abstinence, would you be out skiing?"

Christ! He'd been living in a state of prolonged abstinence for...

He frowned and tried to remember the last woman he'd been with. There was that attorney he'd met at a conference in DC, but that was two, maybe three years ago.

Had he been rosy-palming it for that long?

No wonder he was ready to jump Elle on the side of the road.

He raised his hand to knock again when the door swung open, and he was eye to eye with his brother.

Barefoot and only wearing a pair of track pants, the middle Bergen brother furrowed his brow. "Is everything okay?"

Elle crossed her arms. "Well, we're here."

Brennen glanced between them, looking utterly confused. Elle was right. His brother's blood supply had clearly been diverted south for a prolonged period of time.

Brennen scratched his head. "Yeah, I can see that you're here. But why are you here?"

"Jesus fucking Christ," he said in unison with Elle.

She stared at him with daggers in her eyes. It wasn't his fault they had the same damn response.

Jasper sighed. "You don't even know what day it is, do you?"

Elle crossed her arms. "I told you we should have called."

"I tried to call. The calls all went to voicemail every damn time." He wasn't lying. While she seethed in the front seat, back turned to him, he'd popped in his wireless headphones and tried to call, not once, but four times.

Elle stepped forward. "It's Monday afternoon, Brennen."

"Oh flip!" Brennen exclaimed.

That was the other thing. Bren's sweet schoolteacher fiancée had him talking like a G-rated movie character. But he couldn't fault his brother. Brennen hadn't been this happy and this full of enthusiasm since before their parents had died.

Jasper ran his hand down his face. "Lucky for you, we got here before Gram and Grandad."

"The family engagement ski party thing starts today?" Brennen's eyes went wide. "Come in! Come in!"

They entered the house as another look of confusion crossed Brennen's face.

"Wait! Why did you knock, Jas? You've got a key?"

As if on cue, Abby rounded the corner wearing nothing but a Bergen Mountain sweatshirt and lacy underwear.

Yep, he and Elle had caught the newly engaged couple in full-on fuck mode.

Abby's eyes went wide, and her cheeks grew pink as she took in the scene, then turned on her heel and ran back down the hall.

Jasper met his brother's gaze. "That's why we knocked."

Brennen gave him an easy grin. "What did you expect? We just got engaged."

"And you made it through the man fast," Jasper added, biting back a smirk.

"Make fun of it all you like, big brother. Without the man fast, I wouldn't be standing here half naked, and Abby wouldn't be mortified you saw her in her underwear."

"Did you see me, Jasper?" Abby called from down the hall.

His expression softened. He genuinely liked and respected his brother's fiancée. And he'd be lying if he said he wasn't a little bit jealous. Not that he had any romantic feelings for Abby. He only wondered what it would be like to have someone look at him the way she looked at Brennen. The way his father had looked at his mother.

Jasper cleared his throat. "No, I didn't see you, Abby. You were too quick."

She joined them—now fully clothed—and threw him a bright smile then hugged Elle. "How was the drive up?"

Elle's expression grew stony.

"I'm going to go get my bag," she said, giving Abby a tight smile.

Jasper grated his teeth. "I can get your bag."

She pinned him with that lapis blue gaze. "I don't need you to get my bag."

He leaned in and lowered his voice. "Consider it one of the perks of being under contract with Bergen Enterprises."

Elle reared back. She shot him a scathing glare then stormed out the door. If looks could kill, he'd be as dead as a doornail.

Jasper glanced at his brother and Abby. Abby's lips were pressed together, and Bren just shook his head with an amused expression.

"I'll be right back," Jasper said, his skin prickling.

Eleanor Reynolds made him look like a childish idiot. He was not about to sink into her flippant, irresponsible ways. At least the cottage was enormous. While Elle celebrated with Abby and the rest of his family, he planned on escaping to the study to work.

He stepped onto the porch and watched as Elle yanked on the car's door handle.

"Are you planning on breaking that, too?"

Elle looked up from where she stood, gripping the Audi's handle and pulling violently like somebody trying to shake a vending machine to get a free chocolate bar.

"It's locked!" she called.

"I know. I locked it!"

"In the goddamn driveway with security right down the street?" She scoffed.

"Who doesn't lock their car? Oh wait! Let me guess...you." He scoffed right back.

Elle threw up her hands. "I don't know why you're trying so hard to make me out as the enemy. I wouldn't have agreed to work with Bergen Enterprises if I didn't believe in the company."

This woman.

He released a tight breath, then joined her at the car. "Believing in something isn't enough. I used to believe in Santa Claus and the Tooth Fairy. It doesn't mean they're real. Data and facts are what makes the world go round, Eleanor."

"But belief is what makes it fun. Believing in something is what gives it magic."

"Magic? You're only making my case with statements like that," he barked.

"And what's *your* case?"

"That you're all wrong for Bergen Enterprises. You're too..."

"Too, what?" She took a step toward him.

"Irresponsible. Your car troubles prove that."

She jabbed her index finger into his chest. "People make mistakes, Jasper. Things don't always go as planned. But that's life. Our successes and failures are what makes us human and not just a bunch of hollow bunny robotic sacks of flesh walking around."

His pulse kicked up, and every cell in his body begged him to touch her. He cupped her cheek in his hand, no longer moving of his own rational volition. Their breaths mingled in sharp puffs of white in the cold mountain air as the light snow grew more intense around them.

He brushed his thumb across her bottom lip. "That's the third time you've called me a hollow bunny today. Is that some millennial hipster term real adults don't use?"

She grazed her teeth over the tip of his thumb, and the contact sent a sharp bolt of lust straight to his cock.

What was it about Eleanor Reynolds? Nobody insulted him. No one would dare. He was a rich and powerful man, but that didn't seem to faze her. She saw herself as his equal. Scratch that. She saw herself as better than him.

She bit down harder, and the pain surged through him. Locked in battle with Elle was the most alive he'd felt in years.

She relaxed her bite and ran the tip of her tongue over the pad of his thumb. "You better step back. I'm not sweet like my cousin. I could eat you for lunch if I wanted to."

"I've never liked sweet. I don't even have a favorite ice cream flavor," he growled back.

Snowflakes floated through the air, catching in Elle's dark chestnut hair. One came to rest on the tip of her eyelashes, and he had the sudden desire to kiss each flake from where they landed on her body.

She'd grabbed onto his jacket, her small fists clutching and tightening, keeping him close when the sound of the mountain estate's door creaked open, then shut abruptly.

Fucking hell! They had an audience.

Elle released her grip, and he slid his hand from her face, hating himself for again falling captive to those lapis blue eyes and all the grit and fire and challenge they contained.

"I think Abby and Brennen are waiting for us," he said, doing his best to keep his voice even.

She nodded. "I'm still carrying my own bag."

He reached into his pocket, took out his keys, and pressed the unlock button on the key fob.

He took a step back so she could open the car door and retrieve her bag. "Be my guest."

He followed her back into the cottage where Abby offered to give her a tour, and the cousins set off for the far side of the house. A good plan. He and Elle were likely to start throwing things at each other if they remained together much longer.

His brother bit back a grin. "You and Elle look a little tense."

He stared out the expanse of floor-to-ceiling windows that framed the breathtaking view of Bergen Mountain. "Eleanor Reynolds is impossible and infuriating."

"So, you like her?"

Jasper reared back. The last thing he needed was relationship advice from his younger brother. "Not a chance! Where the hell would you get that from?"

Brennen shifted his weight. "Abby and I think that you each need to get some."

"Get some?" He frowned.

"Laid, big brother. Abby also thinks Elle should go on a *man feast*. You know, the opposite of what she did with the *man fast*."

Jasper shook his head. "Jesus, Bren! Why the hell are you and your fiancée discussing Elle's and my sex life?"

Brennen's eyes went wide. "You guys have a sex life?"

Talking about having no sex life was almost as bad as not having one.

"No! We can barely stand to be together." But just as the words fell from his lips, images of Elle's eyes and her perfect petite curves flashed before him.

"I don't know," Brennen began. "A man feast isn't a bad idea. You're single, and Abby said that she can't even remember the last time Elle got—"

"I'm going to stop you right there. Not only is Elle Reynolds working for us."

"Consulting," Brennen threw out, like there was a damn difference.

"She'll get paid, and my name will be on the check. She's working for us," he shot back.

"I was working with Abby," Bren parried with a sly grin.

"Yeah, and you nearly ruined everything. Listen, Bren." He put a hand on his brother's shoulder. "I'm happy things worked out for you and Abby. She's great, and I'm glad to see the old Brennen, but it's not something that can happen with Elle and me. When we're together, we're about two seconds away from clawing each other's eyes out."

"Or ripping each other's clothes off," his brother offered.

"Jesus, Bren!" He sighed then stiffened as Elle's voice carried up from the lower level.

The women were on their way back, and he needed to quash this conversation fast. But when he saw Elle coming up the stairs, her pinched expression said everything. He'd bet all his shares in Bergen Enterprises that Abby just dropped the *man feast* idea on her.

"How was the tour?" Brennen asked.

Elle smiled, and it was the most relaxed he'd seen her in hours. She hooked her arm with Abby's, and he took in the protective way she looked at her younger cousin. He recognized it because it was how he used to look at Bren and Cam when they were growing up. The weight of being the oldest. The knowledge that you would always hold that sacred position.

"You have a lovely h—" Elle began, but paused when the doorbell rang.

"Is that for you?" Jasper asked his brother.

Bren shook his head. "No, it shouldn't be. Maybe it's Gram and Grandad?"

Jasper opened the door and saw a man in a red Bergen Mountain ski patrol jacket.

He schooled his features. "Can I help you?"

The man smiled past him. "I'm here for Miss Reynolds."

Elle picked up her backpack and slid her arms through the straps. "Oh, that's right! It's been a busy day. I almost forgot."

Jasper frowned. "Forgot about what?" He didn't like this one bit. He needed to know about every interaction Elle had with anything Bergen Enterprises related.

"I wanted to see the cabins your grandparents told me about," she answered.

He pursed his lips. "The ones that aren't open to the public yet?"

"Yeah," she said casually, like she had carte blanche access to whatever her little heart desired.

The patroller turned up the wattage on his grin. "The snowmobile is outside. You can ride with me, Miss Reynolds."

While the Bergen Mountain staff knew about the cabins hidden away on the other side of the mountain, they hadn't shared this information with the public yet. With that part of their property butting up to the National Forest's open space, it was the perfect location for those looking to skirt the resort life and have a more rustic visit to the mountain. Secluded from the rest of the resort, summer guests could enjoy off-trail hiking and mountain biking while winter and early spring guests had access to acres and acres of wild, ungroomed backcountry for skiing and snowboarding.

He'd had no idea Elle had been informed of this and reined in his displeasure. "It's getting late, and it looks like a spring storm might be rolling in."

Elle waved him off. "It's just a quick look. I'll be there and back before you know it, and I'm sure..." She met the ski patroller's gaze.

"Antonio," he supplied, like a puppy dog ready to perform.

She smiled at the man and pulled her gloves and a scarf out of her suitcase. "I'm sure Antonio will take good care of me."

Jasper glanced at Antonio. He looked quite fucking keen on taking *good care* of her.

Jasper wasn't a jealous man. He was a practical, measured adult. A CEO. A respected member of the community. But none of that seemed to matter when it came to Eleanor Reynolds. He clenched his jaw as the muscles in his chest tightened.

"We won't be needing your assistance, Antonio," he said in his fiercest *I own this mountain* CEO tone. "I'll be bringing Miss Reynolds to visit the cabins myself."

CHAPTER 5

JASPER

Elle crossed her arms. "I'm driving the snowmobile."

Jasper passed her a helmet. "No, you're not."

She took the helmet and walked the length of the garage. "I don't understand why you even volunteered to take me!"

Jasper sighed. Neither did he, but he sure as hell wasn't sending her out with Mr. Romeo Ski Patroller.

Things got tense after he dismissed a visibly crestfallen Antonio. Elle had called him a control freak and rattled off her favorite insults for him: tin man, button-up bastard, hollow bunny. He still needed to figure out the last one.

"I'd feel more comfortable if I brought you. The snow's quite deep after that last storm, and another storm could roll in at any minute. Plus, I'm a skilled snowmobile rider."

She narrowed her gaze. "So am I!"

He pulled on his gloves and eased the snowmobile out onto the fresh snow. "This isn't some Sunday sightseeing tour. There are no dedicated trails where we're going."

"I'm fine with that."

"You've taken a sled off trail?"

"In Yellowstone National Park, the Adirondacks, Alaska,

which has some of the wildest terrain anywhere," she added, looking ready to hurl the helmet at him.

Well, shit. He shouldn't be surprised. She could probably also pilot a hot-air balloon and drive a monster truck over a row of crushed Hondas, but he stuck to his guns. "If you want to see the cabins, you'll ride with me. Otherwise, you're not going."

Her lapis blue gaze seared into him. "This is my job, Jasper. I'm not trying to pull a fast one on you. I'm trying to help *you* and Bergen Enterprises."

"By going behind my back and setting up a private tour?"

Her cheeks grew pink. "By following up on an upcoming Bergen resort option I thought people would like to hear about. That, by the way, your grandparents shared with me. All I did was call the ski patrol office a few days ago and let them know I'd be coming up. There's no cloak and dagger antics going on."

He put on his helmet, pulled down his ski goggles, and started the snowmobile.

"This is the only way you're getting up there. Take it or leave it," he called over the rumble of the engine.

She looked around the small garage that housed their snow-mobiles and ski gear. "Why can't I ride my own?"

He mounted the snowmobile and squeezed the throttle, moving the sled forward into the snow. "Because I said I'm taking you. End of discussion."

Elle's mouth moved, but thanks to his helmet and the roar of the snowmobile, all he could make out was a lot of fucks—which he was done giving.

After a minute or two of Elle throwing a fairly decent tantrum, she put on her helmet and slid her arms through the straps of her backpack. She raised her hands in an *are you happy* gesture that bordered on *screw you,* then climbed on the snowmobile and settled in behind him.

Was he happy?

Hell no!

He'd lost a whole Monday. A Monday that should have been

spent doing real work and not babysitting a wayward travel writer. Then her arms wrapped around his waist, and the thought of work disappeared. Her chest pressed to his back. Her thighs brushed against his. He squeezed the throttle, giving the sled a bit too much power, and the vehicle sprang to life, jutting forward and carving deep grooves into the fresh snow. Elle tightened her grip as her helmet bumped into the back of his.

Get it together, Bergen!

Thanks to his father's help, and his years on the Bergen Mountain Ski Patrol, he was an accomplished snowmobile operator. It didn't matter if he was traversing easy trails or the treacherous backcountry. He could expertly maneuver the sled through deep snow, up and down steep grades, and through the densest mountain foliage. But it had been a while—a long while—since he'd last ridden. It took him a minute to get his bearings, but by the time they left the trail leading from the cottage to the mountain and turned off to head for the secluded cabins, he'd found his balance as well as something else.

His smile.

Carving his way through the snow with Elle holding onto him, a surge of euphoria rushed through his body. The speed. The rumble of the powerful engine between his legs. The technical aspect of losing yourself and becoming one with the machine. He'd forgotten how damn fun it was. It had been years since he'd even strapped on skis.

Winter mountain sports used to be everything to him. As kids, he and his brothers lived in the snow: skiing, snowboarding, sledding, snowmobiling, snowshoeing. You name it, if it had anything to do with mountain powder, he and his brothers were there.

But it wasn't just fond memories and the roar of the sled that had his pulse racing. He reached down and squeezed Elle's knee. "Are you okay?" he called back to her.

He felt the pressure of her helmet as she nodded. She tightened her grip on his waist, and for a brief, flickering moment, everything made sense. The snowflakes swirling in the air grew heavier as a fresh blanket of snow lay before them, and all he wanted to do was ride off into the sunset and leave all the guilt and pain he'd carried for so many years behind. Lost in his little fantasy world, he'd hardly realized how far they'd gone until Elle batted at his arm, causing him to overcorrect and bank the sled into a large snowdrift.

He hit the kill switch and pulled off his helmet. "What the—"

Before he could say another word, Elle clapped her hand over his mouth and turned his head toward the wooded area to the west. He blinked. He couldn't believe his eyes.

"They're black bear cubs. I counted two of them," she whispered, slowly taking off her helmet.

"I know they're black bears. Black bears are the only bears we have in Colorado," he answered, watching the dark balls of fluff pull on a tree branch.

"I grew up in Maine, and Maine has the largest black bear population in the continental US," she countered.

Everything was a damn fight with this woman.

"Just because you grew up somewhere doesn't mean you're an expert on its wildlife," he shot back.

"I am on this, tin man," she said sternly. "They most likely just emerged from their den. They've got to be hungry, and their mother can't be far."

As if on cue, the primal grunts of one agitated—and probably ravenous—mother bear cut through the gentle snorts of the cubs.

Holy hell! In all his time in the mountains, he'd seen moose and elk and plenty of deer and mountain goats. Never had he encountered a bear. Scratch that. Bears.

He glanced over his shoulder. The cabin was only twenty or thirty yards away. He pointed up the steep incline. "We're going to leave the sled and work our way up to the cabin."

She nodded and twisted around to get off the snowmobile when her pack fell off onto the other side closest to the bears. Elle turned to try and grab it, but he pulled her back.

"Leave it!"

Her eyes went wide. "No, it's got—"

He took her hand. "I'm not having a bear attack on one of my properties. Leave the backpack."

The mother and one of the cubs headed away from them, back into the National Forest open space, but the other curious baby padded through the snow and headed straight toward them.

"Come on! We'll be able to watch them from inside the cabin," he said, guiding her away from the snowmobile and up the slope.

Elle nodded but kept looking back and forth between him and her pack.

He squeezed her hand. "It's just a bag. Even if your wallet and phone are in there, there's a good chance the bears won't even notice it."

"It's just—"

He lowered his voice. "This is no joke, Eleanor."

"I know. I know," she whispered, tightening her grip on his hand.

He led her through the snow-covered evergreens toward the cabin. It was slow-going. The drifts hit him mid-calf, and each step through the heavy spring snow was more draining than the last.

He turned to Elle. "Can you make it?"

The drifts went to her kneecaps. She nodded, but her red cheeks and heavy breathing told him it was far more taxing on her than it was on him.

"Get on my back, Eleanor."

"I'm fine," she huffed, trudging along.

"That cub is almost to the snowmobile. If its mother comes back for it, she'll be much faster. We need to move."

She shrugged. "All right. Bend over."

He leaned forward, and Elle climbed onto his back.

"Oh shit!" she whisper-shouted.

"What is it?"

"The cub found my pack."

Jasper looked over his shoulder. "What the hell is in your bag that's so important?"

"Don't get mad," she whispered into his ear.

Had she said anything else, the warmth of her breath against his skin might have overtaken him. But that statement—*don't get mad*—usually prompted that exact reaction.

"Eleanor! Do you have a gun or something dangerous in there?"

"No! Of course not!"

"Then, what?"

She cleared her throat. "A jar of honey."

He set her down on the cabin's porch. "Honey? Why the hell would you carry around a jar of honey—especially going out into the wilderness?"

"I forgot it was there. I got it today."

He checked the forest for the mother bear. "As long as it's in a sealed container, it should be fine."

"I don't know how well it's sealed. I got it from an amateur beekeeper this morning."

What kind of life did this woman lead? Amateur beekeeping in the morning. Car repossession just before lunch. And speaking of lunch, he was starving.

The sound of glass shattering echoed through the forest, making him forget his hunger. He whipped around. "What was that?"

Elle grasped his arm. "The cub got my backpack and hit it against the snowmobile."

"What else is in there?"

"Nothing important. My notebook. Some pens. A toiletry case. I left my wallet back at the cottage along with my phone since it was dead."

She glanced up at him. But instead of looking frightened or fearful, she smiled. Wonder and awe sparkled in her eyes, and she leaned into him.

"Look at her. She's amazing," Elle said, gesturing to the cub perched on the snowmobile currently licking honey off her pack.

The snow fell harder, but he could still make out the little bear. "It could be a he."

"The cub?"

"Yeah."

Elle glanced up at him and smirked. "Too smart. It's a she."

He held her gaze. Fearlessness and her zest for life flashed in her lapis blue eyes. He could almost understand why the world was so enamored with this woman until the piercing cries of an angry mother bear cut through the air. With the other cub in tow, she traversed down the mountain, joining her baby perched on the snowmobile.

He nudged her toward the door. "We need to get inside. It's not safe."

She squeezed his arm but didn't budge. "We're fine! I don't think I can compete with something as sweet as honey, and I know you certainly can't. They're not interested in us. And look at those adorable cubs. I bet they're twin female bear cubs—just like my mom and Abby's mom are twins. That's why they're so smart —all females," she added with a smirk.

He glanced at the bears. They were close enough for them to hear their labored breaths.

"This is no joke, Eleanor."

"Jasper, it's okay. We're far enough away."

He unzipped the pocket of his ski coat and retrieved the key to the cabin. "Stop being so irresponsible and reckless."

She let go of his arm. "Maybe you should start enjoying life and learn to appreciate a perfect moment."

He unlocked the door and held it open. "Death by bear mauling doesn't sound like a perfect moment to me—or any other reasonable person. Come on. We need to get inside."

She glanced down at the bears one last time, sighed, then entered the darkened cabin.

She could hate him all she liked. For all intents and purposes, she was a Bergen employee. That made her his responsibility. Ski resorts were already considered a high hazard business by the government agency that regulated occupational safety, and Bergen Mountain Resort had a topnotch rating. He wasn't going to blow that on a *perfect* moment.

He flipped on the lights, illuminating a quaint space with rustic furnishings.

"It's pretty bare bones in here."

Elle nodded and walked the perimeter of the cabin. At only five hundred square feet, it was a tight space. In line with their rebranding effort to show Bergen Enterprises' commitment to the environment, they'd worked with a local architect who'd designed the cabins using sustainable materials. This was the smallest unit, built for two guests and most likely where they were going to stay tonight.

He glanced out the window. Between the spring snowstorm and the bear situation, they weren't going anywhere. He took his phone out of his pocket and shot a text to his brother.

Weather turned fast. Elle and I are going to stay at the cabin and head back in the morning.

True enough. Even without the bear mess, backcountry snow-mobiling in whiteout conditions was a bad idea. And even if the snow let up in a few hours, there was no way they could make it back in the dark.

He was just about to pocket his phone when Bren responded.

Are you guys going to be okay? Want us to send ski patrol?

Jasper thought of Antonio, and a muscle ticked in his jaw. Fuck no, he didn't want patrol.

Don't waste the resources. We'll be fine.

The incoming text dots from Brennen rippled on his screen.

Man Feast fine? Bren wrote, adding a zucchini emoji.

Jasper stared at his brother's ridiculous reply. Man feast! Jesus, Bren!

He found the middle finger emoji and pressed send. Juvenile, but the quickest way to get his point across.

"Is there anything to eat? I'm starving."

He looked up to see Elle opening and closing the drawers in the cabin's kitchenette.

"I'm not sure. Maybe there are some leftovers. We've allowed the resort staff to stay up here to try things out. Kind of like a test run," he said, grabbing a few pieces of wood and starting a fire.

"What are you doing?" she asked.

"I'm making a fire. The power feed to the cabins is still a little spotty, and we'll need it to keep warm if the electricity goes out."

She cocked her head to the side. "How long do you think we're going to be here?"

He set another log in the hearth. "Between the weather and the honey buffet going on next to the sled, we'll need to sleep here tonight."

Her jaw dropped. "We're going to spend the night here, together?"

He hated that the idea of spending the night with Elle brought his cock to life. He shifted and focused on the fire. "I'll take the couch. You can have the bed in the loft."

Elle glanced at the ladder that led to the loft's landing. "We should call Abby and Brennen and let them know."

"I just texted with Bren. They know."

She crossed her arms. "You didn't think to ask me?"

"Under the circumstances, there was no choice. I made a decision."

She threw up her hands. "There's always a choice, and you should have at least asked. What did you think I'd say? Let's head out in zero visibility and hopefully not get eaten by a bear?"

He shrugged. "That's almost exactly what I thought you'd say."

She crossed her arms. "You think you've always got all the answers, don't you?"

He shrugged again. "I usually do."

She groaned and ran her hands through her hair. "There better be some liquor in here," she said as the lights went out almost as if on cue.

Lit by the fire, he watched her search the cabin.

"The staff isn't supposed to consume alcohol here. I've forbidden it."

She pulled a bottle out from behind an end table. "Well, thank the tequila gods, not everyone follows your explicit commands."

He shook his head. He'd check the log when they got back to the resort. Somebody was getting fired.

"And don't even think about firing whoever left it here. It was an act of kindness by the universe," she added.

Damn, it was like she was in his head.

He stood. "An act of kindness for who?"

"For me," she shot back, twisting off the cap and taking a swig. She held out the bottle. "Can you handle tequila, Mr. Fancy Pants CEO?"

"Can I handle tequila?" he grumbled then brought the bottle to his lips and gulped down the harsh liquid. "Jesus! What kind of tequila is this?"

"The cheap kind," she said with a thread of amusement.

He passed the bottle back, and she took it, the tips of her fingers sliding over his. The breath caught in his throat as the fire-light warmed her features, and her tequila moist lips glistened.

Damn this woman for being so infuriatingly alluring.

She took another sip. "You go forage for something to eat. I'll keep looking for contraband."

He nodded and opened the doors on a small buffet table. "Let me know if you find anything top shelf," he called over his shoulder. "We're going to have one hell of a headache in the morning if that's all we've got to drink."

He continued his search when he came upon the motherload. He pulled out the items. "Elle, we've got bottled water, Oreos, tortilla chips, and—"

"Salsa!" she called as a tinny, buzzing sound caught his attention.

"I found a battery-powered radio!" she said and popped an Oreo into her mouth.

He stared at her as she added a chip in with the cookie, closed her eyes, and hummed her satisfaction.

He picked up an Oreo and stared at it. He couldn't remember the last time he'd eaten junk food.

"Eat it!" she said, going for another cookie then washing it down with tequila.

He popped the chocolate treat into his mouth and hummed his own pleasure. "I forgot how good these tasted."

"Now, put an Oreo and a tortilla chip into your mouth at the same time," she instructed.

He grimaced. "That's disgusting."

"Suit yourself! I'll enjoy this salty-sweet feast all on my own," she said, delicately placing a chip on the cookie then attacking the strange food combination with the intensity of a pack of wild dogs.

He held her gaze then picked up an Oreo. He was not one to back down from a challenge.

Carefully, he set a small piece of tortilla chip on top of the cookie and stared at the concoction.

"There you go!" she said through a mouthful of food.

He took a bite. "Jesus, that's good!"

There had to be a rational explanation for why this tasted so fucking amazing. It had been twelve hours since he'd last had anything to eat. Cardboard would have tasted equally delicious. But then he looked at Elle, and he knew he was kidding himself. He chuckled and shook his head, staring at the cookie crumbs dotting her mouth.

He brushed his thumb across her bottom lip. "You eat like a toddler."

She watched him with a mischievous glint in her eyes. "Take off your coat and snow pants."

He was not expecting that.

"Why?"

Good God! Why was he even asking? He had track pants on beneath his snow pants. It wasn't like she was asking him to get naked.

"Just do it," she said, shimmying out of her snow gear.

She turned up the volume on the radio as a catchy little Latin beat filled the cabin. "If we're stuck here, we might as well do some salsa dancing."

He took a long pull off the tequila bottle. "You're kidding." He'd never salsa danced a day in his life.

Still facing him, she walked backward. No, not walked. Wearing only skintight black long underwear, she swiveled her hips to the beat and swayed in the center of the cabin.

"This song is called 'Brujería.' I learned to salsa to it on a trip to Miami," she said, doing a little turn that got his cock's full attention.

He stripped off his coat and removed his snow pants. "What does *brujería* mean?"

She extended her hand and beckoned him with her index finger. "Witchcraft."

Jesus, was it ever!

"Come here! I'll teach you the basic steps."

One hand on her waist and the other holding her hand, he gazed down into her eyes. His body stiffened. He could power the damn cabin with the electricity pulsing between them.

She adjusted his hand on her hip, sliding it a few inches lower. "You can totally do this. Just think quick, quick, slow."

"That makes no sense to me, Eleanor," he said, reasonably sure that was because the majority of his blood supply had abandoned his brain.

But nothing made sense. He didn't like her. She was everything he couldn't stand. She could ruin everything with the rebranding effort. But here he was, captivated and salsa dancing with her.

She chuckled. "Okay, I'll break it down. Step forward with your left foot, then keep your right foot where it is and kind of tap it like a rocking motion. That's the quick, quick part. Now, bring your left foot back to center. That pause is the slow part."

He followed her directions as she did the corresponding movements with the opposite foot.

She beamed up at him. "Perfect! Now, step back with your right foot and do the same thing."

He focused on the steps and her voice guiding him.

Quick, quick, slow.

Quick, quick, slow.

He moved like a thirteen-year-old at a middle school mixer. "I don't think salsa's for me."

She shook her head. "Salsa is for everybody. Don't think about the steps. Close your eyes. Listen to the beat. Let the music tell you what to do."

This must be witchcraft because, before he knew it, he'd closed his eyes and allowed the music to take over.

Elle gasped, and his eyes flew open.

"That's it!" she said through a wide grin. "Jasper Bergen, who would have thought you had rhythm!"

He tightened his grip on her hip, laced his fingers with hers, and repeated the movements.

He was dancing!

"Can I ask you something?" he said, relaxing into the beat.

"Anything."

"What's a hollow bunny?"

She leaned into him and laughed. "I've said that a few times today, haven't I?"

"Only when you were giving me an earful which seems to happen a decent amount."

She sighed. "It's like those chocolate bunnies kids get at Easter."

He frowned. "The gyp ones that aren't solid?"

"Exactly! But I take it back. Anyone who can salsa cannot be an empty shell. And despite your aversion to music, you're not a bad dancer."

He grinned, and the tension drained from his body. "My mom and dad liked to dance. My brothers and I hated it. We'd groan and tell them to stop. But it was really kind of sweet. We'd all be in the kitchen, and if I remember right, it usually happened when my mom was making scrambled eggs. Anyway, some cheesy song would come on the radio, and my dad would whisk my mom into his arms."

"So, you get your rhythm from your dad," she said, eyes twinkling in the firelight.

Warmth settled in his chest. "I guess I do."

Usually, any mention of his parents elicited a stoic, stony response.

But not tonight.

Not in this cabin.

Not with Eleanor Reynolds in his arms.

The song ended, and a slow ballad replaced the quick, quick, slow salsa beat. He pulled her in close, and they swayed together, his hand pressed to the small of her back, her cheek nestled against his chest.

"Did Abby mention anything strange to you today?" he asked before he could stop himself.

She hummed against him, a cross between a sigh and a chuckle. "Are you talking about the antithesis of the *man fast,* otherwise known as the *man feast*?"

He rested his chin on the crown of her head. "Your cousin and my brother really missed the mark on that. It's a crazy idea."

"So crazy," she replied.

"We're totally wrong for each other," he added.

She tightened her grip on his hand. "You're all bank statements and boardrooms."

He rubbed tiny circles against the small of her back. "And you're a fly by the seat of her pants irresponsible quasi-celebrity."

She glanced up at him through her eyelashes. "Quasi?"

He bit back a laugh. "Okay, I'll give you B-list celebrity."

He expected her to throw an insult or a pithy comeback at him, but Elle's expression grew pensive.

"Abby and Brennen might be crazy, but they're not wrong. At least, in my case, it's been a while."

"A while for me, too," he confided.

She chewed her lip. "If anything were to happen, and I'm not saying anything would. It would mean absolutely nothing."

"We're just two people trapped in a cabin," he said, the desire to kiss her growing fiercer by the second.

Her hand glided from where it rested on his shoulder, and she twisted her fingers into the hair at the nape of his neck. "It's biology."

He surrendered to her touch. "Simply the result of an adrenaline rush from almost being eaten by a bear."

"Bears, plural," she added, nodding her head as if they were building a case.

"Right, and a very, very long dry spell when it comes to..." He paused.

She nodded. "The driest. Like a desert. And I should know. I've been to the Sahara Desert, the Great Victoria Desert in Australia, and the Patagonia Desert in Chili. Did you know the Great Basin Desert is the largest desert in the States? It's one hundred and ninety thousand square miles. It borders the Rocky Mountains to the east. You may already know that since you own a good portion of Colorado."

He could listen to Elle Reynolds ramble all night, but his body had other plans.

"Eleanor," he said, breaking into her desert dissertation.

"Yes?" she breathed.

He cupped her cheek and brushed his thumb across her perfectly kissable lips. "Stop talking."

She held his gaze, eyes wide. "Okay."

He leaned in, and she pushed up onto her tiptoes. Her body slid against his, sending a jolt of lust straight through him, and stripped away any last threads of resistance. His lips crashed against hers as the smooth burn of tequila and the sweet bite of the chocolate mingled with her warm breath. It cast a spell, peeling away the layers of the uptight CEO and exposing the man hidden beneath the mask.

She sighed, and her lips parted, making way for their tongues to meet in a heated, frenzied rhythm. In a matter of seconds, this kiss had gone from zero to sixty. Gasping and hands twisting and pulling at their clothes, he guided her down onto the rug in front of the blazing fire. Initially, he'd hated these rugs. Shaggy and fluffy-white, the faux fur décor screamed gaudy Colorado wannabe.

Now, he planned on penning a personal note of thanks to the interior designer.

Elle lifted her shirt over her head and reclined back onto the rug. Her chestnut hair fell around her in gentle waves, and his heart nearly stopped beating. He'd never seen anything more beautiful in his life.

He ran his index finger from the tip of her chin, down her neck, and she arched into him as he worked his way past her sternum. He rested his finger on the lacy bra's clasp and took in the beauty that lay before him.

"Need any help with that?" she asked with a sexy smile.

He gave her his trademark smirk and undid the clasp with one flick of his hand.

She pushed up onto her elbows and gestured with her chin toward the table next to them. "Get the tequila."

He reached over and got the bottle. "Are you thirsty?"

She took the tequila from him, bit down on her bottom lip, and shook her head. "Nope, but I think you're going to be."

She tilted the bottle, sending a thin stream of the liquid between her breasts.

He'd never been thirstier a day in his life.

In the space of a breath, he had her on her back. He licked and sucked the spirits from her skin. Warm and sharp, the sensations rocketed through him as he massaged her breasts and skimmed his tongue over her tight peak.

"I think you've ruined tequila for me," he said against her skin.

"It's not top-shelf." She moaned, threading her fingers into his hair as he licked up every drop.

"This kicks top-shelf's ass any day."

He slid his hand up her body and pressed his thumb to her lips. She opened her mouth and grazed her teeth across the pad, then bit down harder. Pain and pleasure weaved together in a fiery tapestry of lust and carnal need, and a sweet rush of desire washed over him.

He released her breast and gazed up at her. "What was that bite for?"

She pressed a kiss to where she'd just sunk her teeth. "I wanted to remind you that I'm not sweet."

His cock twitched. "Good, because I don't like sweet."

She cupped her breast and massaged herself. "What do you like?"

He prowled her body. "Whatever the hell you are."

Her sexy smile returned. "I think you need to fuck me, Jasper Bergen."

"I think you're absolutely right, Eleanor Reynolds."

He pulled his shirt over his head then went to work, stripping off her long underwear and losing his track pants.

"Wow," she said, gaze locked on his chest.

He glanced down at himself. "What?"

She ran her fingertips across the hard plane of his abdomen. "You. This body. Who knew all this was hidden beneath those stuffy suits?"

"So, I won't hear you complaining about the rigidity of my exercise regimen?"

She held his gaze, and with her other hand, mimicked locking her lips shut with a key.

"Before you lose the key, we need to talk about protection."

She ran her finger down his jawline. "I'm clean and on the pill. Are you—"

"Clean as a whistle," he supplied, a little too eagerly. He was probably cleaner than a whistle for how long it had been.

"Of course, you are. I bet you've got your latest test results saved on your phone."

What the hell was wrong with that?

His expression must have said exactly what he was thinking because she chuckled and shook her head. But she wasn't laughing at him. The opposite.

"Nothing wrong with being a safety-man," she said with a grin.

"Safety-man," he echoed, taking her earlobe between his teeth. "That sounds like some kind of superhero. Do I get to wear a cape?"

She glanced between them and gripped his cock. "No, you don't need a cape. This sword will do just fine."

Sweet Christ!

She caressed him in long, rhythmic strokes as he slid his hand between her thighs. His index finger teased her entrance, slick with desire, and she bucked her hips. He rubbed his thumb over her sensitive bundle of nerves, tracing tiny circles. Elle gasped, riding his hand, but he needed more. He needed to feel her, fill her. Slide inside and experience the grip of her wet heat.

He wrapped his hand around her hand. She stilled and gazed up at him.

"Are you sure you want this? Are you sure it's okay?" he asked.

She watched him, and it was as if she could see into his soul. Then she reclined back onto the rug and lifted her hands above her head.

"Save me, Safetyman," she said in one hell of a mock damsel in distress voice.

He positioned himself at her entrance, his body begging to thrust inside. "I'm going to save you all night long."

"Good, because I could use a lot of saving," she purred.

That was all the consent he needed. He pinned her wrists above her head, putting her perfect breasts on display, and pushed his hard length past her delicate folds. Inch by inch, he spread her open and filled her completely.

All he wanted to do was fuck her hard like an animal, his body so ready, but he held back and met her gaze. "Are you okay, Elle? Am I hurting you?"

She rolled her hips. "You might kill me if you don't start moving."

A wolfish grin pulled at the corner of his mouth. "We can't have you dying on a Bergen property."

"Then you better get to work. I expect the same focus here as you'd give to a spreadsheet in your office."

"Eleanor Reynolds, you are going to get the full CEO treatment."

She laced her fingers with his. "I wouldn't expect anything less."

He pulled back then thrust forward, setting a demanding pace. A sheen of sweat covered their bodies as he worked her, pumping and grinding. Elle writhed beneath him and met him blow for blow, thrust for thrust.

He'd been with other women. He was no virginal light-weight when it came to the bedroom, but no woman had ever gotten his pulse racing like Elle Reynolds. The slap of their bodies coming together. The slide of his thighs against hers. Their hot, tangled breaths, meeting in scorching kisses. It was almost too much.

He pulled back and met her gaze.

She smiled up at him, her eyes telling him everything. Telling him that she wanted him as much as he wanted her.

She raised a hand and cupped his cheek. "Don't hold back, Jasper," she whispered.

Lost in her eyes, he complied. He emptied every ounce of his stoic, stony demeanor and allowed passion and lust to course through his veins. He gripped her ass, changing the angle of penetration and thrust deeper as the friction built between them.

"Yes!" Elle called out, her nails scraping across his shoulders.

Their bodies moved together like a well-oiled machine. Pistons firing. Gears churning. She tightened around him and called out, meeting her release. He doubled his pace, and his sweat-slick body prolonged her bliss, milking every drop of her pleasure until he couldn't hold back. With a primal growl, he pumped his hips and tightened his grip on her ass, owning her, coveting her, claiming her. He flew over the edge, falling, spiraling.

Letting himself go.

Letting Elle in.

After what could have been three minutes or three hundred years, she blinked her eyes open and gave him a sweet, sated smile. "That was…"

He brushed a lock of hair from her forehead. "Did I render the writer speechless?"

She sighed. "Oh, you rendered. You rendered big-time."

They stared at each other as a salsa beat serenaded them from the little radio.

He moved his hips from side to side in time with the beat.

"You remembered the quick, quick, slow," she said, matching the movement.

He kissed her neck. "I can promise you this, Eleanor. We're just getting started, and nothing about what I plan on doing to your body for the rest of the night is going to be quick."

CHAPTER 6

ELLE

Elle sighed as a sleeping Jasper tightened his grip on her hip. She nestled her head into the crook of his neck, shying away from the bright Colorado sunshine streaming in through the window and ran her index finger down the length of his torso. A naughty grin pulled at the corners of her mouth. After last night, if there was one thing she knew for sure about Jasper Bergen, it was that the man was true to his word.

There was nothing quick about the way he feasted on her body. There was nothing speedy about how he bent her over the back of the couch and took her from behind. Nothing hasty or hurried as she rode his cock, staring into his eyes, losing herself in his embrace.

And that ache. That sweet, deep ache between her thighs. She'd forgotten that well-fucked feeling. That place where your limbs hung loose and relaxed and your mind emptied of all its worries.

The last time she'd felt this way, she was with Tate. She tensed as guilt and shame overran the space in her head where peace and contentment had dwelled.

"Hey," came a low, gravelly voice.

Jasper.

"Hey," she echoed.

He ran his hand down her back. "How long have you been awake?"

She swallowed hard and pushed the thoughts of her past back into the dark corners of her mind.

"Not long."

He pressed a kiss to her forehead. "Are you hungry?"

She traced the V of his muscular torso. "A little, but I think we're out of food. You ate the last Oreo off my body somewhere between the couch sex and the chair sex."

He cupped her cheek. "That was one damned good…cookie."

She gasped in mock disbelief. "Is that your most poignant memory from last night? Eating Oreos?"

The dirtiest grin spread across his face, and she sighed. Artists should paint this man. Sculptors should carve him out of marble. No longer clean shaven, Jasper Bergen with a little stubble was the definition of sexy on a stick.

He rolled her body away from him and pressed his chest into her back. His hard length rubbed against her ass as heat pooled between her thighs, and her nipples formed tight peaks. He eased himself inside her, and her body welcomed the sweet penetration.

He kissed her neck. "Doing this is my most poignant memory."

Was it ever! She thought of her sad little vibrator. How was she supposed to go back to that?

Jasper reached around and found her sensitive bundle of nerves, and she forgot all about her pathetic dildo when he cupped her sex. He worked her body in rhythmic strokes as he made love to her from behind. Sweet and slow, their bodies fused. His hard, sculpted angles met her soft curves, melting together, moving as one. There was no learning his body. There was no awkward fumbling. They connected seamlessly, easily, naturally, as if they were made for each other.

Throughout the night, when they weren't tangled in the throes of passion, they'd talked and laughed. She even tried to teach him how to tango, but that ended in the chair sex, which she'd decided was the best way to end a dance lesson.

It was easy to be with this Jasper. The Jasper who wasn't solely focused on carrying the weight of Bergen Enterprises on his shoulders. But she was different, too. She'd let down her guard. She hadn't been in a relationship with anyone since Tate. She'd tried to meet men, tried dating, but nothing clicked. Nobody had come close to scaling the walls she'd erected around her heart until this stoic, stodgy CEO pushed all her buttons, and what she thought was searing hatred toward the man might just be…

No, she couldn't go there.

She rolled her hips and arched her back. Closing her eyes, she pushed away thoughts of what if and focused on the present moment, on Jasper's heated breath, warm against the shell of her ear. She reveled in the flex and release of his abdominal muscles, pressing against her as he thrust. And his cock. His glorious shaft. It fit her perfectly, finding that place deep within her that made her come with an intensity like nothing she'd ever known.

Jasper dialed up his pace, and she was no longer capable of coherent thought. He growled, and the gruff moan blanketed her in goose bumps. The sound, so primal, so sensual, it set her on fire. Like a bow pulled tight, quivering and begging for release, she reached back and weaved her fingers into his hair, anchoring herself to this man before she exploded into a million tiny pieces.

"Eleanor," he breathed, the word no longer reminding her of that pruny aunt. No, his low grumble infused those three syllables with sex and sweat and a yearning so deep it pierced her soul.

"Yes?" she answered.

He pressed his thumb against her swollen bud. "Tell me you want this."

She didn't think it could get any hotter until he busted out the dirty talk.

"I want it. I want it so badly," she answered.

"You won't be able to come again without fantasizing about my cock inside you."

He wasn't wrong.

His scent. His touch. His low, commanding words. He was everywhere. Making love to her. Holding her. Kissing her. Owning her. Worshiping her.

He pulled back, and with his next thrust, she flew over the edge. Weightless and lost in a place where only she and Jasper Bergen existed. Wave after wave of pleasure washed over her body as she tensed around his cock. He joined her, their bodies writhing, demanding more, begging for the rush to never end.

He wrapped his arms around her as their breathing slowed.

"Who would have thought?" he whispered.

She stroked his cheek. "Thought what?"

"This," he said, still buried deep inside her.

He was right. *This* was a lot more than what she'd bargained for when they talked themselves into Brennen and Abby's silly man feast.

And what exactly was this? She turned toward him, and he eased out of her. She kissed his cheek and smiled against the scrape of his beard. Barely twenty-four hours ago, she'd only known the clean-shaven dickhead version of Jasper Bergen.

Boy, what a difference a day makes.

She liked him like this, a little rough around the edges. She wanted to tell him that, but before she could get a single word out, he pressed his finger to her lips.

"Do you hear that?" he asked.

She stilled. "It's a snowmobile."

Jasper reached for his coat and pulled out his phone. "Shit!"

"What?"

"Brennen texted me about twenty minutes ago. He and Abby are coming up to check on us."

"Double shit!" she whisper-shouted, jumping up and surveying the state of the cabin.

Chairs turned over. Pillows and cookie crumbs littering every flat surface. A half-empty bottle of tequila propped against the wall.

"It looks like a cross between a frat house and a sex den in here," she said, grimacing at the sight of the cabin in the light of day.

He came to his feet and kissed the tip of her nose. "You look like a sex goddess."

She tried to run her fingers through her matted sex hair. "I must look a mess!"

His features softened. "I don't think you've ever looked more beautiful."

She cupped his cheek and brushed her thumb across his lips. He held her gaze and rested his hand over hers. He parted his lips to speak, but nothing came out—because there was nothing left to say. What happened here last night was over. Done.

The man feast had ended.

The hum of the sled grew closer.

"We better get cleaned up," he said, but those didn't sound like the words he wanted to say.

The longing in his gaze. The curl of his lips pulling into the saddest smile. Did Jasper want more? Could they extend the man feast? There were no set rules. For Christ's sake, it wasn't even a real thing. Excitement surged through her until she remembered what was at stake.

Her career.

Her livelihood.

Her ability to help her mother financially.

Her heart.

Elle's stomach dropped. She'd screwed the CEO of the company she was contracted to work for on every flat surface of the cabin six ways from Sunday.

She released a shaky breath. "Yeah, let's get dressed. They'll be here any minute."

She found her bra and long underwear then pulled on her snow pants. Silently, they worked their way around the cabin, righting chairs and sweeping up cookie crumbs. Jasper slid the tequila bottle behind the end table, and she repositioned the rug—

the place where their lovemaking had started and ended. Jasper had climbed up to the loft and brought down all the bedding, and that's where they'd stayed, cocooned in blankets and pillows, illuminated in the fire's orange glow.

"Toss me those pillows, Elle."

She glanced up and saw Jasper in the loft.

She nodded and got herself back into the game. "Sure thing," she said, running her hand over the rug's feathery surface one last time.

She threw him the pillows just as a gentle knock came from the cabin's front door.

Jasper climbed down the ladder and came to her side. He cupped her face in his hands, and she leaned in, pushing up on her tiptoes.

"One last kiss," he whispered.

A rush of joy and relief flooded her system. He bent, his lips hovering a breath above hers when another knock ricocheted through the cabin, and they froze.

"Elle! Jasper! It's just us," her cousin said with another gentle tap.

"What the hell happened to the snowmobile?" Brennen added, less gently.

Elle swallowed as Jasper released his hold, and she lowered herself down.

No last kiss.

"We should open the door," he said.

"Yes, we should," she agreed.

The door was only two steps away, but opening it felt like ending something that hadn't been given the chance to begin.

She glanced at Jasper, gave him a little smile, then turned the knob.

"Thank goodness you're all right! That storm was really something!" Abby said, giving her a hug.

Brennen followed his fiancée into the cabin. "What happened next to the sled?"

"What do you mean?" Jasper asked.

"Well, for one thing, you banked it pretty good. And for another, it looks like an animal ripped something apart next to it."

Elle nodded. "That's exactly what happened."

Brennen cocked his head to the side. "What happened?"

"Bears," she answered.

Abby's eyes went wide. "You saw bears?"

"Yeah, a mother and her two cubs."

"That's awesome," Brennen exclaimed.

"Were you scared?" her cousin asked.

"No, but they came up pretty fast, and I wasn't able to get my backpack. It fell off just as one of the cubs was coming over to investigate the snowmobile."

Abby walked into the cabin's kitchenette. "And you guys had to hole up in here. This place is adorable. What did you do all night?"

Elle glanced at Jasper who'd reverted to stony CEO mode. She shrugged. "Not much. The power went out, so we hit the sack early."

"We missed you both," Abby said, walking around the cabin. "We had quite a feast last night!"

At the sound of the word feast, Elle glanced at Jasper just as he looked at her. A spark ignited between them. A delicious secret. A hidden encounter. She felt her cheeks heat then turned her attention to Brennen, who seemed to be sizing them up.

"Harriet outdid herself on the menu," Abby went on. "We had pan roasted filet and seared scallops. Salad with pears and goat cheese with this amazing dressing. And dessert was to die for. There's this little German bakery near Kansas City that makes the most amazing strudels and sticky buns. They had tons of it overnighted to us."

Brennen picked up the carcass that once contained a few dozen Oreos. "Looks like you guys weren't completely without food."

"We survived," Jasper said in his boardroom voice.

"I'm sure you did," Brennen replied, leaning against the wall with a smirk.

If anyone was going to call them out, it was Brennen Bergen. Pre-Abby, the dude was a womanizing douche canoe. But just because he'd changed his ways didn't mean he couldn't suss out two people who'd spent the night screwing each other's brains out.

Abby went over to Brennen, and he wrapped his arm around her shoulder. She leaned into him.

"We should probably get back. Cadence and Bodhi just arrived, and we have our girls' spa appointment. Cadence is so excited for it."

"That's right!" Elle said. She had to shake this sex haze. It was time to work. She'd invited Abby and her cousin's teaching colleague, Cadence Lowry, to try out Bergen Mountain's new ladies' spa package as part of her work on the rebranding. Cadence worked full time and was a single mom to her sweet five-year-old son, Bodhi. If anyone deserved a spa day, it was her.

"Not a bad deal, getting paid to go to the spa," Jasper replied, but there was a naughty twinkle behind his judgmental glare.

A beat passed as Abby and Brennen seemed to be waiting for the Jasper and Elle catfight to begin.

"A girl's gotta make a living, and it sure beats staring at spreadsheets," she threw back.

Fighting with this man used to get her hot around the collar. Fighting with him now got her hot in other ways—far south of the collar.

Brennen clapped his hands. "My fiancée is right! We need to get back. There's a ton of fresh powder, and Gram, Grandad, and I are taking Bodhi out on the slopes. You're welcome to join us, Jas."

Jasper stiffened. "I've already lost a day of work. There's no way I can spend today on the slopes."

"Suit yourself," Brennen said, then gazed down at Abby, tilted her chin up, and pressed a whisper-soft kiss to the corner of her mouth. "Maybe we don't need to leave right this minute. We should think about spending some time up here."

Abby bit down on her lip. "It is quite cozy, and there'd be nobody around for miles."

"Think of all the things we could do here," Brennen added.

"Oh, I've already got a mental list going," she purred.

"Where did you come from?" Brennen asked, staring down at her cousin like he was ready to eat her for breakfast.

She tapped his chest. "You know, silly. Florida."

Abby and Brennen had fallen into a full-blown newly engaged post man fast love fest. Elle turned away. It was far too early to watch another couple's PDA and caught Jasper's gaze. He rolled his eyes, but a flash of amusement graced his hardened expression.

Jasper cleared his throat. "Bren, we get it. You snagged the sweetest girl in Denver, and now you guys are crazy in love. Can you put whatever this is on ice until we get back to the cottage? I've got a conference call in an hour."

Brennen gave his brother a wide grin. "One day, Jas, you won't be laughing at me for acting like this."

"Doubtful, but I'm very happy for you both, nonetheless," Jasper replied.

"Come on," Brennen said, taking Abby's hand and leading her out of the cabin. "We left our snowmobile down next to yours. We'll meet you guys there."

Elle waved to Abby. "Let me just make sure I didn't forget anything. We'll be down in a second."

She stood next to Jasper. "Thanks for always being so kind to Abby."

"I owe her. You know what Bren was like. Jesus, I should probably buy your cousin a mountain. That's how much money she's saved me in paying PR to clean up all of Brennen's messes."

"You called her the sweetest girl in Denver. I didn't think you liked sweet?"

The corner of his mouth raised into the hint of a smile. "I don't. I thought I proved that point five times last night."

"And don't forget about this morning," she chimed, her body buzzing.

His expression softened. "I'll never forget this morning."

"Are you guys coming?" Abby called from just outside the cabin.

Jasper gestured for her to walk in front of him. Elle's chest tightened, and her nose twitched. Was she about to cry? She was not a crier.

She and Jasper had one great night of amazing sex.

One man feast ordered up, and one man feast served. And served. And served.

She blinked and willed back the tears threatening to fall. It was good sex, and it was over. She glanced at Jasper. Placid expression. Stiffened posture. He was back to his old robotic self.

She sighed and passed through the doorway, listening as Jasper closed and locked the door behind them.

She worked her way down the slope toward the snowmobiles when Abby met her gaze and frowned.

"Do you want to ride with Brennen?"

She held her cousin's gaze as an eyeball conversation ensued.

Abby's gaze darted toward Jasper and then to the snowmobiles. It didn't take a genius to decipher her message. Her cousin was trying to give her an out if she'd had her fill of the eldest Bergen brother.

But the butterflies in her belly signaled she hadn't. Not even close. Not even another week locked inside that cabin, eating cookies and making love, would have been too much.

Elle wasn't about to reveal that, so she reverted to her snarky self.

"I've survived one night with tall, dark, and boring. I think I can make it through one more snowmobile ride with him."

"You know I heard that," Jasper said, passing her with a smirk.

"Yeah, I wanted you to hear that," she tossed back.

Brennen started his snowmobile, and Abby nodded. "Okay, if you're sure."

"I'll take good care of your cousin, Abby. Don't worry. I'll get her back to the cottage in one piece," Jasper said, gifting her cousin with a gentle smile.

Elle sucked in a tight breath as those damn tears threatened to fall again. Jasper Bergen shouldn't get bonus points for acting like a human and showing kindness to her cousin. Everyone should be kind to Abigail Rose Quinn. Abby was the closest thing to a saint she'd ever met. But seeing that softer, gentler side of Jasper didn't help her rein in her wildly fluctuating emotions.

The buzz of Brennen and Abby's sled heading back to the cottage pulled her from her thoughts. She joined Jasper at their snowmobile and surveyed what was left of her backpack.

"Looks like they enjoyed the honey," Jasper said, handing her a helmet.

"That it does."

"Was there anything in there that was important?" he asked.

She nudged a scrap of leather with the toe of her boot. "No, just paper, pens, my toiletry case, and you know, a jar of honey."

He nodded and got on the sled. "Are you ready to head back?"

Did he want her to say no? And what if she did say no? Would he toss her over his shoulder and carry her back inside the cabin? She swallowed hard and pushed the thought aside. Thanks to her father and then to Tate, she knew better than anyone not to believe in fairy-tale love stories.

She nodded and got on the snowmobile as Jasper brought the vehicle to life, the steady hum of the engine a welcome distraction. She wrapped her arms around his waist, and they set off, following Brennen and Abby's tracks.

After a good twenty minutes making their way through the snow, they rounded a bend, and the resort came into view. The snowmobile ride went by more quickly than when they'd headed up yesterday, and now that was all in the past as a blanket of fresh powder covered the evidence of their trip up. Jasper remained quiet during the ride, focusing on driving the snowmobile, his hands never leaving the grips.

Elle sighed. He'd made peace with the end of their man feast. She had to, as well. That was all there was to it.

She loosened her hold around his waist and was about to let go when he took his hand off the controls and pressed it to hers, keeping them in place, keeping her close. Despite their gloves, she could feel the heat of him. The warmth that had embraced her all night. She leaned her head against him as he tightened his grip, and that little squeeze set off a contagion of tiny explosions, causing her head to swim with memories of his touch, his lips, the scruff of his beard against her neck as he took her from behind.

They pulled up to the cottage and parked the snowmobile in the lower garage. She started to get off when Jasper turned around, doing a complete one-eighty to face her, and guided her body onto his lap. Elle gasped as their helmets bumped together.

Jasper took off his helmet, and she removed hers.

He gave her that wolfish grin. "I figure we have about three minutes before anyone comes looking for us."

She swiveled her hips. Even through their snow pants, his rock-hard erection pressed between her thighs.

She licked her lips. "What all did you have planned for these three minutes?"

He kept his expression neutral. "I was going to propose an extension to the man feast."

"A three-minute extension?" she asked, heat pulsing in her most sensitive place.

He inhaled sharply and dug his fingertips into her ass. "The number is open to negotiation. Three minutes is what's available now. I'd suggest we capitalize on that and continue negotiations, ideally with my cock buried deep inside you."

Wow! She'd given him a lot of grief for his boardroom skills, but that monotone commanding voice had her wet and ready for him within seconds.

Lust clouded his steel-blue eyes as he stared at her lips. "What do you say, Eleanor? Do you agree to an extension?"

She rested her hands on his shoulders. "I should probably consult my attorney regarding any contract, verbal or written."

His gaze glittered with lust. "That's my kind of dirty talk."

He slid her body flush with his and pressed a kiss beneath her earlobe when the door to the house flung open.

CHAPTER 7

ELLE

"That's the wrong way to ride a snowmobile!"

Elle looked over to see Bodhi Lowry, Cadence's son, staring at them, face scrunched together.

"Thanks for that tip," she answered, trying to scoot off Jasper's lap in the least obvious way possible—which there really wasn't.

The boy's face lit up. "Brennen just told me that he can ski backward! Can you drive a snowmobile backward?"

Jasper shook his head. "No, buddy, you should never drive a snowmobile backward. That would be very dangerous."

Bodhi cocked his head to the side. "Then, what are you doing?"

"Not what I'd like to be doing," Jasper answered.

The boy's eyes went wide. "You guys should come have breakfast. It's not the kind of oatmeal and banana breakfast Mom always makes me eat. It's like cake breakfast!"

A faraway look flashed in Jasper's eyes. "I'm sure it is. My grandparents eat pretty healthy until it comes to celebrations, and then they go a little overboard."

"I just ate a sticky bun the size of my face!" the little boy added.

"Case in point," Jasper replied, easing himself off the snowmobile then helping her down.

Bodhi turned and ran up the steps to the main house. "I'm going to get another before my mom tells me to stop."

"So much for that extension," she said, grazing her fingers over his erection hidden beneath his snow pants.

A twist of a smile pulled at the corner of his mouth. "Don't worry. Our man feast negotiations are ongoing, and I'm confident we'll find a way to reach a satisfactory outcome for both parties."

Holy hell! That sexy boardroom talk really did it for her.

He pressed his hand to the small of her back and guided her toward the steps leading into the cottage. They passed through the mudroom, left their snow gear there, and headed toward the voices coming from the kitchen.

"There they are!" Harriet said, standing in front of the kitchen island teeming with pastries. "Darlings, what a night you must have had!"

Elle bit back a grin. Very few people could pull off the whole "darlings" bit. Decked out in ski gear that cost as much as most people's mortgages and diamond earrings that probably cost as much as a lovely starter home, Harriet Livingstone Bergen could.

"What did you think of our rustic cabins, Elle? Did Jas show you all the energy-saving features?" Harriet's husband, Ray Bergen asked through a bite of strudel.

"Ray, darling, let them get something to eat! Come on, you two, there's plenty."

"There's enough strudel here to feed half the resort," Jasper said, passing by the pastries and taking a plain yogurt from the refrigerator.

"It's not every day that one of my grandsons gets engaged," Harriet crooned, squeezing Abby's hand. "Now eat, you both must be as hungry as a bear!"

"Funny you mention bears, Gram. Jas and Elle saw some around the cabin," Brennen said, cutting a thick slice of apple strudel and handing it to Bodhi on the down low.

"A real bear!" the little boy cried, his mouth stuffed with the pastry.

Cadence entered the kitchen and gave Elle a hug. "What's this about bears?" She glanced at her son. "And Bodhi Adam Lowry, what's that in your mouth?"

"Nothing," the boy said and scampered down the hall.

Elle smiled at the woman. "Jasper and I came upon a mother and her two cubs."

Cadence's eyes went wide. "That's amazing! I didn't know there were any living so close to the resort."

"There's a lake a little over five miles west in the National Forest where they usually congregate. They mostly stick to that area. We've rarely had any trouble with wildlife meandering onto the property," Ray added.

Brennen poured a glass of orange juice. "But isn't that the point of the cabins and why we picked that location? We wanted to give our guests the opportunity to experience a real back-country adventure."

Jasper spread peanut butter onto a slice of toast. "I'm not having the Bergen name and bear attack mentioned in the same sentence. I'll have our people get in touch with the rangers today just to be safe."

Cadence grinned and tapped Elle's arm. "Speaking of the Bergen name, I love that piece you wrote about your first experience with Bergen Mountain Sports."

"What piece?" Jasper asked, tone void of emotion.

Cadence's smile grew forced. "It popped up on my phone from one of the blogs I follow. I think they picked it up from an online magazine."

"When did you read this?" Jasper pressed.

Cadence's brow knit together. "Just this morning. I'm sorry. I didn't think this would upset anyone."

The room grew quiet. Elle glanced around and found all eyes on her. She turned to Jasper and had to stop herself from gasping. The passionate man who'd proposed extending the man feast was gone. Dead eyes. Tight expression. Every ounce of the man who had made love to her evaporated right in front of her.

"Why didn't you mention this, Eleanor? Everything that you write about this company goes through me. I thought you understood that?"

"Now, darling, let's not get ahead of ourselves," Harriet said.

Elle shook her head. "It was nothing, really."

Jasper's tone grew another degree colder. "Everything you write about Bergen Mountain Sports is something, Eleanor."

He stood in front of her in full judge, jury, and executioner mode.

Elle lowered her voice as her skin prickled. "It didn't have anything to do with the rebranding. It was a short piece about my first experience with the outdoors. I'd written it before I'd even signed on to work with your company."

"And you didn't think to mention it?"

She swallowed hard. "Honestly, Jasper, it slipped my mind."

He barked out a laugh. "Why should I be surprised by that."

Her cheeks grew hot. "You should be thanking me. It's a lovely article about what your stores and your ski resort in Fell's Peak, Vermont meant to me growing up. It's a sweet little puff piece. It's not a big deal."

He narrowed his gaze. "*It's not a big deal?* It's my family's reputation, which is quite a big deal."

Screw him. Well, not screw him. Not anymore. But screw him for thinking so little of her, especially after what she thought was a night that had transformed their combative tit-for-tat relationship.

Elle glanced at her audience and held back the verbal assault she wanted to unload, but she wasn't about to back down. "Maybe if you read it, you'd feel differently."

He leaned in, his face inches from hers. "I would have read it, if you'd brought it to my attention."

Unblinking, she held his gaze, as tension hung heavy in the kitchen, until a beeping cut through the air.

Abby patted her pockets then retrieved her phone and silenced the sound. She glanced around the room apologetically. "That's my alarm. Elle, Cadence, we should think about leaving for the spa."

Elle turned to Abby and did everything to block out the micromanaging robot standing beside her. "Thanks, Abs. I'll get my notebook, and then we can go."

Jasper blew out a breath and headed down the hall. "Enjoy the spa, Eleanor. Some of us have real work to do today."

————

"Elle, I'm so sorry. I had no idea Jasper would respond like that."

Elle leaned her head against the spa chair's headrest. "It's not your fault, Cadence. And as much as I hate to admit it, he may have a point. I am under contract with Bergen Enterprises."

She took a sip of her champagne and washed down the words, tasting of shame and regret. She hated that she needed this job. Even more than that, she hated that she'd almost let Jasper into her heart. She knew better than to trust him—or any man—when it came to her well-being. A one-night stand trapped in a cabin wouldn't negate the fact that he was a rigid, robotic CEO, and he'd never be able to give her what she needed. No man could.

"Still, I feel terrible."

The three of them sat with their newly moisturized, glossy hair, their cheeks as soft as a baby's ass, and freshly primped and polished toes and fingernails in the spa's relaxation room. Once they'd arrived for the ladies' BFF package and the staff got wind that Brennen Bergen's fiancée was there, they'd gotten the royal treatment which she usually didn't like, but today, she'd take all the extra cucumber sandwiches and champagne she could cram into her mouth. It was also the first time in three hours they'd been left alone and could chat privately.

She patted Cadence's hand. "Please don't feel bad. I'm serious. This is just the way it is between Jasper and me."

Abby leaned over. "I thought something might have gone on between the two of you last night, you know, with the man feast. This morning you looked really…"

Elle closed her eyes and sighed. "Exhausted? Haggard?"

"Happy," her cousin countered with a hopeful smile.

Cadence sat in the spa chair between the cousins and grasped their hands. "Rewind! What is a *man feast*? Does this have something to do with Abby's *man fast*?" Cadence asked as her phone chimed. She raised a hand. "Hold your explanation. I better check my phone, just in case it's Bodhi."

The woman reached for her cell, and her cheeks grew pink as she gazed at the screen.

"Okay, that is not a *making sure my five-year-old is fine* look. Did someone send you a dick pic?" Elle asked.

A wide grin stretched across Abby's face. "Nope, that's Cadence's *man find* face."

Cadence waved her off. "Oh, Abby, stop! It's nobody."

Elle narrowed her gaze. "I seriously doubt it's nobody. You should see yourself! You're all googly-eyed."

"No, I am not!" Cadence replied, looking very much googly-eyed and turning a darker shade of pink.

Elle threw up her hands. "Okay, ladies. Help a gal out. What the hell is a *man find*?"

Abby giggled. "You know the saying, a good man is hard to find?"

Elle sighed. "Oh, girl! I don't know it. I live it."

"Well, Cadence found one. She talks about him like he's a real find, but he's more like her pen pal. Get it? Her *man find*."

Elle pressed her fingertips to her now petal soft eyelids. "Jesus, Abby! You can't sum up all our man needs into a pithy two-word catchphrase!"

Abby sat back, looking quite pleased with herself. "Can't I? I'm pretty good at figuring out what you need, Elle."

"What do you think Elle needs?" Cadence asked, eyes darting between Abby and her phone.

Abby folded her hands in her lap. "Bren and I say she needs a *man feast* because Elle's had a pretty insane dating dry spell. And you, Cadence Lowery, have *found* a man. You just can't *find* him."

"What the hell does that mean?" Elle asked.

Abby picked up her champagne flute and gestured toward Cadence with it.

Cadence sighed. "I met someone on a mountain sports chat room a year ago, and we hit it off. I just don't know his real name or where he lives or what he does for a living."

"Or if he's a serial killer," Elle added. "Jesus, Cadence! It could be anyone!"

Cadence glanced at her phone then took a gulp of champagne. "It's not like I've shared my address with him. He doesn't really know anything about me other than the fact that I live in Colorado. We just seem to get each other. You know, like everything clicks. He's funny and really knowledgeable. He helped me with the kind of mountain bike I should get, and he knows a lot about hiking. If I had to guess, I'd say he works for the National Parks Service or something outdoorsy like that."

"Or he's holed up in his mother's basement, wiping Cheetos on his T-shirt, and masturbating to your messages!" Elle shot back as Abby and Cadence broke into laughter.

"That would be my luck," Cadence said, wiping giggle-tears from her cheeks.

The door opened, and the spa's director entered the relaxation room. "It sounds like you're having a wonderful time. How were your treatments?"

"They couldn't have gone better! Your staff is extremely knowledgeable and accommodating," Abby said, grinning ear to ear.

Elle smiled to herself. Her cousin was going to be the perfect billionaire's wife.

"And you, Miss Reynolds, how were your treatments?"

Word must have made it to the director that she was here in a work capacity. Elle met the woman's gaze. "I couldn't agree more with my cousin, and don't worry. I'm not here to critique or assess the spa."

"But you will be writing about your experience," the woman said with a cautious expression.

"True, but you don't have to convince me on how great Bergen Mountain is. I'm here because I want to share that information with the world."

The director nodded, her features relaxing a fraction. "It's our pleasure. We work to exceed the expectations of every guest."

"You've done that in spades," Elle answered.

"That's very encouraging," the woman said with a warm expression then turned to Abby and Cadence. "I'm sorry to cut your time short, but Miss Quinn and Miss Lowry's car has arrived to take you back to Bergen Cottage." The woman looked down at the clipboard. "But it looks like you, Miss Reynolds, are staying for a couples' massage package?"

Elle nodded. "Yes, I wanted to try it out so I could write about it accurately. I asked the resort staff to pick someone who worked here to join me."

"Yes, well," the woman said with a nervous smile, "he's arrived."

"Great! I can't wait to meet him."

The director's nervous expression crept back. "And there's another couple booked as well. They'll have their massages separately, but you'll all spend some time here in the relaxation room. I hope you don't mind."

"Not at all. Actually, I'd prefer it," Elle answered.

Some of her most interesting experiences came through the chance meeting of strangers.

"I'm glad to hear that." She turned to Abby and Cadence. "Ladies, I'll see you out, and Miss Reynolds, the staff member joining you is changing into a robe and will be in any minute."

Elle hugged her cousin and Cadence, waved goodbye, then fell back into the pulsing warmth of the spa chair and closed her eyes.

The door opened and closed, most likely her companion for

the couples portion of today's spa-palooza. She sighed heavily, wishing she could sink into the chair and not have to interact with anyone for the next two days.

She kept her eyes closed, listening to the deliberate footsteps of her spa buddy.

"I'm sorry to be rude. I'm Elle Reynolds. I really appreciate you coming to keep me company, but I've had one hell of a twenty-four hours, so I'm just going to veg out here for another minute."

"You and me both," came the low, growly tone of the most infuriating man on the planet.

CHAPTER 8

ELLE

Elle gasped and opened her eyes.

Jasper Bergen stood in front of her.

Her jaw dropped. "What the hell are you doing here?"

He glanced around the room and frowned. "I'm your couple's companion."

"Why you? I told them any staff member could fill in. Man or woman. I didn't care. I thought it would be a good way to get to know someone who worked at the resort."

"Then, I don't see a problem."

"What do you mean?"

"I'm a staff member."

"You own the resort!" she said on a frustrated breath.

Jasper maintained his detached demeanor. "Do you not see how that makes me part of the Bergen staff?"

She stared at the ceiling. If she looked at him, she might punch him in his pretty face. "How did you even know I was trying out the couple's package?"

"When I called the spa to check up on you—"

She shot up, her robe falling off one shoulder, almost exposing her breast. "Wait! You're checking up on me?"

She pulled the robe closed tightly around her body. What did it even matter? A few hours ago, this man was licking tequila off her boobs.

"You work for me. I'm entitled to know what you're doing."

She glanced at him—a glaring giant in a fluffy spa robe. If she wasn't so angry, this might be funny.

"Don't you have numbers to crunch? I didn't think you could spend another day away from doing *real work*."

"I can't have you running around unsupervised."

She grabbed his robe and pulled him down, so they were eye to eye. Unlike back at the cottage, his gaze wasn't cold and muted. Here, alone with her in this room, his eyes burned with intensity. His muscles twitched as if he were preparing to pounce. And sweet baby Jesus, after last night, she knew this man could pounce and pounce.

She blinked. Her chest heaving, she tried to find the words to tell him he was acting like a micromanaging over-controlling ass clown, but nothing came out. The electricity between them, the buzz of having him a breath away, left her mute. All she could think about was his warm breath against her cheek. His ripped torso pressed against her. His glorious cock making her feel things that no vibrator could ever do.

Jasper leaned in a fraction closer and tangled one hand in her hair while the other gripped her robe. "Do you have something you'd like to say to me, Eleanor?"

Damn her body! Damn every inch of her skin that begged for Jasper's touch.

She sucked in a shaky breath. "You are a complete—" she began but stopped when the door opened.

"Elle?" came a deep, familiar voice.

"Allen Parker?" Elle said, still tangled in Jasper's grip.

The attorney's eyes went wide. "Miss Reynolds? Jasper? I didn't realize you two were acquainted."

What the hell was her attorney doing here? The man glanced between them. Faces inches apart and clutching each other, they must look like horny teenagers ready to go at it and not grown adults ready to...

Wait!

What were they about to do? There was no easing into anything when it came to Jasper Bergen. There seemed to be a thin line between despising him and wanting to climb him like a tree and hate fuck him into the ground.

"Allen?" Jasper said as if he couldn't believe the man was real.

"Oh, Jasper, dear! It's so good to see you! It's been ages!" came the singsong voice of a woman entering the room.

"Marla?" Jasper replied. He looked like he was stuck in the twilight zone.

Jasper untangled his hand from her hair, and Elle released her death grip on his robe. He took a step back, his gaze bouncing between the new arrivals.

Elle swallowed hard, and her stomach dropped. Allen wouldn't mention her dire financial situation, would he? No, attorney-client privilege and all that jazz. She steadied herself and pasted on a grin when this Marla lunged forward and wrapped Jasper in a warm embrace.

"Dear, Jasper! It is so good to see you! My goodness! It's been years, hasn't it, Allen?"

Allen Parker nodded, taking a more measured approach to this encounter—thank goodness.

The woman turned to her. "I'm Marla Parker. Allen and I were dear friends of Jasper's parents." She reached up and cupped Jasper's cheek. "You look so much like your father." She turned away from Jasper and met her gaze. "Are you Elle Reynolds?"

"Yes, I am."

Marla pressed her hand to her heart. "It's so nice to meet you. I've read all your books. I'm a huge fan."

Elle released a relieved breath. "Thank you!"

Marla glanced around the room. "Let's sit! What a treat this is! Jasper, I had no idea you were with Elle Reynolds. And aren't they just like Griff and Hannah," the woman said to her husband with a wide, playful grin. "Those two couldn't keep their hands off each other either."

Elle glanced at a shell-shocked Jasper and hooked her arm with his, guiding him over to a pair of couches where they joined the Parkers.

"What brings you to the spa?" Elle asked, keeping Jasper in the corner of her eye.

"It's our fortieth anniversary, and while Allen would rather be up at our ranch tending to the beehives, he's indulging me in this spa adventure."

Allen wrapped his arm around his wife. "I don't think a couples spa treatment every couple decades is too much to bear."

Marla patted her husband's knee. Then her features grew pensive. "Hannah and Griffin would be celebrating their fortieth anniversary this year, too, had they not passed."

Jasper didn't move, didn't blink. Elle reached over and took his hand and held back a gasp when not only did he allow her to hold it, he held onto her as if his life depended on it. The man looked as if he were drowning, and all she wanted to do was save him.

She smiled at Marla and steered the conversation in another direction. "Are you going to get in any skiing while you're here?"

Allen tightened his grip on his wife. "We plan on hitting the slopes tomorrow, thanks to Jasper."

"What do you mean, thanks to Jasper?" she asked.

"I owe Jasper a debt of gratitude," Allen answered. "If it weren't for him, Marla wouldn't be with us today."

"You don't know the story?" Marla asked. "I shouldn't be surprised. Jasper was always so humble. It has to be twelve years ago now. Our family had spent the day skiing here at Bergen Mountain. Allen and our boys were ready to call it a day, but I wanted to get in one more run. It was almost my last."

Elle leaned forward. "What happened?"

"I was coming down Harriet's Descent, one of the more difficult runs on the mountain, but I'd done it plenty of times. Well, a snowboarder came out of nowhere, and before I knew it, I was tumbling down the slope. Jasper was on ski patrol and was the first to find me."

"Were you hurt?" Elle asked, surprised when it wasn't Marla who answered.

"At first, it just looked like she'd had a bad fall," Jasper said, quietly, breaking into the conversation.

Marla nodded. "But then you noticed that I didn't recognize you. I've known Jasper his whole life. He said, 'Mrs. Parker, it's Jasper Bergen. Are you all right?'"

Jasper swallowed hard. "And you said, 'You can't be Jasper Bergen. He's only a baby.' That's when I knew there was a good chance you had a head injury."

Marla smiled. "That's when Jasper radioed in for the sled, and he insisted I be airlifted back to Denver."

"And a good thing he did," Allen continued. "Marla had a subdural hematoma. Had she not gone into emergency surgery as quickly as she did, she probably wouldn't be with us today."

Jasper's grip tightened on her hand. "I was just doing my job."

Marla teared up. "You're the reason my boys still have their mother, Jasper Bergen. That's not just doing your job, dear."

They sat quietly, Marla wiping her eyes and Jasper gripping her hand, when a gentle knock broke through the silence.

"Mr. and Mrs. Parker, your treatment room is ready."

"Oh, my goodness," Marla said, coming to her feet. "I didn't mean to get all emotional. Let's not wait so long to see each other again, Jasper. We'll have to do dinner soon. I don't think we've seen you since..." Marla trailed off.

Allen extended his hand to Jasper. "It's good to see you, son."

Jasper stood and shook the man's hand. "You, too, Allen."

Marla went to Jasper and hugged him, and Elle watched as he robotically reciprocated.

The Parkers left the room, and Jasper dropped onto the couch and leaned forward.

She sat next to him, and before she could say a word, he took her hand and laced their fingers together. This moment felt so raw, so fragile. Holding his hand was like trying to keep a snowflake from disappearing into an avalanche. But he didn't need her pity or her sympathy. He needed her. Every cell in her body was sure of it.

Elle tilted her head, met his gaze, and gave him the hint of a smile. "So, you weren't always a buttoned-up control freak? You actually used to help people?"

Jasper chuckled, his stony exterior peeling away. "I've always been the most reserved of the Bergen brothers, but, yeah, I used to be—"

"Less of an asshat?" she supplied.

"A little less." He caught her gaze, and those steel-blue eyes held her captive. "Thank you, Elle."

"For what?"

He stared down at their joined hands. "You know. For what you did with the Parkers. For steering the conversation away from my parents."

"It seemed like a difficult topic."

His cool CEO exterior vanished, and in its place, she saw a man. A real man with pain so deep it took her breath away.

He squeezed her hand. "I couldn't save them, Elle. I'd helped dozens, maybe hundreds of people the four years I was on ski patrol. I even had EMT training. I'd just been accepted to med school. But none of that mattered. I couldn't save them."

"What do you mean?"

Jasper released a shaky breath. "The world knows that Griffin and Hannah Bergen died in a car accident. What they don't know is that my brothers and I were in the car ahead of them. It was right after Bren had won big in the Winter X Games. Cam, Bren, and I were riding together, and my parents were following behind us. The games weren't at Bergen Mountain that year. We probably should have stayed at the resort and driven home the next morning, but we wanted to get back to the cottage. It was our favorite place as kids, and we wanted to go there and celebrate. We had to take the back roads home because the main pass was closed due to ice. It was just us out there on the road. Bren, Cam, and I were screwing around when a deer came out of nowhere. We stopped as fast as we could, but it caught my dad off guard, and to avoid hitting us, he overcorrected, and their car went off the side of the road."

"Jasper, I'm so sorry."

"I climbed down. They'd fallen a good fifty yards. My dad had no pulse by the time I got there."

"And your mom?"

He rubbed his thumb over her knuckles as if he were trying to rub out the memory. "On patrol, we're taught to check a patient's level of alertness. We ask if they know who they are, where they are, and see if they know when they are?"

"I don't understand the *when they are* part?"

He gave her a sad smile. "Remember how Marla was confused and thought it was twenty years ago when I found her after her fall?"

She nodded.

"My mom was the same way. She thought I was my dad. She kept saying, 'Griff, Griff, check the boys. Check the babies. Check our little stars.' That's what she called us when we were small."

He paused, and she gave his hand a little squeeze, a kinesthetic nudge letting him know it was safe to go on.

He swallowed hard. "The doors were smashed in. I couldn't even get her out of the car. I couldn't start CPR. She died right there, thinking she was talking to my dad, worried that my brothers and I were hurt."

"I'm so sorry, Jasper. I'm so sorry that happened."

He nodded but said nothing.

She met his gaze. "I've been all over the world, and I've met lots of people from many different cultures. There are so many things that separate us, but there's one thread that weaves us all together."

"What's that?" he asked with a whisper.

"Love. Your parents loved you. They wouldn't want you carrying this burden."

He nodded, more to himself than to her. "You always seem to know what to say—even if it's to call me out."

She released a nervous laugh. "If we're taking a time-out from verbally pummeling each other, I should apologize. I'm sorry about the article. It blindsided you, and I should have given you a heads-up."

He rubbed circles into her palm. "I read it after you left."

The butterflies erupted in her belly. She only wrote for one person, but now it looked like there might be two people on this planet whose approval she craved. "And?"

He cracked a wry grin. "It wasn't bad."

"Wasn't bad?" she echoed with mock incredulity.

He took a lock of her hair and stared at it as he twisted it around his finger. "I see why people like you. You're writing pulls them in. It's like you want the reader right there with you, experiencing what you're going through firsthand. Your words are enchanting. You, Eleanor Reynolds, are bewitching." He released the lock of hair and cupped her face in one hand, tilting her head up. He pressed a whisper-soft kiss to the corner of her mouth. "How do we always end up like this?"

She sighed. "Like what?"

"Me, unable to maintain my hollow bunny mask, wanting to peel off your clothes and sink deep inside you."

She hummed her pleasure as he kissed her cheek and then her earlobe. "Remember, asshat, you can't be a hollow bunny if you can salsa. And I would be willing to admit that whatever this is, it's a hell of a lot better than wanting to claw each other's faces off," she answered, melting into his touch.

The pendulum inside her heart had swung again. One minute, she wanted Jasper Bergen exiled to the North Pole, the next, she wanted to wield a sword and protect him from his demons.

"Must be your witchcraft," he whispered.

"Brujería," she breathed as his lips brushed against hers.

Just then—someone who didn't happen to be her or Jasper—cleared their throat. "You must be here for the couple's massage," came a woman's voice with a thick German accent.

They froze.

Jasper smiled against her lips. "I forgot where we were."

"Yeah, me too," she answered, coming back from that place where only the two of them existed.

They pulled apart to find two women grinning at them. Standing almost six feet tall with their blond hair pulled into tight buns, each looked like a poster girl for an eastern European shot put competition.

"I am Helga, and this is Inga. We'll be your massage therapists today."

Jasper tensed. "I'm just here to watch."

Inga scrunched up her face. "We don't allow that at the Bergen Spa, sir."

He shook his head, emphatically. "No! I'm sorry. That sounded creepy. I just don't do massages."

Inga looked at her counterpart. "The reservation says you do."

Elle bit back a smile. "I booked the thirty-minute couple's massage. It's the shortest one they offer. Come on! Push your limits. Take a step out of your comfort zone. You may be surprised by what you find."

He stared at her as if she'd just turned water into wine.

"What?" she asked.

"Someone else has given me that advice before."

The air in the room shifted. This meant something to Jasper. She held his gaze, unable to decipher what he was thinking, then gave him her most bewitching smile.

"It's good advice. You should take it."

CHAPTER 9

JASPER

"People like this?"

"Yes, people like this," Elle answered with a relaxed sigh.

Jasper shifted under the thin sheet separating his ass from mooning Helga as she kneaded his shoulders like they were bread dough. He sucked in a tight breath. He was fine being naked with Eleanor Reynolds. What he wasn't digging was the addition of the massage therapist wonder twins.

"Just close your eyes and focus on your body," she said on a dreamy exhale.

"If I close my eyes, I won't be able to focus on *your* body."

Elle's eyes were closed, but a sexy grin pulled at the corners of her mouth.

That wasn't a lie. The only thing getting him through this massage nightmare without turning into a complete sour puss was that he was lying on a table, inches away from her. Her head rested on her crossed arms as one of the therapists rubbed cream on her back, and he could have stared at her for eternity.

She'd twisted her hair into a loose bun, and he gazed at the curve of her neck, the soft angles of her shoulder blades, and the sweet curl of her lips. She smiled in her sleep, too. He'd stroked her cheek and watched her last night. Lit by the fire, her tousled hair, her lips, red and plump from his kisses, she looked like something out of a dream. A dream he hadn't realized he'd had.

He reached out and tucked a lock of hair behind her ear.

"You're not concentrating," she whispered.

He ran his fingertips down her jawline. "Oh, I'm concentrating."

The dim treatment room smelled of vanilla and honey as a gentle, soothing rhythm of some New Age tune floated through the air. He inhaled and exhaled, taking in the sweet scent, unable to look away from her.

Seeing the Parkers had thrown him for a loop. They'd been a huge part of his life growing up. Birthday parties. Holiday celebrations. He'd skied with their kids hundreds of times during his childhood. But after his parents died, he'd cut them out of his life. Besides work, he'd shunned everything that reminded him of his parents. The fun. The love. The good times. He'd shut them out. He'd never even spoken of his parents' death. His brothers didn't even know their mother's last words.

But Elle did, and surprisingly, that didn't scare him.

In fact, all he wanted to do was take her in his arms and tell her about all the little things. Eating hamburgers piled with pickles with his family on the mountain after a long day racing down the slopes. Cannonball contests in the pool. Nights where they'd snuggle together and watch old movies.

He'd locked it all away, hidden it behind a punishing schedule and a rigid drive in pursuit of one single goal: ensuring the Bergen legacy.

"You are quite tense, Mr. Bergen," the therapist said, massaging the muscles at the base of his neck.

"Yes, Helga, I think Jasper could use some deep tissue work," Elle chimed.

His eyes went wide. "Nothing deep, Helga. Shallow is perfectly acceptable."

Elle chuckled.

"Are you laughing at me?" he asked through a grin.

She opened her eyes and met his gaze. "No, but I think you're starting to grow on me."

"Starting?" he teased.

Inga scooped out a handful of lotion and rubbed it across Elle's back. "We're about finished, Miss Reynolds. I'm applying the vanilla cream. It's completely organic. You could even eat it with a spoon if you wanted to."

Elle licked her lips, and suddenly, he was very fucking hungry.

Helga clapped her hands. "And that is all for you, Mr. Bergen."

Thank Christ!

"What happens now?" he asked.

"We'll give you some time to relax. There's no rush to leave."

Music to his ears and to his throbbing cock. And no wonder he was tense! Lying next to a naked and moaning Elle—unable to have her—while a large German woman squeezed his appendages for thirty minutes constituted as torture in his book.

The massage therapists left the room, and Elle pushed up onto her elbows. "Are you thinking what I'm thinking?"

He gave her a wolfish grin. "If you're thinking we need to make sure that cream is edible, I'm your man."

She gestured with her chin toward the fancy container containing the vanilla lotion. "What are you waiting for?"

He slid off the massage table, wrapped the sheet around his waist, and picked up the delicate jar. Twisting off the lid, he set it aside and dipped his index finger into the cream.

"Well?" she asked.

"You tell me." He pressed his finger to her lips. Elle opened her mouth and sucked on the tip of his finger, sending a jolt of lust straight to his already aching balls.

"Mmm," she hummed. "It's sweet. You should try it."

"That's what I'm about to do." He traced a line with his tongue from the nape of her neck down to the base of her spine.

Fucking ambrosia.

She looked over her shoulder. "What do you think?"

What did he think? He couldn't think. All his senses on overload, he reveled in her taste, her touch, her scent. Years spent shunning pleasure had left him dry and withered—a man dying of thirst in a desert of his own design. He pressed a kiss to each of her shoulder blades, and she sighed, the sound washing over him like sweet summer rain, soaking his wilted soul.

"I think this is the best part of the massage," he answered.

She sat up. "You know how après-ski is when everyone has drinks after a day on the slopes."

He nodded, unsure of where she was going with this.

"Maybe you're just an *après massage* kind of guy."

He sat down next to her and kissed her shoulder. "I couldn't agree more."

A devious twinkle sparkled in her eyes. "But I don't want you to abandon massage altogether. Can we try something?"

"Does it involve that cream?"

The tip of her tongue wet her lips. "Yep." She stood and patted the massage table. "I need you to lie down on your back. You'll also need to lose the sheet."

That was not a problem. He pulled at the thin fabric, allowing it to pool at his feet and stood in front of her.

"Somebody's ready for a happy ending. I had no idea Helga had such an effect on you," she said, staring at his hard length.

"Helga did not do this to me," he countered.

She cocked her head to the side. "No?"

He bit back a grin. "It was Inga."

She gasped in mock surprise. "Did Jasper Bergen make a joke? Is there a sense of humor buried deep beneath that growly CEO exterior?"

He cupped her cheek. "Would you like to know what I would like to be buried deep inside?"

A sexy smile pulled at the corner of her mouth. "Oh, I've got an idea. Lie back."

He reclined onto the table, finally able to relax now that Inga and Helga were gone. But it was more than that. It was Elle. With her, he was different. The one-dimensional life he'd lived these past ten years couldn't exist on the same plane as Elle Reynolds.

There were no tasks to be marked off a list—no cost-benefit analysis.

Everything here was fresh and unscripted. Multidimensional and layered. For Christ's sake! He'd salsa danced last night, and this morning, he'd nearly made love to her on the snowmobile.

"Are you ready?" she asked, holding up the jar of edible cream.

"Do I have any say in what's about to happen?"

She dropped the sheet draped around her body. "Nope."

"Would you like a suggestion?"

She walked around the massage table. "You're not the CEO in here, Mr. Bergen."

He bit back a grin. "I technically am."

She stood at the end of the table then climbed onto it, scaling his body before settling herself on his torso. She raised her hands and started waving them around as if she was cleaning off some invisible surface.

"Should I be concerned?" he asked, skimming his hands over her ass.

She grinned. "I'm erasing your story."

"It's that easy?"

She met his gaze. "Dean Largecox entered Jemima Sex Kitten's office."

"Who the hell are Dean and Jemima?"

She winked. "That's us."

He chuckled. This woman! "Are you narrating a porno?"

She lifted her hips. "This, Mr. Largecox, is a work of *erotic* fiction." She took him into her hands and positioned the tip of his hard length at her entrance. "Names, characters, places, and incidents are either the product of the author's imagination or are used fictitiously."

Holy fuck! She was making a legal disclaimer sound sexy as hell.

She lowered her body, enveloping him in her tight heat. "Any resemblance to actual events, locales, or persons, living or dead is entirely coincidental."

He pressed his fingertips into her supple skin. "What does Dean Largecox do for a living?"

Elle closed her eyes and rolled her hips. "He's a lumberjack."

"What about Jemima Sex Kitten?"

A naughty grin bloomed on her lips. "She's the CEO of the lumberyard."

It wasn't that much of a stretch. Buried deep inside her, he was ready to give her the controlling shares of Bergen Enterprises.

She picked up the jar, dipped her finger inside, and rubbed the cream onto his chest. "Your skin gets so dry chopping down all that hard wood. Let's get you nice and moist."

She rocked her body, riding him in smooth, measured strokes. Her back arched and her breasts bobbed gently with each thrust.

She was poetry in motion.

Or in their case, erotica in motion as he guided her body, dialing up the pace as his thumb rubbed her sensitive bundle of nerves.

"I see you've brought me a special piece of your hardest wood." She moaned.

"Elle?" he bit out, growing closer to release.

"Yeah?"

"I secretly always wanted to be a lumberjack," he growled, setting a heated, frenzied pace.

"I can tell," she replied and pressed her palms to his chest as their bodies met in a feverish, sensual slap of skin on skin.

"Look at me, Eleanor," he demanded, the pressure building.

She met his gaze.

"I want to watch you fall apart," he whispered, tightening his grip on her ass.

Her lips parted as her body tensed, and she flew over the edge and met her release. Listening to Elle moan his name, he followed her as wave after wave of warmth rushed through him. He pumped his hips, lengthening her orgasm as they hovered in that place made only for the two of them, gazes locked.

No one brought out this side of him. He didn't even know he had this side of him.

"Jasper," she breathed, part prayer, part demand.

She rolled her hips once more, then collapsed onto his chest. Breathing hard, she tucked her head in the crook of his neck, and he wrapped his arms around her. Still connected, they stayed like that, blanketed in vanilla and honey and cocooned in the golden glow of the treatment room.

"You're a very convincing lumberjack," she whispered against his neck.

He sighed and tightened his grip. "You're a damn good CEO, Jemima Sex Kitten."

"Did you like that?" she asked.

He stilled. He liked it more than she'd ever know. It was as if she'd taken his hand and allowed him to step outside himself. Outside the pain. Outside the guilt. She'd opened a window and bathed him in the light of letting go.

"Yes," he whispered.

She shifted her body and stroked his cheek. They gazed at each other, frozen in time until a gentle knock cut through their delicious sex haze.

"Your car's here, Mr. Bergen," came a voice from the other side of the door.

"Thank you. We'll be right out," he called, harnessing his CEO tone as Elle's body tensed. He stroked her hair. "What is it?"

"We probably shouldn't mention this to anyone—especially Abby or Brennen since they already think…" she trailed off.

She was right. This was insane but so was cutting himself off from anything that brought him even an ounce of pleasure—and then he remembered their arrangement. The man feast.

He shifted their bodies and sat up, keeping Elle on his lap.

"There's nothing to mention. This is the man feast extension we discussed."

"Right! An extension. Like if you happened to sneak into my bedroom tonight. That would be…"

He kissed her neck. "Simply an extension of the man feast extension."

She bit her lip. "A double extension."

"Is that something you'd be open to, CEO Sex Kitten?"

"Oh yes," she purred.

"You know all those pastries my grandmother had flown in?"

She nodded.

"I'm going to sneak into your room tonight, and we're going to reenact the Oreo situation."

She traced his abdominal muscles. "Except with strudel?"

He ran his hand down her silky-smooth back. "Every last slice of it. The man feast is on."

CHAPTER 10

JASPER

J asper opened his bedroom door and stepped into the darkened hallway. It had been years since he'd been here with a house full of guests. They'd grilled hamburgers and chicken breasts, and the savory smell lingered with the scent of the hickory wood popping and crackling in the fireplace.

He and Elle had gotten back just as the group had gathered to eat. He'd worried someone would have inquired as to why they'd returned to the cottage together. But no one said a word. With the excitement of Brennen and Abby's wedding plans and everyone enjoying having Bodhi in the house, no one seemed to notice Elle's kiss-swollen lips and mussed hair.

But holy fuck, he did.

The entire group had stayed up chatting, sitting around the fire pit, roasting marshmallows like they used to do when he was Bodhi's age.

The blessing of being a closed-off hollow bunny was that no one expected him to contribute much to the conversation. In the firelight, he'd watched Elle all evening. Watched her gesture and hold the group's attention as she enchanted everyone with her tales of travel to Tibet and Thailand.

Brujería. Witchcraft. Whatever the hell it was, it worked.

A little over a day ago, the thought of this woman contributing anything worthwhile to Bergen Enterprises seemed as likely as a blizzard in July. And while he couldn't relinquish all creative control, he knew that was because when he was with her, her witchcraft transformed him into someone else. Something more than the hard-driving workaholic.

It made him whole.

This silly man feast. This crazy contractual way to justify being with her, touching her, making love to her, was one of the smartest business decisions he'd made.

He took his phone out of his pocket and checked the time. At almost quarter to one, he was reasonably sure everyone had fallen asleep until the door next to his swung open and a wild-haired Bodhi Lowry stared up at him.

"Where's my mom?"

He patted Bodhi's shoulder. "She's asleep, buddy—just like you should be."

The boy scrunched up his face. "Why aren't you asleep? Did you have a bad dream, too?"

Jasper scanned the darkened hallway. "No bad dreams. I was…thirsty."

Not a complete lie.

The boy's eyes widened. "I'm thirsty, too! Will you get me some milk? Mommy always gets me a glass of milk then sings me a song when I wake up from a bad dream."

Jasper glanced down the hallway at Elle's door. "How about this. I don't think I'm as good of a singer as your mom, but I can help you out with the milk."

"Okay," Bodhi answered, taking his hand.

Jasper stilled as memories of his father came back to him. How many nights had he walked hand in hand with his dad down this very hallway after waking from a bad dream? Like Bodhi, he'd had nightmares as a child. Run of the mill generic monsters under his bed or something scratching in his closet, but his father was always there, gently waking him, softly letting him know he was safe in bed.

Bodhi looked up at him. "Will you stay with me?"

"Sure, bud," he answered, guiding the boy down the hall and into the kitchen.

He flicked on the light then stopped. Elle met his gaze, holding a plate piled with apple strudel slices.

She glanced at Bodhi and bit back a grin. "Are you guys here for a midnight snack, too?"

Elle's hair hung in loose waves, and she wore a pair of sleep shorts, fuzzy slippers, and a worn gray Fell's Peak Ski Resort T-shirt, and his pulse kicked up.

She'd never looked more lovely.

His mind flashed to Sunday mornings. A day no different than any other for him. Up early. Punishing workout. Starched shirt. Yogurt and peanut butter toast. But instead, he pictured those slippers thrown haphazardly on the floor next to his bed—the bed where she slept in his arms, her hair tickling his chin as she sighed in her sleep and cuddled in close to him.

"Jasper, can we have a snack with Elle?" Bodhi asked, pulling him from this alternate universe where Elle Reynolds belonged to him.

"Yeah, let's have some milk and strudel, too," he answered, unable to pull his gaze away from her.

Elle led Bodhi over to the couch in the great room overlooking Bergen Mountain while he poured three glasses of milk.

He carried the cups into the room and found Bodhi cuddled in close to Elle. Outlined by the moonlight, she patted his head and hummed softly. This is what he must have looked like on the nights when his mother would join them on the couch after he'd woken up from a nightmare. He'd tried so hard to stay awake, wanting to savor the moment, warm and safe tucked between his parents, watching the beams of light from the snowcats traversing the dark side of the mountain.

He sat down next to Bodhi and handed the boy his glass.

The youngster took it with two hands and gulped down the milk.

Elle patted his knee. "You're a thirsty bird."

Bodhi rubbed his wrist across his mouth, wiping away the milk mustache. "My mom says I'm a milk machine."

Jasper held up his glass. "I'd say she's right. Do you want mine, too?"

With a nod of his head, Bodhi handed Elle his empty cup and started in on his second glass. He drained the liquid, pulled the cup from his lips, then released a rather impressive burp.

Elle chuckled. "Do you feel better?"

The boy nodded, eyes growing heavy.

"Do you want me to take you back to bed?" Jasper offered.

Bodhi shook his head. "I'm still scared."

Elle rubbed the little boy's shoulder. "What was your bad dream about? My mom always says talking about a bad dream will make it less scary."

"In my bad dreams, I'm falling and falling," the boy answered.

Elle pursed her lips. "And then you wake up before you hit the ground, right?"

He nodded.

She wrapped her arm around him. "You don't need to be frightened by that one. It's just a skydiving dream. Do you know what skydiving is?"

A look of wonder crossed Bodhi's face. "Yeah! Have you ever done it?"

Elle nodded. "A bunch of times! I did it not long ago when I was in Thailand for my job."

Bodhi turned to him. "Have you ever done it, Jasper?"

"No, Bodhi, I like riding in airplanes. But you'll never see me jumping out of one."

"So, you'll never try it?" the boy pressed.

"No."

Jasper schooled his features. Honestly, was life so boring that people needed to jump out of planes? The entire skydiving industry seemed like a giant liability.

Elle leaned in toward Bodhi, conspiratorially. "Jasper just doesn't know what he's missing. Now, I'm going to tell you what it's like, and you're going to tell me if your falling dream is similar."

Bodhi nodded.

"When you skydive, you put on a harness and wear a back-pack called a rig that holds your parachute. That's important! That part probably isn't in your dream," she said, tapping the boy's nose.

The child grinned. "Nope, no harness in my dream."

"That's okay. Let's keep going. First, you get on a little plane that fits about four people and a pilot, and then they take you up way into the sky." Elle raised her hand, mimicking a takeoff.

Bodhi copied the gesture with sound effects.

Elle grinned. "Once the plane is high in the sky, and you're about ten thousand feet up, all the buildings and cars look teeny-tiny, and it's also very peaceful."

"Peaceful?" the boy parroted back.

"Yep! You see the land stretched out for miles and miles. And that gets you thinking about all the nice people in all the different places around the world."

"I have a globe in my room at home."

"So, you know it's a big world."

The boy nodded sagely.

"Then it's time to jump. You hang out of the plane. It's windy, and your tummy gets all ticklish. And then, you let go."

"Like jumping off the high dive?"

"Just like that," Elle agreed.

Bodhi's smile disappeared. "But on the high dive, I know I'll land in the water."

Elle's expression grew serious. "With skydiving, what's different is that you fall a little longer and then a parachute brings you safely to the ground."

Jasper cleared his throat, and Elle shot him a glance.

Bodhi didn't look convinced.

"Do you want to know what I like to think about when I'm skydiving?" she asked.

Jasper bit back a grin. "I hope the parachute works?"

She threw him another look, but the playful glint in her eyes softened the rebuke.

She smiled at Bodhi. "I pretend I'm a bird."

"Like an eagle soaring?" he asked.

"That's right! I feel the air all around me. I have the best view of the whole city, and I imagine that I'm free of anything that scares me or makes me nervous. So, the next time you have that falling dream, instead of being scared, you can pretend you're a bird."

Bodhi yawned and leaned into Elle. "I could be a California condor or a hawk."

"That's right," she said as the boy yawned again.

He closed his eyes. "Or a falcon."

"Or a seagull," Elle whispered to a now sleeping Bodhi. She stroked the boy's hair then glanced up at him. "This isn't what you were picturing when you proposed the midnight man feast extension."

Jasper was about to answer when Bodhi shifted in his sleep. He scooted in closer to keep the boy from tipping over. Shoulder to shoulder with Elle, he wrapped his arm around her, then glanced at the plate teeming with strudel. "I'm not sure what you were expecting to happen with all that."

"You said you wanted to reenact the cookie scenario," she answered, innocently.

He chuckled. "You've got to have about a pound of strudel on that plate."

Her lips curved in a sexy grin. "I know you've got the stamina."

He twisted his finger into her silky hair. "There's always the extension to the extension to the extension."

"I can agree to those terms." She glanced at the little boy. "But I think we're on Bodhi duty tonight."

"The timeline for the extension is open to negotiation. Not to mention, we're staying in the same mountain house, and I'm currently residing in your building in Denver."

She held his gaze. "Wow! You've thought this through."

Jesus! Had he? Yes, she'd been all he could think about, but there couldn't be anything more than the man feast, could there?

"You really wouldn't try skydiving?" she asked, leaning her head on his shoulder.

"No, someone in my position can't behave like that."

She tensed.

Dammit! He'd done it again—dished out that buttoned-up bullshit she'd called him on.

"But I used to pretend I was a bird when I was a kid," he added, trying to soften the blow.

She relaxed a fraction. "You did?"

"Yeah, when I skied with my brothers. I loved slicing through the trees. The icy air. The speed. Finding that narrow twisting trail and flying down the mountain. I used to find it exhilarating."

"You don't do it anymore?"

"What, ski?"

"Yes, ski."

He shook his head. "No, not anymore."

"Do you miss it?"

That was a loaded question. His wants and desires disappeared the day his parents died, and obligation and duty to the Bergen brand took over.

"That's not how my life works."

"Even CEOs are entitled to miss things, Jasper."

The muscles in his chest tightened. He'd miss this.

He'd miss her.

Elle sighed, her slow breaths matching Bodhi's. "Maybe you just haven't found anything you want worth the risk."

He wanted to give in. He wanted to allow her witchcraft to set him free. But as he gazed out at the mountain he was responsible for running, his throat tightened.

Nights hidden away in cabins.

Days spent at the spa.

This wasn't his life.

His life was Bergen Enterprises. The rebranding project would end, and she'd go back to her world of travel and excitement, and he'd go back to boardrooms and bottom lines. The man feast was simply a respite, an anomaly created out of temporary circumstances—and the childish extensions had to end.

He stared out at the gliding points of light dotting the mountain then shifted his gaze to the faint outline of the three of them reflected in the window. Despite knowing the man feast couldn't go on, he tightened his hold on Elle and released a pained breath.

The problem wasn't that he didn't have anything in his life worth the risk. What sent a shiver down his spine was that he just might have found it. But he couldn't have Eleanor Reynolds, and the only way to end it was to revert to his hollow bunny ways and break her heart.

CHAPTER 11
ELLE

Elle cracked open her eyes then blinked away the sleep. She stared out the windows as the white expanse of Bergen Mountain sparkled in the morning sun and rubbed at a kink in her neck. That's what she got for spending the night on the couch. She shifted her body as something warm nuzzled into her, but it wasn't Jasper.

"We had a sleepover," came Bodhi's groggy voice.

She sat up and patted the boy's back. "We sure did."

The house was quiet, and the clock on the wall read half past nine.

Bodhi hugged a cushion and yawned. "Where's Jasper?"

Good question.

She glanced around the room. Where was Jasper?

"How about we head into the kitchen and see if anyone else is up."

Bodhi's eyes lit up. "Sticky buns!" the boy said and was off like a shot.

She followed several steps behind him and smiled to herself as thoughts of Jasper crept into her mind. His scent. His touch. His taste. And while last night didn't garner the naughty strudel feast they'd planned, seeing him with Bodhi, experiencing this softer, gentler side, made that tiny kernel of hope she'd held in her heart spark to life.

Maybe fairy tales did come true. Maybe their man feast had turned this Bergen man-beast into a Prince Charming.

Maybe all men weren't like Tate and her father.

She rounded the corner into the kitchen and came to an abrupt stop. Clean shaven and pouring a glass of milk, Jasper stood, dressed in a suit and tie. He handed Bodhi the glass, and the boy settled himself on a chair at the kitchen's large center island. She smiled, but he didn't even glance at her.

She tucked a lock of hair behind her ear. "You're up early."

"This is actually quite late for me," he answered sharply.

She tried again. "You can bend the rules a little. We're on vacation."

He frowned, and her stomach dropped. She recognized that frown—that callous, judgmental, downward twitch of his lips.

"I don't have time for *vacations*, Eleanor. There's an issue at our Fell's Peak resort in Vermont that I need to address."

She bristled at his robotic tone.

The way he said *vacations*, you'd never guess the man owned and oversaw several vacation resorts for a living.

"Are you heading back to Denver?" she asked, waiting for his expression to soften, hoping the warmth would return to his eyes.

He opened a cabinet and took out a jar of peanut butter. "No, I'm flying to Vermont this morning."

Her jaw dropped. "This morning?"

What the hell had happened to him?

Last night, she'd fallen asleep next to the man who'd bared his soul to her. He'd opened up and talked about his parents. He'd kissed her and touched her with such tenderness. They'd made love, and he'd played along with her silly role-playing game.

He'd shed his hard CEO shell, hadn't he?

She would have sworn she'd peeled back the layers and had seen the real Jasper Bergen. But the man mechanically spreading peanut butter onto a piece of toast wasn't the same man who'd held her close. It wasn't the same man who'd wanted to spend last night eating pastries off her body.

What could have happened? It wasn't even like she could have said something to set him off! She'd been asleep for Christ's sake!

Elle clenched her jaw and willed herself to keep it together. Anger replaced shock as resentment twisted in her belly.

She'd almost allowed this man into her heart.

The mistake was hers.

"Good morning," Abby said, padding into the kitchen.

Jasper nodded, and Elle gave her cousin a tight grin. God knows what would come out if she opened her mouth.

Her cousin took in the tense scene, then turned to the boy happily gulping down a glass of milk. "Hey, Bodhi! Your mom is looking for you."

His shoulders slumped. "Do I have to take a bath?"

"She did have a fluffy towel, but I also saw a big bottle of bubble bath in her hands."

Bodhi set down his glass, beaming like a new man. "Bubble bath!" He bounced off the stool and headed down the hallway.

Abby turned her chipper teacher charm on Jasper. "You look awfully nice. Are you headed back to the city?"

"No, to Vermont."

Her face fell. "I'm sorry you have to go so soon."

Jasper's expression softened a fraction. "Yes, I apologize for leaving your engagement celebration early, but the matter at hand needs my attention."

Abby nodded. "I'm sure it does." She turned. "Elle, would you mind helping me with the clasp on my necklace? I left it in the powder room."

Elle met her cousin's gaze, and a round of eyeball talks ensued.

Abby's gaze darted to Jasper, and then she lifted an eyebrow.

Elle rolled her eyes. Jesus! They weren't children. "Where's that necklace, Abs?"

"Just down the hall in the bathroom," Abby answered, gifting Jasper with a smile before she turned and left the kitchen.

Elle glanced over at the entity that aliens had left in the place of the man she fell asleep next to last night.

Nothing. Not a smile. Not even a nod of his head. Zero acknowledgment.

She'd never seen anyone focus so intently on a piece of toast and a cup of plain yogurt. She huffed then left the kitchen to find her cousin, who was waiting in the doorway of the bathroom. Abby pulled her inside and shut the door behind them.

"What the f is going on, Elle?"

"What the *f* do you mean?" she threw back at her cousin.

Abby cocked her head to the side. "Do you want to start from the beginning and tell me the truth?"

"Abs, please don't talk to me like I'm a six-year-old."

"Sorry, I just thought you two were…"

"Man feasting our brains out?"

Concern clouded Abby's expression. "Well, yeah. He couldn't keep his eyes off you last night."

"He couldn't?" she asked as that damn spark of hope longed to ignite.

"No, he looked mesmerized. I mean, you were in *full Elle Reynolds* mode."

Elle raised her hands. "Um, full stop there, Miss Quinn. What the f is *full Elle Reynolds* mode?"

"You know," Abby said, morphing into a wide-eyed, deranged Disney princess. "In Tibet, I visited the grand Potala Palace and met the Dalai Lama. In London, I attended a gala and befriended a duchess in the loo."

Elle pressed her hands to her hips. "That stuff really happened."

"I know."

"Do I come off like some loudmouth?"

Abby shook her head. "No, not at all. You're amazing. You're riveting. Your enthusiasm for the people you've met and the places you've visited is contagious."

Elle stared at a tile on the wall. "Maybe that's all it was. He was just being polite."

"No, his expression wasn't like everyone else's. He looked completely enamored. I was waiting for cartoon hearts to pop out of his eyes. Bren saw it, too," her cousin added.

Elle pressed her fingertips to her eyelids and leaned against the sink. "I don't know what's going on. I thought…"

"What?" Abby pressed.

Elle wanted to scream.

I thought he cared for me.

I thought I could trust him.

I thought he trusted me.

"I misjudged our situation," she said instead.

"So, there was a situation?"

"*Was*, my dear cousin, is the operative word."

Abby frowned. "You guys seem so perfect for each other."

Elle's jaw dropped. "Abs, where would you get that? Half the time, we're seconds away from ripping each other's throats out."

"Bren says he's not like that with anyone."

"Then you're mistaking affection with loathing."

Abby grinned. "You push his buttons."

"All the wrong buttons," Elle shot back.

"I woke up early this morning. I saw the three of you."

Elle swallowed past the lump in her throat. "We were there for Bodhi. He had a nightmare, and we all fell asleep on the couch."

Abby tapped her chin. "Let me get this straight. Both you and Jasper just happened to hear Bodhi in the middle of the night and came to his aid before he got his mother's attention."

Elle shook her head. "I'm an idiot, Abs."

"You're not. Jasper's just…"

"A toast eating, buttoned-up, massage-hating, data crunching bag of dicks," she blurted.

Abby gave her a sympathetic smile. "You really like him."

The cousins kept straight faces for a beat before Abby cracked and they broke into giggles.

Elle wiped away a tear. "At least he's off to Vermont. I'll have a few days of peace before I fly out to the Bergen resort in California."

"Is Jasper going with you?"

Elle leaned her head against the wall. "Not as far as I know."

Abby tucked a wayward lock of hair behind her ear. "We'll make sure your next few days here are relaxing and free from bags of dicks."

They started another round of giggling when a soft knock cut off their laughter.

"Abby Rose, it's just me," Brennen said through the door.

"We'll be right out," she called back.

Elle lowered her voice. "Can he not be without you for five minutes?"

"Yeah, I heard that," Brennen said through a chuckle. "And it's not Abby everyone's looking for. It's you, Elle."

Elle stared at the door. "Who, me?"

"Yes, you," Brennen answered.

"Couldn't be! Then who?" Abby busted out, then blushed. "Sorry, it's from the 'Who Stole the Cookie from the Cookie Jar' chant. We sing it a lot in first grade."

Elle stared up at the ceiling. "Remind me to download some decent adult music on your phone."

Abby opened the door, and Brennen peeked his head inside. "Everything all right?"

Elle lifted her chin. "We're peachy. Is your Eeyore of a brother still here?"

"Yeah, he needs to leave, but my gram says he needs to wait for you."

"For me?"

"Yes, you."

Elle turned to Abby. "Don't you dare start singing that cookie song."

Abby mimed zipping her lips.

Elle stepped past her and joined Brennen in the hallway. "Do you know what this is about?"

"It's something that has to do with that piece you wrote going viral."

Elle shook her head. "Bad viral or good viral?"

There really was no bad publicity—unless, you were being paid to enhance the brand of a company looking to accentuate their positive attributes.

Brennen patted her shoulder. "I don't know. They were still talking when I left to find you."

"They?"

"Jas and my grandparents."

The Bergen power trifecta. Fan-fucking-tastic.

"Okay, thanks for coming to get me, Bren."

She started down the hall, listening to snippets of the conversation.

"It makes perfect sense, Jas, darling."

Harriet.

"Our marketing and PR people agree we need to capitalize on this."

That was Ray.

A frustrated groan.

And there was the buttoned-up tin man himself, Jasper Bergen.

Elle lifted her chin and entered the kitchen. "Good morning! Brennen said you were looking for me."

"Elle, darling!" Harriet said, beckoning her to have a seat. "Our PR and marketing people have a wonderful idea."

Elle glanced at a clench-jawed Jasper.

Ray took a sip of coffee then nodded. "It's about that piece you wrote about your first experience with Bergen Mountain Sports. It's gone viral."

Elle glanced between the company's founders, who looked extremely pleased.

What the hell was wrong with Jasper? How could he not like a viral post spewing the positive attributes of *his* company?

Harriet handed her a cup of coffee. "That line you used. *I am Bergen Mountain Sports.* It's brilliant. People are posting their childhood pictures online of themselves with the I am Bergen Mountain Sports hashtag."

"You seem to be trending," Jasper said, finally joining the conversation.

She nodded. "Is there a problem with that?"

"Not at all!" Ray replied with a grin. "The piece centered around your experiences at our Vermont store and your first time skiing at our resort at Fell's Peak. We weren't planning to send you there but after this article and its viral success, our PR people want to get you there to capture some footage."

Harriet leaned in. "And since it's so close to the end of the ski season, they want you there as soon as possible."

"And you could visit your mom, Elle," Abby said, entering the kitchen with Brennen.

"I thought you were from Maine?"

The tin man spoke again.

She met his icy gaze. "I am, but my mother recently moved to Fell's Peak."

"Does she live in town?" Harriet asked.

"Yes."

"Well, that settles it," Ray said, refilling his mug. "You can go with Jasper. The Bergen jet is already at the Eagle County airport."

Jasper looked at his watch. "I've got a ten a.m. departure time. I need to leave now."

"Jasper, darling, that's the beauty of owning your own plane. Pick up your phone and tell the pilot you need to push it out an hour to let Elle take a shower and get packed," Harriet said with a wave of her hand.

Elle glanced at Jasper.

A muscle twitched in his jaw. Even a minor tweak to his schedule had him ready to crack a molar.

How predictable!

"I know we hadn't discussed bringing Fell's Peak into the fold, Elle. It's one of our smaller operations, and we'd only discussed sending you to our largest resorts around the world," Ray added.

Elle shook her head. "It's not a problem. It makes perfect sense for me to visit Fell's Peak now."

Harriet clapped her hands. "Wonderful! You should call your parents and let them know you're on your way."

"It's just my mom, and I'll be sure to let her know," Elle added and shared a look with Abby.

Her cousin knew about her mom and dad's divorce. Abby had been surprised. They'd always seemed like the perfect family.

Seemed.

Elle took a sip of coffee and felt the hairs on the back of her neck rise. She looked over to find Jasper watching her.

Was there something between them?

They'd connected—and it was more than just man feast sex. It was deeper. More intimate.

Wasn't it?

She held his gaze and warmed her expression as his chilled.

He turned his back to her. "You should start getting ready. I don't like to be kept waiting."

CHAPTER 12

JASPER

J asper rolled his neck from side to side, trying to work out the kinks, and glanced toward the front of the plane. The Bergen Learjet 45XR seated eight and offered a double-club seating configuration. A damn good thing! It allowed him to set up camp and work in the back portion of the plane while Elle had the front four seats all to herself.

What he didn't expect was for her to extend the pull-out table and start working, too.

He checked the flight display. They'd be landing at the Morrisville-Stowe airport in Vermont within the next half hour, and Elle had barely lifted her head during the entire flight. Focused on her laptop and jotting notes on a pad of paper, whatever the hell she was doing, she was completely engrossed.

They hadn't spoken. Not one word during the car ride to the airport. Not one word when they'd boarded the plane. And not one word since the jet took off.

She'd put on a pair of reading glasses, or maybe she'd forgotten her contacts.

Did she even wear contacts?

He'd bared his soul to her. Made love to her. Held her in his arms. And he didn't know if she wore glasses or contacts. Fuck! She hijacked his thoughts—even when she was ignoring him.

Elle glanced up and caught him watching her.

"What?" she asked on an exasperated breath.

"I didn't think you worked," he blurted out like an idiot.

She shook her head and barked out a laugh. "Right, because nobody could work as hard as the super CEO, Jasper Bergen."

"That's not what I meant."

She narrowed her gaze. "Did you mean to imply that you were surprised to find me researching and planning?"

She had him there.

"I wasn't sure what you were doing."

She blew out a breath. "Normal humans ask. They say, 'Hey, what are you doing?' And then the other human answers. It's called basic communication. You should look into it."

He swallowed hard. Her anger was justified. Yesterday, they'd had sex on a massage table. Last night, she'd fallen asleep in his arms. But there was no way forward for them. As much as he craved her touch, he couldn't forget that he was responsible for the financial health of Bergen Enterprises—a job that required his complete focus.

In the very least, he owed that to his parents.

She stared at him and drummed her fingers, waiting.

"What are you doing?" he asked, amending his statement to her human response requirement.

She sat back and crossed her arms. "I was researching Fell's Peak. I know the town well, but it's been ages since I skied there. I wanted to familiarize myself with anything new. I've also prepared a schedule for the production team, so we can be as efficient as possible and still touch on all the places I mentioned in my piece. I also wanted to make sure I emphasized how the resort has evolved—throw in the energy efficiency and environmentally friendly improvements and highlight how those changes would be a draw for women in the age range your rebrand effort wanted me to target."

Holy fuck!

"Oh," he answered like he had shit for brains.

"What did you expect me to say? Did you think I was watching cat videos and trolling my exes on social media? Maybe getting in a little online shopping for a cute pair of espadrilles?"

She had him reeling.

"I don't know what espadrilles are."

She feigned mock surprise. "Look at that! Something Jasper Bergen doesn't know. They're shoes—just in case you actually cared."

He held her gaze. "I didn't know you wore glasses."

"There's a lot you don't know about me." Her tone was sharp, but the slight quiver of her bottom lip told him she wasn't as indestructible as she tried to appear.

"Elle, I—"

She waved him off. "No, don't say anything. This man feast experiment extension—whatever the hell you want to call it—was a mistake. Don't waste some *I'm too wrapped up in work to be with anyone* explanation on me. You made yourself crystal clear this morning. I'm not a moron."

He schooled his features. "I know you're not."

She held his gaze, and they were locked in another staring contest.

"This again?" he asked.

She leaned forward and widened her eyes.

She infuriated him.

She challenged him.

Nobody in his orbit dared behave like this with him.

It made him want her all the more.

A tight smirk pulled at the corners of her mouth when a chime sounded, and the pilot's voice filled the cabin.

"Mr. Bergen, Miss Reynolds, we've been cleared to land. I've also been notified by the tower that you've got a visitor meeting the plane. Go ahead and buckle up. We'll be wheels down in the next ten minutes."

Elle broke their connection and closed her laptop, and Jasper released the breath he hadn't realized he'd been holding.

"The person meeting the jet is probably just the driver to take us to Fell's Peak."

Elle nodded indifferently as she finished packing her papers, then fastened her seatbelt.

He glanced out the window and found Fell's Peak in the fading light. After their late takeoff and losing two hours flying to the East Coast, it was almost seven o'clock. His family owned a luxury duplex unit on the resort's grounds. He'd take one half, and she could have the other. And they could have their own space where he didn't have to worry about impromptu staring contests.

Or impromptu salsa lessons.

Or an impromptu night, cuddled in next to her, comforting a young boy just as his parents used to do for him.

He shook off the sentimental bullshit and buckled his seatbelt.

It was too late to visit the resort's administrative offices tonight. He'd spend the rest of the evening going over the resort's maintenance records and the bids for the new ski lift, order dinner in, and go to bed—alone.

A routine he was well accustomed to following, which now, after the last two nights with Eleanor Reynolds, seemed like a foreign concept.

It had only been a handful of days.

She couldn't have worked her way into his life in that brief amount of time.

Unfortunately, or fortunately—he wasn't sure which—it didn't matter.

Her sharp retorts and glaring eyes told him her defenses were up and on high alert.

He'd destroyed what had grown between them with his callous demeanor this morning. He had to do it. He just hadn't expected it to hurt so damned much.

The jet touched down, and he caught Elle gazing out the

window. Her hardened expression had softened, and the hint of a smile pulled at the corners of her lips.

After reading her piece, there was no doubt she loved Fell's Peak and the Bergen Mountain Sports shop in town. In the article, she'd painted the picture of herself as a girl, going with her mother to pick out her first pair of skis. The piece recounted Elle and her mother, riding the lift, enjoying hot cocoa on the mountain, and chasing each other down the rolling slopes of Fell's Peak.

Then it hit him. There was nothing about her father.

The jet came to a stop in front of the small terminal, and the co-pilot opened the aircraft's door. Jasper exchanged a few words with the woman, while Elle got her suitcase and shoulder bag and climbed down the stairs to the tarmac.

His gut twisted. Why the hell did it hurt so much to see her walk away?

He knew the answer but pushed it aside.

He grabbed his things, thanked the pilot, then got off the plane.

"Elle!" he called.

She stopped but didn't turn around.

He caught up to her. "We might as well ride to Fell's Peak together."

She glared at him. "Great idea! We do so well traveling in cars together. Like two peas in a pod!" She shook her head. "I'll call for the Fell's Peak shuttle."

They entered the small terminal, and Jasper scanned the crowd for his driver.

Elle glanced around and started down the hall.

"Where are you going?" he asked.

She slung her bag over her shoulder. "The bathroom, if that's all right with you? I'm pretty sure using the restroom facilities is allowed per my contract with Bergen Enterprises."

He nodded. He deserved everything she could dish out. And Christ, could she dish it. But he wasn't about to leave for Fell's

Peak without making damn sure she was in a car—any fucking car she picked—and headed to the resort.

The one-runway airport was fairly busy during the ski season, and groups of people lingered in the terminal, waiting for their flight. An older woman caught his eye and surprised him when she waved.

He glanced around. Was she waving to him?

The crowd parted, and the woman moved toward him slowly, using a walker.

Did he know her? Was she part of the Fell's Peak staff?

As she closed the distance between them, he saw the color of her eyes and the breath caught in his throat.

"You look just like your picture on the Bergen Enterprises webpage," she said, stopping in front of him.

"I'm sorry to sound rude, but do we know each other?" he asked. He had to be sure.

"Not formally. I'm Eleanor's—"

"Mom?" came Elle's surprised voice from behind him.

"Sweetheart!" the woman said, her lapis blue eyes shining with tears.

Elle went to her mother. "Do you want to sit, Mom?"

The woman shook her head. "No, no. I'm fine."

Elle glanced between him and her mother. "What are you doing here?"

"Abby called. She said you and Jasper Bergen were on your way to Fell's Peak. I was so excited. I threw a chicken in the Crock-Pot and went to the store and got your favorite ice cream."

Elle squeezed her mother's hand as the woman steadied herself with the walker. "Mom, you didn't need to go to all that trouble. I was going to call you after I finished my work here."

"Nonsense! You haven't seen the house since I moved in. The craftsmen finished modifying everything for me." Her mother paused. "I did want to ask you about Monty. I tried to call him to make sure I was using the right checkbook for the trust, but I wasn't able to reach him."

Elle glanced over her shoulder at him, then patted her mom's hand. "It's nothing to worry about. I have a new lawyer named Allen, who's helping with all that. I'll get you his information."

Was she talking about Allen Parker? Elle and Allen did recognize each other when they'd bumped into the Parkers at the spa.

Elle's mother reached out to him, and he took her shaky hand. "Where are my manners. I'm Lila Reynolds, Eleanor's very proud mother. It's so lovely to meet you. I hope you like chicken!"

His gaze bounced between Elle and her mother. He'd never seen Elle like this. He was used to the sharp-tongued, fearless version. This Elle had lost her hard edge and worry clouded her expression.

He pasted on a placating smile. "I'd hate to trouble you. I was going to order in and do some work. I've got business to attend to at Fell's Peak tomorrow morning."

The woman narrowed her gaze, her lapis blue eyes just as intense as her daughter's. "There's no substitute for a good, home-cooked meal. I insist you join us. Tell him, Eleanor."

"My mom does know her way around a Crock-Pot," Elle answered.

He held her gaze, then turned to Lila. "I'd be honored to join you for dinner."

Christ! Did he just agree to spend the evening with them? Damn that Reynolds witchcraft!

"Then it's settled!" Lila beamed. "Come on! I'm parked right outside."

"Let me help you, Mom," Elle said, shifting her shoulder tote, while also trying to pull her roller bag, and help her mother at the same time.

He put his hand on her shoulder, and she stilled. Had he not been watching her so closely, he would have missed the fraction she'd turned into him—neglected the barely perceptible amount she'd leaned into his touch as if she'd wanted him there, needed him there.

He lifted the strap off her shoulder and took her bag. "I'll get our luggage so you can walk with your mom."

"Thank you," she replied, the raw honesty of her words cutting into his heart.

He took out his phone and shot off a text, informing the car service that he didn't need to be picked up, and followed a few steps behind Elle and her mother. He'd had no idea Elle's mom was…

What was she?

Was she sick or maybe recovering from an illness or surgery? The woman was by no means elderly, but she was weak and moved cautiously, relying on the walker to keep her upright.

And it wasn't just Lila Reynolds's condition that had him perplexed.

Elle's whole demeanor changed the moment she saw her mother. Not that Elle wasn't a nurturing person. He'd watched her last night as she comforted Bodhi. But this was different. This was a level of devotion he understood. A level of commitment he'd had no idea they had in common.

"Here's the car," Lila said as they approached a Mercedes SUV parked in a handicap spot.

Elle pulled a set of keys from her mother's purse. "Why don't you let me drive, Mom."

"Go ahead, sweetheart! I'm still not used to driving such a fancy car."

Jasper loaded their bags into the back of the Mercedes and listened to Elle and her mother discuss the car. It sounded as if Elle had purchased the vehicle for her. And then he remembered her question about a trust.

Was Elle supporting her mother?

Her words flashed through his mind.

There's a lot you don't know about me.

Elle was right. There was.

He went to get into the back seat when Lila stopped him.

"Jasper, take the front seat. I'm barely five foot three. You've got to be well over six feet tall. You'll need all the leg room."

Elle met his gaze. "Can you put her walker in the back with our bags?"

He softened his expression. "Sure."

Lila sighed. "Eleanor, you don't need to fawn all over me. I get around quite well on my own."

"I know, but I'm here," she answered, helping her mom into the back seat.

He closed the back hatch then slid into the passenger's seat. Elle started the car, and the dashboard illuminated her face as she released a heavy breath.

He wanted to reach out and take her hand—do something to help shoulder the pain she carried.

"When was the last time you visited Fell's Peak, Jasper?" Lila asked, breaking into his thoughts.

He shifted his focus from Elle to her mother. "It's been a while. I've always loved Fell's Peak. My mom grew up not far from here in Stowe."

"So this area is in your blood. Eleanor and I fell in love with this place from the first moment we arrived, right, sweetheart?"

Elle backed the SUV out of the parking spot and nodded. "We sure did. I just wrote a whole article about it recently."

Lila pressed her hand to her heart. "I saw that! My friend's eight-year-old grandson set up some kind of alert on my computer that sends me messages anytime something about you pops up on the internet."

"That's terrifying," Elle said through a laugh.

"Not at all. I'm so proud of you, Eleanor."

He'd thought of Elle in so many different ways: infuriating, maddening, irresponsible, sexy, sensual. She exuded confidence and self-reliance. But he'd never thought of her as someone's daughter. He'd never considered there was a vulnerable side to this powerhouse of a woman.

Fell's Peak came into view, and Elle maneuvered the vehicle onto the quaint main street. They passed the Bergen Mountain Sports shop then turned down a side street. She slowed the car when they came to a sprawling ranch-style home a few blocks from the Fell's Peak city center and parked in the attached garage. He got their bags from the back and followed Elle and her mother into the house.

The home had a cozy feel as the comforting scent of roast chicken lingered in the air. Stacks of books and framed photographs were scattered throughout the kitchen and living room. It reminded him of his grandparents' home.

Jasper set their bags by the door, then walked over to the bookshelf. Jane Austen. Virginia Woolf. William Faulkner. Even a copy of Margery William's *Velveteen Rabbit* sat on display. He removed the hardback of Woolf's *To the Longhouse* from the shelf.

"That's a first edition you've got there, Jasper. It's from 1927," Lila said, opening a drawer and taking out a stack of cloth napkins.

"It's well preserved," he replied, appreciating the binding and craftsmanship.

"Books are my passion. I was a librarian."

"You are a librarian," Elle corrected, removing the chicken from the Crock-Pot.

Her mother smiled. "I volunteer at the Fell's Peak Public Library now."

He carefully slid the book back onto the shelf and picked up a framed photo of two young girls.

"That's a picture of me and my twin sister," Lila said with a grin.

Jasper gazed at the image of the young girls with their arms wrapped around each other. "Abby's mother?"

Lila nodded, and Jasper set the picture frame back on the shelf.

"Is there anything I can do to help?" he asked.

"Could you get the salad out of the fridge?"

The three of them moved around the kitchen. Lila had set her walker to the side and navigated the space well without it. She still moved slowly, but in her home, she seemed self-sufficient.

With the table set, they sat down, and Lila poured three glasses of wine.

"A toast to my daughter and her friend, Jasper. It's such a lovely surprise to have you both here."

Jasper clinked his glass with Lila's then turned to Elle. They tapped their glasses together, and he held her gaze, trying to read her, trying to understand her.

"So, Jasper, which book of Eleanor's is your favorite?" Lila asked as they started in on the meal.

Out of the corner of his eye, he saw Elle press her lips together, holding back a grin.

"I haven't read any of your daughter's books yet."

Lila cocked her head to the side. "You must have seen the movie they made of her novel?"

Elle took a bite of salad, her cheeks growing pink.

She was laughing at him, albeit, trying to hide it. But damn, if it didn't send a rush of warmth through his body to finally see the worry she'd carried since her mother met them at the airport dial down a notch.

"I don't have a lot of free time."

Lila turned to Elle. "Then, he doesn't know."

Jasper's gaze slid to Elle. "Know what?"

Lila took a sip of wine. "The story of how Eleanor started writing."

"Mom, Jasper's not interested in that." Elle's eyes went wide as she flashed him a *knock it off* look.

Now it was his turn to bite back a grin. "Actually, I'd be very interested in hearing that story."

Lila sat back. "It all started about ten years ago before we knew I had Multiple Sclerosis."

He nodded solemnly. That explained the walker.

"We weren't sure what was going on with my health. I was

tired and growing weaker. I stopped skiing and hiking and then travel became too taxing."

Elle's eyes grew glassy, and she took a long sip of Chardonnay.

"That's when Eleanor became my personal storyteller. Tell him, honey."

Elle took another sip of wine. "There's not much to it. It started when I did a semester abroad in Costa Rica. I'd write to my mom about my experiences."

Lila waved her off. "It was more than that! Eleanor would weave together her experiences with the history, the geography, and the culture. It was as if I was right there with her, ziplining across the jungle or meeting a village elder."

Jasper leaned in. "That's how I felt reading the article that went viral about her first experience with Bergen Mountain Sports and Fell's Peak."

Elle's lips parted, but she didn't say a word.

Lila nodded. "That's Eleanor's magic. Everywhere she goes, she sends me pictures and postcards. I've got them all over the house."

Jasper glanced around the room. Postcards from New Zealand, Italy, Switzerland, South Africa, and Morocco were tacked to a large corkboard, and all the framed pictures were of Elle or shots of exotic places.

Lila patted Elle's hand. "I'd take Eleanor's letters with me everywhere I went. I'd share them with my friends who started telling their friends about them. Soon, strangers were coming up to me in the grocery store, asking to hear them. I was at a coffee shop when a friend of a friend came up to me. He was a literary agent and had heard about Eleanor's letters."

"That's quite a story," he replied, mentally kicking himself for being so damned rigid in his opposition to her working for Bergen Enterprises.

"It is," Lila continued. "Not only do Eleanor's books help people find the hidden gems in the places they visit, they also stress one vital thing."

"And what's that?"

Lila smiled. "Living. Living for now. Living for today. Taking the plunge. You never know what life will throw at you." she added, blinking back tears.

"And this is why we limit my mom to one glass of wine," Elle said with a teary shake of her head.

But when Elle met her mother's gaze, the bond between mother and daughter was palpable.

"I think I've had about all the Crock-Pot chicken I can handle," Elle said, taking her plate over to the sink.

"Honey, don't worry about the dishes. You and Jasper should take a walk up to town." She turned to him. "Is it true? You don't have a favorite flavor of ice cream?"

"Um, no," he answered.

"That's what Abby said," Lila replied, pursing her lips. "We can't have that! It's a lovely evening. Finish up your dinner, and then you and Eleanor can take a walk up to town and get some ice cream."

He nodded and made a mental note to hire Lila Reynolds. There was no way he could say no to her—and he was the king of saying no. Now he saw where Elle got her commanding presence.

Elle picked up her mother's plate and set it in the sink. "Mom, Jasper needs to get to the resort. I'm sure he's got work to do."

"It can wait." He could hardly believe he'd uttered those words.

Elle narrowed her gaze. "Are you sure?"

This conversation went deeper than just discussing a trip to an ice cream parlor.

He swallowed past the lump in his throat, past the guilt he'd carried all these years.

"I'm sure."

CHAPTER 13

ELLE

Elle pulled up her hood and inhaled the crisp night air.

New England cold was a different kind of cold compared to Colorado. Instead of the dry Rocky Mountain air she'd grown used to since she moved to Denver last year, Vermont's chilly nights, with the hint of humidity, always made her think a snowstorm was just around the corner.

She listened to the sound of her footsteps next to Jasper's and hated herself for finding comfort in their rhythmic beat.

What the hell was happening? How did Jasper Bergen end up eating dinner at her mother's kitchen table?

She knew the answer to that—her sweet as honey cousin. If she didn't love Abby like a little sister, she'd be itching to wring her neck.

Abby may be over the moon in love with her Bergen brother, but that did not mean that she'd wanted one for herself too.

Or did she?

She released a breath and watched as the condensation appeared and disappeared in the glow of Main Street as they approached Fell's Peak's town square.

Separated by a few miles, the town of Fell's Peak was located just off the main highway while the Bergen Ski Resort was situated closer to the base of the mountain.

"Your mom's great," Jasper said, breaking into her thoughts.

She glanced up. "Yeah, she is. She's doing well now."

"What do you mean, now?"

"We didn't know what was wrong with her for many years. Luckily, she was referred to a really good neurologist, and that's when we found out she had Multiple Sclerosis. It's a condition where your body starts attacking your nervous system. That's why she needs the walker."

"That had to be hard to learn."

She shook her head. "No, it was a relief to finally have an answer. She started treatment and has been stable for a while now. She doesn't let it hold her back. She's the strongest person I know."

"You're a lot like her," Jasper replied.

"I'm not so sure about that," she answered.

"Is your dad around?"

She resisted the urge to spew profanity. "Oh, he's around."

"In Vermont?"

"No, Paris."

"Paris?"

"Yes, he's a genetics researcher. He's shacked up with one of his doctoral students there."

"Jesus, I'm sorry, Elle."

She shook her head. "Don't be. We're better off without him."

"What do you mean?"

"Six years ago, I was in London. He was doing a guest lecture series at Cambridge, and I'd decided to go there and surprise him. Except I was the one who got the surprise."

"What happened?"

"Giselle happened."

"The doctoral student?"

"Yep, they were making out in the parking lot like teenagers. My first instinct was to get out of there and try to process whatever the hell that was. This was right after my mom got her Multiple Sclerosis diagnosis, and I think that's what threw me over the edge."

"What did you do?"

"I walked right up to them and tapped my dad on the shoulder."

"Christ," Jasper replied.

"He was shaken—to say the least. He took me to a coffee shop and swore it was just a fling and that he'd end it. He said he didn't know how to deal with my mom's condition and that he'd made a terrible mistake. He begged me not to tell my mother, and I didn't—until I caught him again."

"Was it the same woman?"

She nodded. "My dad always traveled a lot for work. Speaking engagements. Collaborating with other researchers. When I was growing up, he could be gone for months at a time, but he always called, and things seemed okay between him and my mom."

She glanced up at Jasper. He nodded, giving her space to keep going.

"Almost a year ago, I did the same damn thing. I showed up to one of his lectures unannounced, and there was Giselle. He saw me in the back of the auditorium, and his expression said everything. Then, I did a little bit of digging and found out they were living together. I flew back to Maine that day. I told my mom everything, and then I called my business manager and had him transfer funds into a trust in both of our names. She filed for divorce a few months later."

"You're supporting her?"

She shrugged. "My mom didn't want anything from my dad, and she couldn't manage on her own. They had some money set aside, but researchers—especially ones with mistresses—don't have a lot of cash on hand and helping her out is the least I could do. With my dad gone so much, she put her career aside to raise me. She didn't want to stay in the house she shared with my dad in Maine. So, I asked her, if she could live anywhere, where would it be? She said Fell's Peak. This was like our second home. My dad didn't ski, and he was gone so much anyways, this became our special place. That's why I freaked out when my hat blew off when we'd stopped on the side of the road."

"The Fell's Peak hat?" he said, connecting the dots.

She sighed. The day on the side of the road felt like it had happened months not days ago.

"My mom got me that hat on what turned out to be our last ski trip. After that, she started having health problems, and we never skied together again."

Jasper nodded but remained quiet.

"That was probably more information than you wanted. Even Abby doesn't know all the ugly details."

He offered her his arm, and she took it without thinking. He was only being kind, but it steadied her, nonetheless.

"We're kind of alike in that way," he said.

"Good at holding it all inside?" she asked.

He gazed down at her. "Something like that."

They turned onto Main Street and blended in with all the tourists in town for the last few days of the ski season. They passed the Mom and Pop hardware store when the hanging sign for the Lucky Scoop Ice Cream Parlor came into view.

"You really don't have a favorite fl—" she began but stopped at the sight of a woman holding a baby.

"What is it, Elle?" Jasper asked.

The woman's features hardened. "Tate!" she called.

A man got out of a parked car, accompanied by a young boy. "What is it, Laura?"

Elle froze and cursed karma. She'd just outed her father as a cheater and had just exposed Giselle as a harlot sleeping with a married man.

Elle stared at the glaring woman. This must have been the way she'd looked at Giselle.

The revulsion.

The disgust.

But she deserved it, too.

Tate and the boy joined them on the sidewalk.

The man looked from his wife to her, his Adam's apple straining as he swallowed. He glanced over his shoulder at Lucky's. "We were about to get ice cream."

The banality of those words underscored that this was the first time she'd seen Tate since Laura had caught them together.

She tightened her grip on Jasper's arm. "Do you live in Fell's Peak?" She had to ask.

"It's none of your business where we live," Laura said, lip trembling.

Tate put a hand on his wife's back. "No, we don't live here. We're on vacation. It's our last night in town."

Laura sniffed. "If you must know, we live in upstate New York. And we're very happy, no thanks to you!"

The four adults stood silent. Humiliation tore through her. If it weren't for Jasper reaching over and covering her hand with his, she might have imploded like one of those dilapidated buildings deemed unworthy.

Jasper met her gaze with more kindness than she deserved. "We need to get going," he said, then turned to a dumbfounded Tate and his scowling wife. "Enjoy your ice cream, and your last evening in Fell's Peak."

And it was over.

Jasper led her away from Tate and his wife. "It's okay," he said in a low voice as they continued down the street.

She willed herself to stop trembling, then pointed to a dive bar across the street.

"That's exactly where I was headed," he answered, his even tone calming her frayed nerves.

They crossed the street and entered the tavern. Classic rock layered with sounds of conversation and laughter surrounded them as Jasper took her coat then gestured to a stool before joining her at the bar.

"Tequila?" he asked.

She held his gaze. "I'm waiting for you to make that face."

"What face?"

That judgmental, rigid, *I know better than you*, CEO face.

He signaled to the bartender. "Whatever the hell that was back there, I think we're well past that face."

She slumped forward.

"Two tequila shots," Jasper said, but she stopped him.

"Just a club soda for me."

He eyed her wearily.

"I might be able to drink a crew of Somali pirates under the table, but I can't be hung over on camera tomorrow."

He turned to the barman. "Club soda for the lady. I'll still take those two shots."

She leaned onto her elbows. "I'm sure you've figured out by now that I slept with that woman's husband."

"It certainly didn't look like you were old friends," he replied, his expression neutral.

The fight drained from her body. Whatever lecture he had in store for her, she deserved it. She released a heavy sigh. "You must think I'm a hypocrite."

He rolled up the sleeves, exposing the muscular forearms that had held her close, and undid the top button of his dress shirt. Looking all deliciously business casual, he held her gaze. "I think things are more complicated than they seem."

She closed her eyes, as if that could keep the memories at bay. "I didn't know he had a family."

The bartender placed their drinks in front of them.

She lifted the glass and took a sip. "Tate's a photographer. I got paired with him to work on a project for a travel magazine about five years ago. It seemed like a dream assignment, traipsing across Italy, going vineyard to vineyard. By the end of the first week, we started sharing a hotel room. When you spend so much time together, things can get intense quickly."

He stared at her, biting back a grin.

Of course, he understood. They'd embarked on their man feast Monday, and today was only Wednesday.

She took another sip of the club soda, wishing she could drown herself in tequila.

"Tate's wife showed up at the little bed-and-breakfast we were staying at in Siena. The magazine booked two rooms, but we'd always stay in his." She steadied herself as the images of that day flashed through her mind. "The innkeeper let her into the room, and she caught us in bed. It turned out, she was also pregnant. She was there to surprise him with the news."

Jasper watched her with that same neutral expression, giving her nothing. Without a word, he knocked back one shot, then the other, then got up and disappeared into the crowd of people surrounding the bar.

She sat there, dumbfounded. What was she supposed to do, laugh or cry? She'd spilled her guts to a man who made her crazy in every way. One minute, she was ready to hand him her heart, then next, the stoic, stuffy bastard was lucky she didn't punch his lights out.

She folded her arms and dropped her chin to her chest. Even Elle Reynolds, piss and vinegar fueled Elle Reynolds, wasn't completely bulletproof. She gave herself a moment, then lifted her chin, ready to leave the tin man's ass at that bar. She knocked back the last of her club soda and headed toward the exit when the eighties rock ballad booming through the speakers cut off abruptly.

She glanced over at the dance floor where couples and groups of people once swaying to Steven Tyler stood with their mouths hanging open, looking around like goldfish plucked out of the water. The confusion grew when the catchy sound of lively trumpets woven with a spicy Latin beat and that unmistakable quick, quick, slow salsa rhythm floated through the air as the first lines of "Brujería"—their song from the cabin—resonated over the sound system.

Conversations stopped as everyone in the bar stilled—except for one person.

In the middle of the dance floor, hand extended toward her, was Jasper Bergen salsa dancing.

"Are you going to make me do this all by myself?" he called as the patrons watched their exchange.

All the shame and humiliation she'd carried over Tate and all the anger and disappointment she'd felt toward her father lifted as tears threatened to fall. She blinked them back, her heart in her throat. She walked toward him, and the crowd parted like a bad chick flick, making a path straight to Jasper.

She'd given him such shit. Called him a robot. A hollow bunny.

She was wrong.

When she needed him the most, he was measured and balanced. Composed and pragmatic.

She closed the distance between them, one shaky step at a time, took his hand, and let him lead as they salsa danced alone under a lopsided disco ball.

"Am I doing this right, Eleanor? Last time we did this, I'd had considerably more tequila."

"You're doing fine." She shook her head in disbelief. "How in the hell did you get them to play this song?"

He bit back a grin. "I found the owner of the bar and offered to buy the next round for the entire place."

"And?" she pressed. They were in rural Vermont. Blasting salsa music in a locals' dive bar would take a hell of a lot more than buying a round of drinks.

"And I agreed to pay his lease this month."

She cocked her head to the side.

A sly smirk pulled at the corner of his mouth. "And the next month."

She stared at this man who seemed to know exactly what she needed. "Why would you do all this?"

He pulled her in closer. "I needed you in a better headspace so I could tell you something, and you'd believe me."

"And you thought salsa dancing was the way to do it?" she asked, her words infused with wonder.

His expression grew earnest. "I'm improvising. Going off-plan. I'm stepping out of my comfort zone because this is important."

"What's so important?"

His gaze softened. "You're not your father, Eleanor. And that man's wife may blame you for her husband's infidelity, but she's wrong. He kept you in the dark. I know that if you had known he was married, you would have never gotten involved with him. It's not who you are."

She held his gaze, her vision growing glassy.

He stopped dancing and leaned in. "You are a remarkable woman. You're talented, and you're not only devoted to your mother. I know how you took in Abby when she first got to Denver. I know how you were the catalyst in getting my brother to shape up and be the man your cousin deserves. You're selfless. You're also a giant pain in my ass. You make me question everything." He cupped her cheek in his hand and brushed away her tears. "You are the most infuriating person I have ever met, and I wouldn't change one damn thing about you."

"You wouldn't?" she whispered.

"No, and now, I'm going to kiss you."

"Is this another man feast extension?" she asked.

He shook his head. "We're done with that. It's over."

The song ended, and no one in the entire bar moved a muscle.

He brushed his thumb across her trembling bottom lip. "I've been under your spell from the moment I laid eyes on you, Eleanor. I'm tired of fighting it. I'm tired of denying my feelings for you. I'm tired of pretending whatever it is between us is something that can be flicked on and off like a light switch. Say you want this. Say you want me just like I want you."

She stared into his eyes as the disco ball cast them in a blanket of twinkling lights. A week ago—no, three days ago—she would have laughed in the face of anyone who said she and Jasper would end up like this, professing their feelings for each other while salsa dancing in Vermont.

"Kiss him, Eleanor!" came a loud shriek from the bar.

Elle looked around at the dozens of pairs of eyes glued on them.

"Yeah, Eleanor! Go for it!" came another voice from the crowd.

She bit her lip, giddy with excitement, her heart about to burst.

"Girl, if you don't want him, I'll take him!" came another shout.

She held Jasper's gaze. "I want him."

A mischievous glint sparked in his eyes. "Are you sure? There will be spreadsheets."

She stared at this man who surprised her at every turn. "I'm sure."

The sweetest smile bloomed on his lips, then his expression darkened, and his gaze grew heated. She barely had a second to take a breath before their lips met in a crash of relief and desire and anticipation as the crowd broke out into cheers.

And then it disappeared, and all that existed was the two of them.

She wrapped her arms around his neck, melting into his touch, as he lifted her off the ground.

This was a kiss for the ages.

A kiss out in the open for all to see.

They weren't hidden away in a cabin or holed up in a private massage room. This wasn't some man feast where they were supposed to get their fill and then move on like nothing ever happened. The butterflies in her stomach and the electricity pulsing through her body told her one thing: This was the real deal.

She sighed and after God knows how long, Jasper paused and pulled back a fraction. "I think we have an audience."

She glanced around the room at the smiling faces—half of them recording the encounter on their phones.

Jasper gave her his million—no his billion-dollar grin then turned to the crowd. "Eleanor Reynolds has just made me the happiest guy in Vermont. Drinks are on me!"

The place erupted again, and everyone rushed the bar.

"I thought drinks were already on you?" she asked, unable to stop smiling like an idiot.

"It doesn't hurt to milk it a little from time to time. Call it my dramatic flair."

She narrowed her gaze.

"You should probably know that this will most likely be the first and last time I do anything that could be characterized as having a *dramatic flair*."

"You never know," she answered, still in his arms, toes dangling above the dance floor.

He set her down, then took her hand. "Let's get out of here."

"Where to next?" she asked as he helped her into her coat.

He captured her with those steel-blue eyes. "Wherever the hell I can have you all to myself."

CHAPTER 14

JASPER

Elle unlocked the door to a small cottage located on her mother's property and they entered the cozy space. She turned on a lamp and took off her coat, resting it over the back of a chair.

"I had this guesthouse built in case I needed to hire someone to care for my mom full time. I'm pretty sure she's asleep, but I didn't want us to..." she trailed off.

He stared at her. She'd always been beautiful. Those lapis blue eyes had always made his pulse race. But now, she looked different. Without the guise of the man feast, this wasn't just some erotic tryst between two sex-starved individuals.

It was the two of them. Their scars exposed. Their secrets revealed.

Her brow knit together. "Say something."

The excitement of his salsa escapade thrummed through him. It killed him to see her so shaken, so raw. And then he'd remembered dancing with her. Holding her. And his mind went to their run-in with the Parkers and how she'd held his hand. She hadn't pitied him. She'd been herself. Her snarky, smart as a whip self. And he'd told her everything.

His greatest pain was no longer his greatest secret. Elle knew it all, and she didn't judge him. And now the tables were turned, and all he wanted to do for her was what she'd done for him—and show her the way forward.

"I was just thinking about tonight," he answered.

They'd walked back to her mom's place hand in hand, neither saying a word, neither wanting to break the spell that had been cast on the dance floor.

He'd professed his feelings in the middle of a bar while salsa dancing.

There wasn't much more out of character for him than that.

But that's what Elle did. That was her magic, her witchcraft. She gave him that extra nudge. She pushed him that extra inch.

"Are you second-guessing yourself?" she asked, a slight shake to her voice.

He took off his coat, set it on top of hers, then cupped her face in his hands. "No, I'm not second-guessing anything."

"Then, this is real," she whispered.

He tilted her head and met her gaze. "It's always been real, Elle. The only thing that's different now is that we both believe it. I know I do."

"I do, too," she answered and melted into his touch.

He stroked her cheek. "I never thought I'd find anyone. I'd resigned myself to a solitary existence. But I don't want that life, Eleanor. I want you. I want all of you."

"Then kiss me, because I'm yours."

Their lips came together, and she sighed, her sweet moan owning him. The sound went straight to his cock as his body ached for her touch. He unbuttoned his shirt and threw it onto the ground, then fell to his knees and unzipped her jeans. He peeled them off her body, along with her boots, and tossed them aside.

He needed this. They needed this. The drive to be inside her, to claim her, raged through him like wildfire. He was a measured man—until it came to Eleanor Reynolds.

She sank onto the ground next to him, and he pulled her sweater over her head then feasted on her breasts, unclasping her bra as he massaged and sucked her tight peaks. She arched into him and threaded her fingers into his hair, twisting and tugging, her desire matching his as her gasps and tight breaths fueled the fire within him.

"Yes!" she gasped.

He lifted her into his arms and carried her into the bedroom. Laying her down gently on the bed, he hooked his fingers into the band of her lacy G-string and pulled the garment down her thighs. The moonlight streamed through the window and cast her body in a milky glow as he took off his pants and boxers, then stood at the end of the bed and took in the splendor.

Her smooth skin.

Her soft curves.

He climbed onto the bed, prowling her body, dropping kisses along the way. First, her ankles. Then, her inner thigh. He licked a slow trail to her sweet center then pressed two fingers to her tight bundle of nerves, rocking them in a rhythmic circular motion.

"Jasper," she cried, bucking her hips.

He could listen to her call out his name all night long.

Working her with his mouth and tongue, he feasted on her most sensitive place.

Feasted.

This was their new definition of the man feast. In every other aspect of his life, he was reserved and cautious. But not here. Not with Elle. In this place, their place, he let go and surrendered to hunger within.

"Jasper, I need you inside me," she called out, gripping the bedsheets.

His cock throbbed between his thighs, happy to oblige. He met her gaze and positioned himself at her entrance.

They stared into each other's eyes, and the significance of the moment hung in the air, heady and fragrant. They'd slept together, but not like this. Not as a couple. Not as two people made for each other.

She cupped his face in her hand. "Make love to me, Jasper. Show me this is real. Show me I'm yours."

He pushed past her delicate folds, and she moaned, taking all of him into her sweet wet heat. He held her gaze as their bodies came together. No words were spoken, but a promise more binding than any contract passed between them.

She was his.

He was hers.

Despite their differences. Despite trying to hide it. They belonged together.

"You're mine, Eleanor. Every beautiful, maddening part of you is mine."

"Show me," she whispered, tightening around him.

He pulled back then thrust his hips, meeting her body in a sensual rhythm. He laced his fingers with hers and rolled his hips, working her slowly, and their bodies came together in perfect synchronicity.

Each gasp, each growl, each thrust of his hard length, strengthened the bond between them like an invisible thread, encircling them, tethering his heart to hers, binding their souls.

Dialing up his pace, their bodies grew slick with sweat, and he brought her to the edge. She called out, writhing beneath him, riding the waves of her orgasm.

But he wasn't done making her body sing with carnal pleasure.

He released her hands and gripped her ass. Pumping deeper and faster, he balanced on the precipice between pleasure and pain and waited for her to join him. She grabbed the back of his neck and pulled him to her. Their lips and teeth and tongues met in a fiery exchange as the waves of their release crashed over them, rolling and turning and tossing them around in an ocean of ecstasy.

He'd spent so much of his life wielding control, exercising caution, and denying his wants and desires. With each glorious pulse of their mutual release, he reveled in her body and worshipped her spirit, her energy, her zest for life.

In her arms, he was reborn. The part of him he'd locked away tore through him like the rumble and roar of an avalanche.

Relentless.

Merciless.

All-encompassing.

Their breaths mingled together as they drifted back from the throes of their release. He steadied himself on his elbows, careful not to crush her under his weight. She sighed deeply, tracing her fingers along his jawline.

"What comes next for us?" she asked with a sated smile.

He brushed a lock of hair from her cheek, completely under her spell. He met her grin with one of his own and remembered his thoughts of Sunday mornings, waking up with her beside him, their bodies tangled together as they made love in the warmth of the late morning sun.

No schedule. No action items looming. Just Elle's smile. Elle's laugh. Elle's sighs. Elle's body welcoming his weeping cock.

He pressed a whisper-soft kiss to the corner of her mouth. "Everything comes next, Eleanor. Everything, and then after that, even more."

———

"Is everything all right, sir?"

Jasper glanced up from his laptop as heat pulsed through his veins, the word *everything* evoking memories of making love to Elle last night.

He turned to his assistant. "Everything's fine. The numbers look good. The bids for the new ski lift are in line with what we were expecting."

Collin had flown in the day before to prep the Fall's Peak management team for their meeting which had just ended on a good note.

"Do you see a problem, Collin?" he asked.

They were the last two left in the conference room.

The man shook his head. "No, I don't see a problem. It's just…"

"What?"

"You're smiling, sir."

Jasper schooled his features. "Do you have an issue with smiling?"

His assistant handed him a file, a bewildered look on his face. "No, no, there's nothing wrong with smiling! I've just never seen you do it."

Jasper glanced out the conference room window that overlooked the mountain and found Elle in the sea of skiers and snowboarders, making their way down the run. She wasn't hard to spot with a camera crew at her side.

Collin looked out the window then down at his tablet. "Miss Reynolds leaves tomorrow morning for California, right?"

He nodded, his chest muscles tightening. "Yes, we're sending her to our properties near Lake Tahoe then on to British Columbia to visit our resort in Whistler. She'll hit Australia next and finish up with our European properties."

Elle had five weeks of travel ahead of her, and he had five weeks jam-packed with work back in Denver.

Collin finished packing. "The numbers are already looking good from that article that went viral."

It had only been a few days, but they'd seen a marked increase in the rebranding target group Elle was brought on to engage in retail sales and in purchasing season ski passes to their resorts for the upcoming season.

Jasper smiled. "It looks like she's got the magic."

She certainly did over him.

He closed his laptop. "What's next on my schedule, Collin?"

"Actually, that's it."

He stood and crossed his arms. "We worked through all the action items I wanted to get through?"

The assistant nodded. "We did. It was a very productive meeting. You were more..." his assistant trailed off again.

"Collin, say what's on your mind."

"You were receptive to the management team's ideas. Usually you—"

"Bark out orders like a drill sergeant?"

"Or a dictator."

Jasper narrowed his gaze. "Don't push it, Collin."

His assistant bit back a grin then glanced out the window. "I have Miss Reynolds's schedule here. It looks like they should be finishing up soon."

He turned his attention to the slope and the beautiful brunette surrounded by cameras, and an idea hit him. "Collin, would you call down to the pro shop and have them pull some gear together for me? They should have all my sizes in their system."

His assistant's eyebrows shot up. "You're going to ski down the mountain?"

"I'm certainly not going to be skiing up the mountain."

His assistant blinked once then twice. "You're serious?"

He patted the stunned young man on the shoulder. "Completely. And would you mind making sure my laptop and briefcase are returned to the Bergen townhouse? I won't be coming back to the office today."

Collin pulled his phone from his pocket. "Of course! Enjoy your afternoon."

Jasper glanced out the windows toward the main plaza and watched as a gust of wind blew a ball cap off a young girl. An older woman—perhaps her mother, her aunt, or just a friend—ran forward and scooped it off the ground and handed it back to her. They continued walking, and Jasper lost sight of them.

"One more thing, Collin. Call Bergen Mountain and ask some of our guys to head out to mile marker 249 off the I-70 interstate."

"Why?"

"To look for a hat."

"A hat?"

"Yes, a faded blue Fell's Peak Ski Resort ball cap."

"There's a Fell's Peak cap laying around somewhere near the highway in Colorado?"

"Yes, right around mile marker 249. It blew over the guardrail."

"Is it important, sir?"

He glanced at Elle. "Very important."

Jasper left the conference room feeling lighter than he had in years. Perhaps running himself ragged and putting in hundred-hour workweeks while micromanaging every aspect of Bergen Enterprises wasn't the most efficient way to lead a company.

Elle had rubbed off on him.

Today he'd listened rather than lectured. Delegated responsibilities rather than adding new tasks to his already overloaded schedule. He'd loosened his grip on the reins of Bergen Enterprises and found increased productivity and efficiency.

A sentimental pang in his chest told him this would have made his father proud.

He left the resort's administrative building and stepped out onto the main plaza. It was a bluebird day. The weather was mild, and there wasn't a cloud in sight. Piped in music floated through the air as people relaxed in the Adirondack chairs scattered in groups at the base of Fell's Peak, laughing and sharing stories about their day on the mountain.

Did you see me kill it on the double black?

Dude, you were ripping today!

He smiled to himself. He, Bren, and Cam used to try to out-do each other on the runs, nearly busting their kneecaps cruising through the jarring moguls or finding the spots where they could catch the best air.

He entered the Bergen Pro Shop just as a salesclerk set a helmet next to a stack of gear.

"Hello, Mr. Bergen! The guys in the back are just adjusting the bindings on your skis. By the time you change, we should have everything ready to go."

He picked up the items and thanked the clerk.

It was not a bad day to own a mountain sports empire.

He changed into his gear, picked up his boots and skis, and headed toward the lift when he saw Elle coming his way, chatting with one of the Fell's Peak camera crew. Decked in a pair of ski goggles, a neck gator, and his helmet, she didn't recognize him, and passed him without a second glance.

"Elle Reynolds, can I have your autograph," he called after her.

She froze, then turned.

If he'd had the power to stop time, he would have chosen that moment. The light caught her lapis blue eyes, turning them almost lavender in the afternoon sun. And her smile. Holy fuck, that smile deserved a chorus of angels—and it was all for him.

Elle said a quick goodbye to the camerawoman, then joined him. "What are you doing here? I thought you had a meeting?"

"It ended early."

"Early?" she echoed, jerking her head back in surprise.

"Yeah, it turns out when you don't spend fifty percent of the time trying to do everyone else's job, shit gets done quick."

She stepped back. "Is that really Jasper Bergen under there? I need to confirm I've got the right Bergen brother."

He lifted his goggles and rested them on his helmet. "You've got the right one."

She blushed. "You're right. I do."

He glanced at the ski lift. "I know they worked you pretty hard today, but do you think you're up for one more run with *your* Bergen brother?"

Her expression grew wary. "How do you know they worked me hard?"

"The conference room looks out onto the runs. You're not too bad on the blacks."

She narrowed her gaze. "Not too bad!"

He shrugged playfully.

She pulled down her goggles. "You're on, mister."

They clicked into their skis and glided across the snow-covered pavilion to the lift. They grabbed the next chair, and he wrapped his arm around her as they dangled their ski-clad feet, soaring above the mountain.

"How was your day?" he asked.

It had been a decade since he'd donned ski gear and rode the lift. Fresh air. The big sky. He'd nearly forgotten the joy it was to ride the lift, to watch the skiers and snowboarders sail down the trail below. He'd had some of his best talks with his parents riding the lift. Nowhere to go. No distractions. Just you, your lift-mates, and a little time to talk that often turned out to be the conversations that mattered the most.

Elle rested her head on his shoulder. "It was a good day with the crew. We got some great footage, and I have some ideas on how I'd like to shoot when I get to Northern California. Are you...?"

She paused, and he knew what she was thinking.

Was he going with her? Did he still think she needed to be monitored?

He pulled her in closer. "I think we both know that you've got this."

"Yeah?" she asked.

"Yeah, I'm always slammed with work at the end of the ski season. We've got management teams flying into Denver from all over the world. I need to be in Colorado for the next several weeks."

She gave him a wry grin. "It looks like we're going to have a *man fast* of our own."

He chuckled at the reference to Elle's cousin's name for swearing off men which thankfully didn't end with Abby kicking his brother to the curb.

He rubbed her shoulder. "Oh, hell no. There will be no fasting—man or otherwise. We're utilizing video chat. A lot."

She grinned. "That could be fun."

The lift made it to the top. They got off, then skied to the top of the run.

He gazed out at the snow-covered peaks. "I haven't done this in ages. Are you going to go easy on me?"

She gave him a sexy little smirk. "Never!" she answered, pushing off and flying down the steep incline.

His pulse kicked up, and muscle memory took over.

He straightened out his skis and leaned into the run, building speed like a freight train coming down the mountain. Despite the cold, warmth radiated through his body. His thoughts scattered like a mosaic, a mishmash of days on the slopes with his family overlapped with his time on ski patrol. His heartbeat thrummed in his chest as he followed behind Elle, tracing her elegant tracks.

She maneuvered her body and did a one-eighty, skiing backward like she was born to do it.

"Showoff!" he called.

"Let's see what you've got!" she replied, flipping forward.

He checked the terrain and found a sweet spot to catch some air. He picked up speed, hit the bump, and shot up. Adrenaline surged through him as he extended his legs and arms like he used to as a kid and rocked a flying eagle jump.

"Woo-hoo! Bergen's CEO has got his groove back," Elle called, carving a quick turn in front of him.

He followed her lead, heart racing, breaths coming fast.

It wasn't from exertion. It was her. The magic. The witchcraft.

Elle disappeared into the trees. He trailed behind but slowed when she came to a stop.

"Do you need some help?" she asked.

He looked past her and saw a little girl with her skis off, poles staked in the snow, and dried tears on her cheeks.

She shook her little pink helmet head and blinked back tears. "I can't talk to you. My mom says I can only talk to people who work here. Like if we go to the supermarket and I get lost, I can ask the man who works in the deli or the cashier for help."

Jasper unclipped his boots from the ski bindings then went to the girl. When he was on ski patrol, at least half his day was spent reuniting lost kids with their families.

"I work here," he said, crouching down to meet her gaze.

She pursed her lips and gave him the once over. "You're not wearing a ski patrol jacket."

"You're right. I'm not. My name is Jasper Bergen. I own this ski resort."

She narrowed her gaze. "Prove it."

He bit back a grin, unzipped his jacket, and handed her his ski pass.

The girl's eyes went wide. "Are you the Bergen burger guy? I had a Bergen burger for dinner last night."

He shared a glance with Elle then schooled his features. "I am. Did your Bergen burger have eight pickles? That's the magic pickle number."

The girl nodded. "Yes! I counted. There were eight." Her face fell. "But my brother stole one when mommy and daddy weren't looking, so I only got to eat seven of them. He's the one who left me here. He was supposed to stay with me, but he went ahead, and I got scared skiing through the trees."

"Are you hurt?" Elle asked.

The girl eyed her. "I can't talk to you unless you work here, too."

"I do! Did you see the people with the cameras on the mountain today?"

The girl nodded.

"I was working with them to make a commercial for Fell's Peak."

"Is your last name Bergen?"

"No, it's not. My name is Eleanor Reynolds."

The girl lit up. "My name is Eleanor MacCaffrey!"

"It's nice to meet you, Eleanor MacCaffrey," Elle said with a warm grin. "Would you like Jasper and me to ski with you and get you through the trees and back onto the run?"

"I'm supposed to find a ski patroller if I get lost."

"There's a patrol building not far from here. How about we take you there?" Jasper offered.

They helped Eleanor MacCaffrey with her skis and poles then worked their way through the trees. The little girl traced Elle's tracks as he followed behind. It only took a few minutes to get back onto the open, winding run before they'd found the patrol station and Eleanor MacCaffrey's relieved parents and apologetic brother.

He and Elle skied to the bottom of the run, carving S-curves and cruising down to join the rest of the skiers where the trails merged near the base of the mountain.

She lifted her goggles and stared at him.

"What?" he asked, clicking out of his skis.

"You! First, it was Bodhi and then Eleanor MacCaffrey. Who would have thought the stuffy suit Jasper Bergen was so good with kids?"

He grinned. "I guess I'm a sucker for an Eleanor."

She took off her skis and balanced them on her shoulder. "You're really okay with me visiting all the Bergen properties on my own?"

He inhaled a tight breath as the part of him used to total control bristled. He exhaled and cast the familiar feeling aside.

Old habits die hard.

He couldn't expect a personality transplant overnight. She had Bergen Enterprises' best interests at heart. He knew this.

He gathered her skis and carried them along with his. "You'll be submitting your articles to us prior to publication."

She nodded cautiously. "To the marketing and PR team. Do I need to cc you as well?"

His father's words came back to him.

Great things happen when you push past your comfort zone.

He had this woman. This intelligent, feisty, passionate woman who cared for him. They'd shared their darkest secrets and their greatest regrets. If he couldn't trust Elle, he couldn't trust anyone.

He reached down and held her hand. "You don't have to run anything by me. I trust you."

Her gaze softened. "Thank you. I know it isn't easy for you to give up control." Then her expression grew playful. "Can you trust me with one more thing?"

"What?"

Jesus! In addition to handing Elle creative control, he'd smiled in his meeting this morning. And he'd fucking delegated. He'd just about hit his limit for relinquishing control.

They walked together hand in hand toward the Bergen townhouse when a man appeared at the door of his unit carrying a large cooler with *Lucky's* written on the side.

"That's for us," Elle called to the man. "We can take it from here."

He nodded, left the cooler on the porch, then headed back to his delivery truck.

Jasper frowned. "What's this all about?"

"My favorite flavor of ice cream is chocolate super fudge. We never figured out your favorite flavor," she said, a naughty bend to her words.

Jasper leaned their skis and poles against the side of the townhouse then lifted the cooler's lid. "There have to be over twenty different pints of ice cream here. What are we going to do with all this?"

"Market research. I thought we'd have you taste each flavor." She unzipped her ski jacket. "Off my naked body. A kind of ice cream feast before we parted ways tomorrow."

His gut twisted at the thought of being away from her, but this was one hell of a way to celebrate their last night together.

He schooled his features, reverting to his hollow bunny persona. "I get to choose the order and what part of your body I want to eat it off of."

"Are we negotiating the ice cream taste test trial terms?" she asked, now popping the button on her ski pants to reveal the hint of lace panties.

He hardened his gaze. "No, I'm setting the terms. I want complete and total access to every part of you."

Her gaze dropped below his belly. "You drive a *hard* bargain."

"Take it or leave it," he growled, his body buzzing in anticipation. He'd forgotten how fun it was to go toe to toe with her, even if it was in jest.

She pulled down the zipper halfway on her base layer, and the hint of a matching black lace bra peeked out. "I have one little condition."

"I may be inclined to entertain one condition."

She gazed up at him through her lashes. "No Eleanor or Jasper. It's Jemima Sex Kitten and Dean Largecox for the next twelve hours."

Twelve hours!

His cock answered before his brain could even form a complete sentence. Just the mention of Jemima Sex Kitten had him ready to take her right there on the damn ice cream cooler.

"I can agree to those terms, Miss Sex Kitten."

She smiled and held his gaze. "We better get started. I know you're a very busy lumberjack."

"How am I going to make it five weeks without you?" he asked.

She opened the door then gazed back over her shoulder. "We'll just have to make enough memories tonight to sustain us." She glanced down to where he sported a raging hard-on. "And I don't think that's going to be a problem for Dean Largecox or Jemima Sex Kitten."

CHAPTER 15

ELLE

"Miss Reynolds, I'm sorry to wake you."

Elle blinked open her eyes to see the smiling face of the private jet's flight attendant. She sat up and ran her hand through her sleep-tangled hair. "Are we home? Did I sleep through the whole flight?"

"Not yet. I just wanted to let you know that there's been a change to the flight plan."

Elle nodded, still groggy. "Thank you. Is it going to be much longer?"

"Another hour at the most. I just wanted to make sure you were okay. You fell asleep right after we left Switzerland. It's been almost eight hours."

Elle reached for her water bottle and took a long sip. She could have slept for eight more.

Damn, she was tired. In forty days, she'd traveled to three continents, five countries, and multiple Bergen resorts and properties. She'd written numerous articles, filmed spots, and if she had to get another spa treatment, she was going to cut somebody with a pair of cuticle scissors.

"Oh, and I almost forgot," the woman said. "You fell asleep so quickly. I wasn't able to give you this."

Elle knew what the flight attendant was talking about even before she produced the pint of Lucky's chocolate super fudge ice cream. She left it along with a spoon, gave her a knowing grin, then headed to the front of the cabin.

Elle had flown with this crew a few times as she traversed the globe, and they'd become used to Bergen CEO's requests for them to play salsa music over the intercom after take-off or stock the plane with actual hollow chocolate bunnies.

Jasper Bergen, her once rigid buttoned-up suit, had turned out to be quite the skilled long-distance romantic. From Denver, he orchestrated hotel rooms bursting with flowers and always had a pint of Lucky's chocolate super fudge waiting for her on each flight.

But the teddy bears were her favorite.

At each new destination, she'd find a plush animal perched on her bed. The first was a black bear and two little stuffed cubs, and it only got sweeter from there. A salsa bear. A bear riding a snowmobile. A bear in a business suit—presumably him. A bear holding a book—presumably her. A ski bear. Lots of skiing bears.

But the last bear she received a few days ago threw her for a loop.

Decked in sunglasses and a Hawaiian shirt, this bear was ready for the beach—a far cry from the ski runs and snow-capped peaks she'd come to know well over the last five weeks.

And then there was her favorite bear. Dressed in a red flannel, jeans, and suspenders—her lumberjack bear with the name Dean embroidered on its paw.

She glanced at Dean, wielding a tiny plush ax on the seat next to her. "We're going home, Mr. Largecox, and then we're going to hibernate. I know it's spring, but this mama bear is planning on getting into bed and staying there."

She glanced at the pint of chocolatey fudge bliss and her stomach twinged. "And I think I'm going to pass on the ice cream today," she said, still talking to the stuffed animal.

He didn't have much of an opinion.

"I could go for Jasper's favorite ice cream," she continued. Strange because she was a chocolate gal through and through. She smiled, remembering their last night in Fell's Peak.

She'd never eaten so much ice cream or had so many earth-shattering orgasms. And the added bonus—the taste test worked! After sampling eleven different flavors on four different parts of her body, they'd succeeded in finding his favorite flavor.

Lucky's *Dulce de leche.*

It seemed her Rocky Mountain boy liked his dancing and his ice cream with a Latin kick.

She bit her lip, remembering his touch, his tongue, his hard length.

It was no wonder Abby and Bren were going at it like rabbits after their man fast ended. She couldn't wait to get back to Jasper. All she wanted to do was fall asleep in his arms.

Sweet sleep.

She plucked Dean from his chair and snuggled back into the plane seat that reclined into a bed.

"We'll just rest our eyes for a few minutes, Dean," she sighed, pulling the blanket up to her chin.

————

"Dean the lumberjack is one lucky bear."

Elle shifted beneath the blanket.

Dreaming. She had to be dreaming. There was no way Jasper Bergen had materialized into the jet's cabin when they were cruising at thirty thousand feet.

But there was no mistaking the warm hand cupping her cheek and then tucking a lock of hair behind her ear.

She opened her eyes. "Jasper? How did you get on the plane?"

He grinned. "The stairs. The plane landed twenty minutes ago."

She sat up. "It did?"

He nodded. "The crew said you were exhausted. I told them

I'd sit with you until you woke up. I also had some ice cream." He held up the empty pint of chocolate super fudge—his second favorite flavor. "We couldn't let that go to waste."

She reached up, threaded her fingers into the hair at the nape of his neck, and guided his lips to hers.

He pressed whisper-soft kisses across her lips. "I missed you."

She hummed with contentment. "I missed you, too."

He pulled back and observed her carefully. "Are you hungry? The flight attendant said you didn't eat a thing during the entire trip."

She rubbed at a kink in her neck and yawned. "I may have caught a little bug somewhere between the French Alps and the Swiss Alps. You know, the jet-set life of the travel writer."

He frowned. "Are you all right, Eleanor?"

She stood and waved him off. "I'm fine, but I could really go for some tacos from that food truck that's always near The Dalton. It may be parked closer to Larimer Square. What time is it?"

"In Denver?" he asked.

"No, in Hong Kong! Yes, Denver! I'm plotting a food truck excursion, and then we're going straight to bed."

He stroked her cheek. "I'm completely on board with going straight to bed. But we're not going to be able to visit your food truck—that is unless they deliver, and their delivery zone has a two-thousand-mile radius."

"Why would they need that?"

"Because we're not in Denver."

"We're not?" She whipped around and looked out the window, expecting snow-capped mountains and instead found slim arching trunks with lush, broad green leaves.

Palm trees.

"Nope, we're not," he answered with a sly grin.

She spun around. "The bear! The beach bear!"

"I wondered if you were going to figure that out, but it looks like the flight crew and your Sleeping Beauty nap kept it a surprise."

She wrapped her arms around his neck. "Where are we? The Cayman Islands? I know your family has a place there."

"Not the Caymans. We're in Miami."

"Miami!" she exclaimed.

"When you're in the resort business, you know others in the industry. We've got a penthouse overlooking the ocean in the heart of South Beach waiting for us."

She gazed up at him. "I never pictured you in any place tropical."

"Must be my icy demeanor?"

She shook her head then leaned in and kissed him. "Nope, like I said, nobody who can salsa like you can be a complete ice man."

"Speaking of salsa," he said, one hand on the small of her back while the other held her hand up in a dance position.

She cocked her head to the side, her eyes going wide. "Are we going salsa dancing in Miami?"

His grin said they were.

"You remembered I learned to salsa here." She blinked back tears.

What the hell was wrong with her? She was not a sappy kind of gal. She was probably the only woman on the planet who didn't get misty-eyed over *The Notebook*.

He pulled her in closer. "I remember *everything*."

He led her off the plane to a sleek black Mercedes parked on the tarmac.

When it came down to it, she was a small-town girl from Maine who could rough it in the mountains sleeping under the stars or car camp her way through Utah. But on a day like today, when she'd just completed a whirlwind trip of long days on location and even longer nights knocking out articles, it was not bad to be dating a billionaire Bergen brother.

"A girl could get used to this," she said, biting back a grin as he helped her into the car.

He bit back a grin of his own. "It's more efficient to have the car meet the plane directly."

They drove north from the Executive Airport and crossed the bridge over to South Beach. Elle inhaled deeply. Early April was the perfect time of year in South Florida—not too hot and with just the right amount of humidity. She'd been used to the dry mountain air and welcomed the balmy Florida heat, heady and fragrant with jasmine.

Art Deco buildings in pastel pinks and blues and yellows lined the boulevard, and it wasn't long before Jasper pulled up in front of one of these iconic structures.

"We're here," he said, giving her a quick kiss before the valet opened her door.

She looked over his shoulder at the vast expanse of the ocean. "This is so thoughtful of you. All of it. The flowers. The bears. The ice cream—and now the beach."

"Just don't let anyone know I'm not a hollow bunny."

She gazed into his steel-blue eyes. "Your secret's safe with me."

Elle glanced at the building. This wasn't a hotel. It was a luxury condo complex. The valet went to work collecting their luggage while a doorman greeted them as they entered a stylish lobby. Jasper led her to a bank of elevators. He swiped a black keycard across the panel and the light for the penthouse floor illuminated. And just like that, the doors opened, and they headed to the top.

The elevator car set off for their floor just as a wave of nausea passed over her. Swaying, she braced herself on the wall and held on to Jasper's arm.

"Elle, are you going to be sick?" he asked, keeping her upright.

She released a shaky breath. "I'm okay. I just need a little fresh air."

The elevator opened into the penthouse, and Elle went straight for the veranda that overlooked the ocean. She threw open the doors and inhaled the fresh sea air.

Jasper joined her and rubbed soothing circles on her back. "Maybe we should stay in tonight."

She shook her head. He'd gone to all this trouble to plan a surprise Miami getaway. She could push through the exhaustion and the sour stomach. She'd done it plenty of times. She'd patch herself up with some Pepto Bismol, hydrate, and then she'd be as good as new. But she was all out of her stomach meds. She'd used up the last of her travel sized bottle in the Alps.

She leaned into him. "There's a drugstore a few blocks away. I think I'll walk over and pick up something to help me feel better."

"I can have someone do that for you. The building has full concierge service," he answered, continuing with the soothing circles.

She rested her hand on his chest and glanced inside the penthouse at the gleaming, fully stocked bar. "Why don't you make us some mojitos? After that flight, a little walk would do me good."

He tightened his grip. "I can come with you."

She stepped out of his embrace. "No, it's okay. Get settled here, and I'll be right back."

He frowned. "Do you think you need to see a doctor?"

She waved him off. "It's nothing. Probably just a bug I picked up on the road."

He nodded, but he didn't look happy. "Here." He pulled another keycard from his pocket and handed it to her. "Are you sure you know the way?"

She patted his cheek. "You still haven't read my books."

He blushed.

"If you had, you would have known that I stayed not far from here when I wrote the Miami and Key West travel guides."

He pressed a kiss to her forehead. "I almost forgot I was in the midst of a seasoned travel professional."

She cupped his cheek and stroked her thumb across his jawline. "I'll be right back, and those mojitos better be ready."

He walked her to the elevator, and she pasted on a sweet smile. But as soon as the doors closed, she released another shaky breath.

Jesus! This trip really took it out of her.

The elevator doors opened to the lobby, and she steadied herself and left the complex.

Walking down South Beach's main drag, teeming with camera-clad tourists and cheerful beachgoers, she tried to let the tropical air settle her stomach. But by the time she made it to the store, not only was she nauseous, she was also lightheaded.

Browsing the aisles, she picked up a bottle of Pepto then froze when she saw the pregnancy tests stacked in a neat row nearby. A wave of nausea merged with a pang of anxiety, and she swallowed past the bile in her throat.

Her birth control pills had been in her toiletry case. The same case the bears had torn apart.

"Oh shit," she whispered and rested her head against the cool metal shelf.

She hadn't gotten a new pack. They'd gone straight from Bergen Mountain to Fell's Peak. From there, she'd flown to California, and her lightning-fast romance with Jasper hadn't given her any time to call her doctor or refill her prescription.

She picked up one of the pregnancy tests, paid for the items, then went into the store's restroom.

Two minutes later, she knew why she'd been suffering from bouts of nausea.

Dazed, she put the test into the bag with her stomach medication and headed back to the penthouse.

What was she going to say to Jasper?

She'd told him she was on the pill. And she was! She was until life raced into hyperdrive, and a night spent drinking tequila and salsa dancing with the man she'd once considered her polar opposite changed everything.

Her stomach twisted as the gravity of the situation sunk in.

This was bigger than Jasper's reaction.

This was a baby—a child.

What would this mean for her career?

How would this impact her financially?

She released a tight breath. She'd go back to the penthouse and tell him—and not just about the pregnancy test. She'd tell him everything: why her car was repossessed, why her mother was asking about the trust. She'd come clean, and they'd figure it out. He cared for her, maybe even loved her. It had to be love, right?

But an unplanned pregnancy?

What would that mean to someone like Jasper?

Someone who stressed personal responsibility. A man who thrived on order and routine. But he'd changed. He'd opened up. He'd pushed past his self-imposed hard limits—*for a few days*.

Jesus! The entirety of their time spent physically together spanned five days. Not even a week! Yes, they'd been in touch while she traveled. Yes, he'd been sweet, and the phone sex had been thrilling, but he'd gone back to his life, his routine.

Would they make it as a couple if they weren't trapped by hungry bears or forced into couple's spa trips?

She stopped in front of the building. The doorman wasn't there—a good thing. She needed another second to order her thoughts.

"Elle Reynolds!" came a loud bark just as she started to open the door.

She released the handle and looked over her shoulder to find a man she didn't recognize. He held out his phone and started filming their exchange.

She clutched the plastic bag and smiled apologetically. "I'm sorry, but I'm not able to do an interview right now."

He took a step closer. "Is it true that you've lost all your money and are now trying to bag a billionaire to fund your extravagant lifestyle?"

Her jaw dropped. "Who the hell are you?"

He held out another phone and played a video. Elle watched the screen and saw herself in Jasper's arms, salsa dancing in the Fell's Peak bar.

That's right! All those people had their phones out. She hadn't even thought a video of them dancing would go viral.

She schooled her expression. "Are you a journalist?"

She needed to know who she was dealing with.

A slimy smile oozed on the man's face. "I'm from the Tattle Zombie blog."

Dammit! She'd heard of them. A loose network of so-called *fact finders* who specialized in creating and fabricating the worst, most salacious internet clickbait stories.

"That's not a credible news organization." She turned to enter the building but reared back when Jasper appeared at the door.

He joined her on the sidewalk, looking back and forth between her and the clickbait blogger. "I saw you from the veranda. What's going on? Who's this guy?"

"You're Jasper Bergen," the man said, jamming his phone into Jasper's face.

Jasper swatted it out of the way. "Miss Reynolds and I aren't answering any questions."

"Come on, man!" the guy pressed.

Jasper narrowed his gaze and morphed into his hollow bunny facade, and a chill ran down her spine.

He took a step toward the blogger. "If you even think about putting that phone in my face one more time, you're going to regret it," he answered, his tone as cold as jagged ice.

Exhilaration glittered in the creep's eyes. "Did you hear that! Did you hear that! Billionaire CEO Jasper Bergen just threatened me, and I've got it on tape!"

Jasper took her hand. "Let's go inside."

"What do you think about Elle Reynolds losing all her money in the Monty Morris scandal? I think she's with you because she's some gold-digger trying to cash in," the man yapped just as Jasper opened the door.

Jasper tensed then released her hand and faced the brazen blogger. "Get your facts straight and go peddle your lies somewhere else."

"You don't know?" the man asked.

A muscle ticked in Jasper's jaw. "I know that this is over." He took her hand and led her into the lobby as the man stood at the window, recording their departure.

They entered the elevator, and as soon as the doors closed, he turned to her.

"What the hell was that?"

She shook her head but didn't meet his gaze. "Some moron who thinks he's an entertainment reporter."

The doors to the elevator opened, and she headed for the penthouse's kitchen.

It was too much. This whole situation was too much.

She opened several cabinets looking for a glass. Despite the humidity, her throat had gone dry. She found the cupboard containing the glasses, and with a shaky hand, turned on the tap and filled the cup.

Jasper crossed his arms. "Eleanor, talk to me."

She took a sip of water then set the glass and her bag from the convenience store on the counter. "With or without that guy ambushing me, I was going to tell you everything."

His expression hardened. "That asshole was telling the truth?"

She leaned against the counter, needing its support. "My former money manager, Monty Morris, tricked me into investing in what they call a pump and dump scheme. I lost nearly eight million dollars."

His stony exterior cracked as surprise lit his face before he reverted to his muted CEO mask. "That's why Allen recognized you at the spa. He tried to play it off, but I could tell, you two weren't strangers. He's the best financial fraud litigator in the city. Is he your attorney?"

She nodded. "Yes, I saw Allen right before I ran into you in The Dalton's parking garage. I wanted to see if he could help me recover what Monty had taken."

"And could he?"

She shook her head.

"Christ, Eleanor! Why didn't you tell me this when your car was getting repossessed?"

Anger edged out shame, and she lowered her voice. "Because it was none of your goddamn business."

His expression grew tighter. "Not my business? You're a central figure in our rebranding efforts. And now, you're going to be embroiled in some financial scandal. How is that not my business?"

She felt her cheeks heat. "That's where your mind goes first? You're not at all concerned about me and how some shyster asshole stole almost all of my hard-earned money."

He looked away and shook his head. "I shouldn't be surprised by this."

She blew out a frustrated breath. "Why? Because I'm *so* irresponsible? Because I don't live my life in preplanned increments? That didn't seem to bother you when you were screwing my brains out."

He stiffened. "How much money were you looking to get out of me?"

"You bastard," she bit back. "I wasn't *looking* to get anything other than what I earned. You know how hard I work. And I know that your numbers have improved thanks to me."

He stared out the windows at the ocean. "You should have said something, Eleanor. This needed to be disclosed. You had ample opportunities to communicate this information."

Her vision went red. "Go fuck your ample opportunities! I'm leaving!"

She snatched the plastic bag off the counter and the contents scattered onto the floor. The positive pregnancy test skidded to a stop between them like a landmine.

Jasper didn't move, his gaze laser-focused on the life-altering piece of plastic. "Is that what I think it is?"

She picked up the test and threw it at him. "You can add that to the Elle Reynolds irresponsibility file. I'm sure it's a mile thick by now."

"You said you were on the pill. I asked you specifically if we needed protection," he replied, his tone jagged and rough.

She threw her hands up. "You want to know what happened? The bears ate my birth control pills. The pills were in my pack that got torn to shreds. I figured it would be fine. I didn't think a couple of missed pills would matter. And everything was moving so fast. It was like living in some alternate universe where I thought we were falling in…"

She stopped. Christ, she loved him! But there was no way in hell she was going to tell him that. Not when he'd gone all hollow bunny.

She started over. "Where is the man who filled my hotel rooms with flowers and sent me ice cream and teddy bears? Where is the man who said *everything* starts now?"

"That man didn't know that *the everything* also meant having a child," he shot back.

She stared at him. The tin man. The hollow bunny.

Where was the man who had kissed her so tenderly? Who had played Dean Largecox and Jamima Sex Kitten with her?

Gone—swallowed up by the one-dimensional caricature of a button-up, rigid CEO.

She pushed past him and found her suitcase. "I'm leaving. This is over."

"We need to discuss how to address the situation."

She whirled around to face him. "*The situation*? I'm not some number on a planning forecast. This baby isn't a situation! And just in case you believe that I'm some gold digger trying to get a piece of the Bergen fortune, rest assured, I don't want a damn thing from you. Not one cent."

He opened his mouth to speak, his gaze softening. But she was past the point of letting him take back his cruel words.

She pressed the elevator call button.

"Elle," he said, pain laced in the word.

She met his gaze, and that sliver of emotion in his eyes nearly had her. But she held strong.

"Let me tell you something, Jasper Bergen. A strong, proud woman raised me. My father was never around. And now that

I'm an adult, I know that was a godsend. He didn't want a family. His absence was a blessing." She lifted her chin. "I don't want your help. And I certainly don't need it. You don't have to do a cost-benefit analysis on me or this baby. We don't want a damn thing from you. Go back to your spreadsheets! Let them keep you warm at night."

"Eleanor, I'm just trying to be pragmatic. For just one second, try to put yourself in my shoes. I am responsible for Bergen Enterprises," he answered, a slight shake to his voice.

She huffed an exasperated laugh. "Try thinking about this: I'm supporting myself and my mother—and I'm going to raise this baby on my own. Bergen Enterprises could cease to exist, and you'd still be sitting on a giant trust fund. You'll never know what it's like to have people who really count on you."

He stared at her but said nothing.

She glanced out at the water—so peaceful and enduring—and steadied herself.

She flicked her gaze back to him. "What it comes down to, Jasper, is that I can handle this—the loss of my savings, the prospect of being a parent. I will rise to the challenge. The damn shame is that you won't. You're scared. You can't take the plunge, and that will forever be your Achilles' heel."

Again, he watched her, lips parted, and said nothing.

The elevator doors opened, and she stepped inside. "And as far as your responsibility to your company and your precious rebranding. You don't get it! People don't go to Bergen Mountain to be carted to the top of a mountain and ski down like mechanical wind-up toys. People don't go to the spa like cars going in for an oil change. They do these things to connect. To grow. To push their limits and make the kinds of memories that can't be boiled down into a number. Your grandparents understand that. You think I'm a liability to your business? If anyone in this room is going to sabotage the success of Bergen Enterprises, it's you."

He stared at her, eyes wide, unblinking, and held her gaze.

Another staring contest.

Their last staring contest.

Unwavering, she held strong until the doors shut. And then she crumpled to the ground, her hand pressed to her stomach as tears streaked her cheeks.

"These are the first and last tears I'm going to cry for Jasper Bergen. What matters is us. He is irrelevant," she whispered.

The elevator doors opened to the lobby, and she pulled herself up and straightened her shoulders.

She knew this was the way it had to be. Now, she had to convince her shattered heart to believe it, too.

CHAPTER 16

JASPER

Jasper stood, agitation prickling in his veins, and surveyed his desk. "Collin! I asked you to get me the numbers for the Bergen Lodge renovation five minutes ago!"

His assistant ran into the office and handed him a file. "Sorry, I was on the phone with one of the contractors getting an updated bid."

Jasper narrowed his gaze. "That should have been done yesterday!"

Christ! Was he the only competent person in the damn building?

"Where are we with the summer transition?" he pressed.

A glazed look crossed Collin's face.

"I emailed you last night. You know that the summer is just as busy for us as the winter. I need to make sure our hiking, mountain biking, climbing, and water sports programs are ready to go at all our North American and European properties."

"Doesn't our Mountain Education Department take care of that, sir?" Collin asked meekly.

Jasper pinned the man with his gaze. "They do. My job as Chief Executive Officer is to determine if they've done it correctly."

"I'll get on that right now," Collin nodded but didn't move.

"Is there something else?" he barked.

"Nina had asked a few days ago if you were able to get her book signed by Miss Reynolds?" the man asked, gaze trained on his shoes.

Jasper stared at his assistant. If he didn't have the strongest ice man game in town, he might have lost his shit.

"Do I strike you as the kind of person who has time for that, Collin?"

"No, sir. I'll get you that information," he answered and darted out of the office.

Jasper glanced at the calendar, and a muscle ticked in his jaw.

Twenty days.

Twenty days since his blow out with Elle. Twenty days since his world turned upside down.

He'd tried to contact her. He'd left messages. Sent emails. He'd even waited outside her apartment. They needed to talk. They needed a plan. Contracts. Schedules. Arrangements. Every facet of their situation needed to be addressed.

But she'd rebuffed him at every turn. Ignored his every attempt to get in touch. And he could no longer hold her contract with Bergen Enterprises over her head. It had ended the same day she walked out of the Miami penthouse. She was no longer tethered to him except for…

He sat down in his chair and rubbed at a kink in his neck.

Wake up. Complete a punishing run followed by an arduous weights circuit. Work twenty hours. Sleep. Repeat.

That's how he'd spent the last four hundred and eighty hours.

He'd reverted into the robotic, unrelenting, unstoppable working machine that had insulated him from pain for the last decade.

But it wasn't working with Eleanor Reynolds.

Why?

Because she was fucking everywhere—needling into the space he'd crafted to protect his scarred heart.

He glanced at the muted big screen television in his office which was always tuned to CNBC or Bloomberg so he could stay abreast of business and financial news. And there she was, smiling and speaking with the host thanks to her former financial planner.

The Monty Morris scandal did make headlines. But he'd miscalculated the fallout.

Nobody blamed Elle or any of the other celebrities who had been conned by the duplicitous money manager.

While most of Monty's targets waved off reporters or gave no comment, Elle embraced the situation.

She'd collaborated with a reputable financial expert, and together, they wrote a piece on how to protect one's assets and identify the warning signs of financial fraud.

Sympathy for Elle's situation and gratitude for her openness to share about her financial peril only made the public love her more. All the major business networks interviewed her. It didn't matter if he changed the channel. Those lapis blue eyes would show up sooner or later.

But it didn't matter. He had no choice but to put Bergen Enterprises first. He couldn't take a step back. Couldn't give an inch.

Those who were entrusted to lead didn't have that luxury.

He loved his brothers, but neither were up to the task for what being CEO entailed—and what it meant giving up.

Under Elle's spell, he'd forgotten this and succumbed to her witchcraft. He'd lost sight of the vow he'd made to continue his family's legacy.

This was his sacrifice. This was the price he had to pay for not saving his parents' lives.

For a handful of days, he'd thought he could have it all. The warmth of her body in his arms. Her breath on his lips and that charge of electricity that surged through him the millisecond before they kissed.

Everything had seemed possible with her by his side.

But fatherhood—a baby? How the hell was he supposed to do

that? And what the hell would someone like him have to offer a child? He'd had in-depth medical training as a ski patroller and all he could do was watch his mother die, inches away, right before his eyes.

A knock pulled him back to reality.

"Do you have a minute?" his grandfather asked, standing in the doorway.

Jasper schooled his features. Did he have a minute? He had back-to-back meetings with his operations managers, a video conference with his VP of Hospitality, and then a string of calls to make to their suppliers overseas.

He wasn't even going to break for lunch today. But he couldn't blow off his grandfather. The last thing he needed was a Harriet and Ray Bergen tête-à-tête where they counseled him on finding balance and not working himself to the bone.

He stood and waved him in. "Is everything all right?"

Ray Bergen kept his expression neutral. "How about we sit down."

His grandfather stepped aside, and Allen Parker entered the office.

Shit! This could not be good.

Jasper kept his CEO mask in place, shook Allen's hand, then gestured to a table. Jaw clenched, he took a seat and joined the men.

Despite Allen being his father's oldest friend, he was also Elle's attorney. Did she send him here with a list of demands? Is this how it was going to be between them?

"What brings you here today, Allen?" he asked, keeping his tone neutral and detached.

Allen leaned forward and steepled his fingers. "It concerns Elle Reynolds and her contract with Bergen Enterprises."

He held the man's gaze. "Let me guess. She wants more money?"

Allen frowned. "No, quite the opposite. She doesn't want any money."

His grandfather sat back in his chair. "Allen came to me with this first. It seems Elle would like us to give what we owe her to charity. She doesn't want any of it. Not even the tax write-off for the donation."

Jasper could feel the heat rise to his cheeks. She'd made the threat, but he didn't think she'd follow through on it.

He shook his head. "How is she going to survive? Everyone on the planet knows she's lost almost everything."

Allen's expression grew pensive. "You don't need to worry about that, Jas. She's been offered several book deals, and a movie studio has optioned another one of her novels. This will all become public knowledge in a few days. I don't think she'd mind me sharing this with you."

Jasper released a tight breath. He was a damn fool.

"She's pregnant."

Ray and Allen looked at each other.

"You didn't know?" Jasper asked. "That's why I thought you were here, Allen. I thought you wanted money for that."

"Elle Reynolds is pregnant, and the baby is yours?" his grandfather asked with a creased brow.

He nodded. "Yes, and of course, I'll provide financially for the—"

"Jasper, this is wonderful news!" his grandfather said, cutting him off. "Why aren't you with her? Why haven't we seen her?"

"This wasn't planned, Grandad. This could jeopardize everything with the business." He turned to Allen. "She must have told you."

The attorney shook his head. "I had no idea."

Concern flashed in his grandfather's eyes. "What happened, Jas?"

He ran a hand through his hair and sighed. "I didn't handle the news of her pregnancy well. I was concerned about how it would impact the company."

He expected the men to glare at him, maybe even chastise him, but the two looked at each other and broke out into laughter.

He frowned. "I don't see anything funny about this situation."

"Well, you wouldn't," Allen said, laughing so hard, he was nearly crying.

Ray clapped his hands. "No, he couldn't!"

Jasper watched the men who seemed to have lost their fucking marbles.

"What the hell is going on here? Would somebody like to clue me in on how an unplanned pregnancy is a good thing?"

"You sound just like your father," Allen said.

"My father?" he repeated.

"You remember what he was like," Grandad said, grinning ear to ear.

Allen nodded. "He thought he had it all figured out. Cocky as hell and all that ego!"

His grandfather sat back in his chair, still chuckling. "He was damn lucky Hannah didn't kick him out of the house!"

Jasper waved his hands. "I need you both to slow down and explain what the hell you're talking about."

Allen sighed. "You know that I was one of your dad's closest friends, Jasper. Let's just say, when your mother told your father she was pregnant with you, his first reaction wasn't one of jubilation."

Jasper's jaw dropped, and his muted CEO mask disappeared. "Wait! I wasn't planned?"

Ray shook his head. "No, Jas, you weren't. Your parents were traveling all over, going to Europe and Australia and New Zealand setting up the mountain education programs."

Allen nodded. "Your dad loved the freedom of being able to travel the world with your mom."

"But how do you know I wasn't planned?" Jasper asked.

This still didn't make sense.

Allen and his grandad looked at each other, their cheeks turning pink. "The eggs!" they said in unison and fell into another bout of giggles like a couple of preteens at a Justin Bieber concert.

"What do you mean eggs?"

This was getting ridiculous.

Allen caught his breath. "Your dad told your mother he didn't believe her. He said she couldn't be pregnant because he wasn't ready."

"Jesus!" Jasper gasped.

Allen leaned in. "That's not all. He told her that he wasn't sure he even wanted children because their life was so busy and focused on expanding Bergen Enterprises international properties."

Holy fuck! This was not at all the loving, devoted father who had raised him. This douche bag sounded like...

Shit! It sounded like him.

Allen slapped his leg. "Then he asked her how it happened. Oh, Jas! From what your dad told me about that morning, your mother was livid. They were in the kitchen, and she was making scrambled eggs when this all went down. Your mom started explaining the mechanics of how one gets pregnant and when she got to the part about the egg and the sperm, she made sure the point hit home by pelting your father with all the eggs left in the carton."

"He was covered nearly head to toe by the time he made it out of the house," his grandfather added.

Jasper felt lightheaded, remembering how his parents seemed the most in love when they danced together in the kitchen while she made—scrambled eggs.

"How do you know all this?" he asked.

"Allen and I were there," his grandfather answered. "We showed up to get Griff so the three of us could go mountain biking. I pulled up just as he ran out of the house! I damn near hit him with my pickup truck."

"He had egg in his hair," Allen added.

Granddad nodded, laughing. "Egg running down his face."

"When he told us what had happened, we couldn't stop laughing. We called him the ultimate Denver omelet," Allen said.

Ray turned to Allen. "Remember, we made him ride in the bed of the truck."

"Oh, the smell!" Allen replied, covering his nose.

Stunned, Jasper opened and closed his mouth like a goldfish. His father, the man who always had time for him and his brothers, was…

Was just a man. An imperfect man.

"What's going on in here?"

Jasper looked over to see his grandmother.

Fucking fantastic!

"The employees are worried, darling. They've never heard laughter come from your office before."

Ray stood and pulled out a chair for his wife to sit. "We were telling Jasper about when Hannah told Griff she was pregnant."

Gram looked between the men. "What brought on that story?"

He might as well tell her. What was the point in holding back now?

"Elle is pregnant, Gram, and the baby's mine."

The hint of a smirk pulled at the corner of his grandmother's lips. "Ah, so you knocked her up out of the blue just like your grandfather did with me and your father did with your mother."

"Jesus, Gram!" He turned to his grandad. "You didn't plan on having dad? Are we just a family of men who haphazardly impregnate women and then act like complete morons when we hear the news?"

Harriet tapped her chin. "Let's see. When I told your grandfather I was pregnant, Bergen Enterprises was starting to pick up steam. We'd just bought the mountain and were swimming in debt with the store expansion."

Ray took Harriet's hand. "I don't think I'd ever been so afraid in my life. We were stretched razor thin as it was. The thought of a baby sent me reeling."

"What did you do?" Jasper asked.

"I took my pack, headed to Bergen Mountain, and started walking. I hiked nonstop for two days before it hit me."

"What?"

Ray smiled at Harriet. "That your gram and I were a team, and there wasn't anything life could throw at us that we couldn't handle. But that doesn't mean you don't get scared or instantly start doing everything right."

"The opposite, for sure," Harriet continued. "It means that you love each other enough to work through the hard times. It means you trust in each other."

Jasper nodded. He'd never given a second thought to his birth or even his father's. His dad and grandad were such caring, loving fathers. Dedicated to the company, but equally devoted to their family.

"Well, darling, now you have to tell us. What did you do when Elle told you she was carrying your child?"

Jasper ran his hands through his hair again. "Basically, what dad did, just on a larger scale. I told Elle she was irresponsible and that a child would interfere with my job."

His gram, grandad, and Allen all cringed.

"I know. I screwed up. I just never thought I'd…"

"What darling?"

Jasper paused, dumbstruck.

"I never thought I'd fall in love. I was ready to commit my life to the company. To Mom and Dad's memory. I got scared."

He stopped. Elle was right. He'd thought he'd been driven by dedication, but maybe it was fear. Fear of love. Fear of not being in control. Fear of the possibility of losing someone. Fear of not being able to fix every situation. Control every outcome.

Would Bergen Enterprises be what it was today without family? Would it have had the heart and spirit that had drawn people to their stores and their resorts—the very things that had made them so successful?

His parents and grandparents had built Bergen Enterprises into what it was today. And they didn't do it by shunning their family. They did it by embracing it. And they'd done it with the person they loved. The person they promised to honor and to cherish.

For him, that person was Eleanor Reynolds.

"How did Dad patch things up with Mom?" he asked. He needed a plan—a plan that didn't involve contracts and cash payments.

"First, we hosed him off," his grandad said with a chuckle. "Then we had a long talk, very much like the one we're having now. After that, we went to the grocery store."

"Why the grocery store?" Jas asked.

"Eggs," Allen replied.

Jasper stared at the man. "Eggs?"

Ray nodded. "It was your dad's idea. He bought ten cartons of eggs and went home. He apologized and told your mother she could pelt him with as many eggs as she liked, but that he was ready for whatever life had in store for them as long as she was by his side."

Jasper bit back a grin. While his mother was a kind and forgiving person, she wasn't a pushover. Not even close. "How many eggs did mom throw at dad?"

Harriet grinned. "Three dozen."

Jasper chuckled, imagining his father dripping with egg. But he understood why his dad did it. To get Elle back, he'd gladly endure being pelted by three dozen eggs. Hell, thirty dozen! Three hundred dozen!

Jasper looked around the table at the people who had known him for his entire life. "I'm in love with Elle Reynolds."

Harriet patted his hand. "I had a pretty good idea you were when you told us you could marry her."

Jasper frowned. "When did I do that?"

"In this very office. We were talking about Abby joining our family, and you said Elle wasn't family because you could marry her if you wanted to."

"I did, didn't I?" He shook his head. "I screwed up. I screwed up big time. What should I do?"

"Go to her, Jasper. Talk to her," his grandfather offered.

"But she won't talk to me. She hasn't responded to any of my calls or emails."

"This might get her to talk to you, sir."

Jasper looked up to see his assistant standing in the doorway, holding a box.

He schooled his features, switching back to CEO mode. "Have you been listening to this entire conversation, Collin?"

His assistant gave him a sheepish smile, when Jasper caught movement behind the man, just outside the doorway.

He leaned back in his chair, looked past Collin, and saw at least twenty of the Bergen staff standing outside his door.

What the hell were they doing?

Before he could ask, Collin took a few steps forward.

His assistant gave him a hesitant grin. "After you got back from Fell's Peak, you were like a new person. Everyone in the office noticed."

Jasper crossed his arms. "Was I the topic of office gossip?"

Collin shrugged. "Usually, people talk about how scary you are. And then we all saw that video of you and Miss Reynolds dancing. You're not half bad."

Jasper narrowed his gaze.

Collin swallowed hard. "Anyway, I think you'll want to see this. It was just delivered. It's the hat you'd asked me to have our guys go look for off the highway at mile marker 249."

Jasper stood and took the box from Collin.

"It's hers," his assistant said softly.

Jasper touched the brim of the worn Fell's Peak cap. "How did you know that?"

"Look on the inside."

He turned the hat over and saw *Eleanor Reynolds* written in faded permanent marker. He rubbed his thumb over the worn letters, then turned to his grandparents. "This is it. This hat is like dad's eggs."

Everyone stared at him, confusion marring their expressions.

"I think she'll see me if I tell her I've got her hat. It's important to her."

This hat, her hat, was a sign. Witchcraft, coincidence, a twist of fate. This was his call to action. This was his dad sending him his version of a carton of eggs. He grabbed a pen and scribbled a note onto a piece of paper and handed it to Allen. "I need you to take care of this for me," he said, passing the attorney the slip of paper.

"What are you going to do, Jas?" his grandmother asked.

Determination surged through him. "I'm going to win her back." He turned to his assistant. "Cancel the rest of my day, Collin. I'm going to scour this city until I track down the woman I love."

CHAPTER 17

ELLE

"All right, Miss Reynolds. Everything seems to be in order. Go ahead and have a seat. The nurse will be out to get you soon."

Elle slid her insurance card into her wallet and nodded to the receptionist. She glanced around the waiting room where couples sat together, most of the women in various stages of pregnancy.

There was a young couple, heads bent over the book *What to Expect When You're Expecting*. Another couple sat with an open box of saltine crackers between them, the man passing them to his partner dutifully, while a grinning couple smiled and spoke in hushed tones as the husband patted his wife's round belly.

She'd arrived for her appointment early—too early. Abby had called in for a half-day substitute for her class and had promised to meet her there, but Elle was too jittery to wait around in her apartment at The Dalton.

She'd gotten back to Denver last night after spending the last ten days in New York City, and life was moving quickly.

After the Monty Morris scandal broke, she had two choices: shy away from it or face it head-on.

After she'd spoken with her mother and explained the situation, there was only one choice. Grab that bull by the horns and hold on tight.

She met with financial experts and wrote a series of articles on her experience with financial fraud.

And then it exploded.

The world embraced her. Sympathized with her. Talk shows wanted her. Business and financial channels reached out. And with this tornado of publicity came a seven-figure deal to write a full-length book about the scandal, as well as a studio optioning another one of her books.

To anyone on the outside looking in, Elle Reynolds appeared to have it all. And she was grateful. She was. Ironically, all the publicity from the Monty Morris scandal had made her more money than she'd lost. As long as she was careful, she didn't have to worry about money, and there was plenty to care for her mother.

She should have been on Cloud Nine.

Should have been.

She picked a seat away from the couples, next to an older woman paging through a garden magazine. Elle settled herself into the chair then glanced into her bag and stared into the glassy eyes of her lumberjack bear with Dean embroidered on his little paw. She stroked the letters then closed her eyes.

She hated how much she missed Jasper. Hated how honey and Oreos and ice cream all made her want to crumple up on the floor and cry. Hated how her heart skipped a beat every time he texted or called or emailed. But she hadn't responded. She couldn't. Not yet. He didn't want this baby. He'd made that and his disappointment crystal clear.

"Hey! Am I late?" Abby said, sailing into the waiting room. "I thought you said your appointment was at ten."

Elle glanced at her watch. It wasn't even nine thirty. She tried to smile. "I felt like getting out of my apartment. That's all."

Abby took the seat next to her. "How are you doing? You just got back, right?"

"Yeah, last night."

Abby scanned her from head to toe. "Is the nausea better? You look good. The color's returned to your cheeks."

Elle nodded. "I contacted an herbalist I met last year when I was in China doing the piece on the Dali Torch Festival. She suggested dandelion root tea and these ginger chewy things. They seemed to do the trick."

"I'll have to remember that," Abby replied.

Elle's jaw dropped. "Are you...?"

Abby's eyes went wide. "Oh no! Bren and I want kids, but we've got too much going on planning a Bergen wedding."

Elle pulled her cousin in for a hug. "I'm happy for you, Abs. I'm happy things worked out for you and Bren."

Abby watched her, concern clouding her expression. "Have you talked to Jasper yet?"

Elle glanced at the teddy bear in her bag and shook her head. "No, I've been really busy."

Abby cocked her head to the side. Her cousin didn't believe her bullshit answer.

Elle sighed. "I'm just not ready."

Abby leaned in. "You said it all happened quickly. The creep reporter. The pregnancy test flying out of the bag. I'm sure he regrets how he responded, Elle. Anyone could tell by the way he looked at you that he—"

Elle shook her head. "It's more than that, Abs. I can't be with him."

"You don't even want to hear what he has to say?"

Elle took a breath and harnessed all the resoluteness she could muster. "I can't be with someone who doesn't want a child or a family. That's my dad. When things got hard with my mom's health, he took the easy way out. He was gone all the time—and he, he cheated on her. I caught him, twice."

Abby's jaw dropped. "Why didn't you tell me?"

Elle sat back and stared at a picture on the waiting room's wall of a smiling family. "The first time I caught him, he'd promised to stop. When I caught him the second time, it wasn't worth the effort to try to make him be a devoted and loving husband. He'd had his chance. He blew it. After that, I told my mom everything. That's why she filed for divorce and moved to Vermont."

"I thought maybe they just grew apart," Abby said.

"No, he couldn't deal with her illness, and you know, his work always came first. It didn't really even matter that he'd cheated. He'd checked out on me and my mom long before that."

Abby gave her a hopeful smile. "But Jasper cares for you, Elle. I know he does."

Elle released a tight breath. "You didn't see his face, Abs. The disdain and disappointment. I have to figure out a way to do this on my own."

"Have you told your mom?"

"No, not about the baby. And she likes Jasper. She'd probably tell me to—"

"Talk to him?" Abby finished.

"Yeah, but I can't," she answered, her gaze returning toward the happy couples sitting in the waiting room.

Her father had hidden his cheating ways. Tate had hidden his marriage.

At least with Jasper, she knew where she stood.

Abby took out her phone and started texting. "Well, you're going to stay with Brennen and me in our bungalow. At least, for a few days. I won't take no for an answer."

Relief flooded her system. A few days at Abby's place would do her good. "I'd like that, but who the hell are you texting?"

"Bren. I told him to go to your place and grab your bag. We've got your spare key."

"How'd you know I haven't unpacked yet?"

"I lived with you, remember?" Abby answered. "Oh, and where's your lucky hat? I figured you'd be wearing it today."

"I lost it."

Her cousin's expression grew pained. "When?"

Elle crossed her arms. "Chalk it up to another Jasper Bergen disaster. It blew off while we were having a fight on the side of the road on the way to your engagement weekend."

"Oh, Elle," Abby said. She patted her hand, then peered into her purse. "Hmm, it looks like you might have a new good luck charm."

Elle zipped her bag. "It's nothing, Abs."

"It's from him, isn't it?"

She gave her cousin a resigned nod. But that bear didn't represent the Jasper Bergen she'd left in Miami. That bear was from the man who'd broken out of his comfort zone, who'd smiled and laughed and made her feel cherished, adored, *loved*.

Abby reached over and rubbed her shoulder. "I wish I could spend the day with you, but I've got parents coming in this afternoon to celebrate the end of our first-grade poetry unit."

Elle sighed, happy for the change in topic. "What's that sound like? Roses are red. Violets are blue—"

"You should talk to Jasper, I know deep down he cares about you," Abby said, cutting her off.

Elle stared at her purse with the plush Dean Largecox hidden inside. "Maybe he does, maybe he doesn't, Abs. But he'd need to do something pretty freaking huge for me to think he'd ever change."

Abby grinned. "Never say never when it comes to the Bergen brothers. Bren really knocked it out of the park proving his feelings for me."

She was right. Brennen had knocked it out of the park, professing his love to her with a TV camera crew in tow for the whole world to see. She glanced at her purse. She wanted to believe Jasper was capable of that, but thoughts of her father and Tate tamped down that hope.

Abby had gotten her Bergen brother, but she couldn't see a way forward with hers.

Elle started to reiterate this to her cousin for what seemed like the bazillionth time when a nurse stepped into the waiting room.

"Eleanor Reynolds?"

"That's me."

She and Abby followed the woman into an exam room. The nurse gestured for them to sit and glanced down at a chart.

"I see you had your initial blood work done two weeks ago to confirm the pregnancy. It all looks normal. Your hCG levels are a little high, but that's nothing to worry about. How are you feeling?"

"Better."

"And from the information you provided at your first visit, you should be close to ten weeks along. The doctor will confirm all that with the pelvic ultrasound."

"Pelvic ultrasound?" Elle repeated.

The nurse nodded and gestured to a long device attached to a piece of medical equipment. "Yes, the doctor will insert the probe into your vagina to check the baby's development."

Abby and Elle looked at each other, wide-eyed.

Elle crossed her legs. "I'll take the ultrasound you see the doctors doing on TV. You know, the belly one."

The nurse chuckled and went to the door. "Don't worry. You'll be fine. The pelvic ultrasound is the best way to see the baby this early in your pregnancy. Go ahead and take everything off below your waist and have a seat on the table. You can cover up with the sheet."

The woman left, and Elle turned to Abby. "Why doesn't anyone talk about the giant vagina probe?"

Abby took a closer look at the machine and gasped. "Elle, there's a bunch of condoms in a container next to it."

Elle took off her yoga pants and set them on the chair. "Jesus! Isn't it a little late for those now?"

Abby held up the probe. "Good gravy! Do you want to come back to school with me once this is over? You may not want to be alone after this."

Elle sat on the table and arranged the sheet. "I wish I could, but I've got work."

"You have to work?" Abby asked, eyeing the probe.

"Yeah, this was scheduled ages ago. I'm going skydiving."

Abby's head whipped toward her. "You're going skydiving while you're pregnant?"

"No, of course not, Abs! I'm writing a piece for a Colorado magazine about a Buddhist monk that runs a skydiving business near Boulder called Buddha Jump."

"Buddha Jump?"

"Yeah, he's a former Buddhist monk who now jumps out of airplanes. I'm going up in the plane to interview him and watch him jump."

"Gotcha," Abby said, gaze locked on the probe.

"Will you put that thing down!"

Abby held it out. "I guess it's not that bad. I mean, Bren is about—"

Elle put up her hands. "No, no, no! If you're about to say anything about your fiancé's penis, I'm going to stop you right there."

Abby gazed at the vag probe as if she were assessing the quality of a piece of fruit. "I was just thinking, since Bren and Jasper are brothers, there's a good chance that—"

Elle scooted forward and bumped her knee on one of the table's stirrups. "Ouch! Abby! Do you want me to jump off this table half naked and hit you over the head with that probe?"

"Ooh! There's a giant tube of lube next to the condoms," her cousin said, ignoring her threat and biting back a giggle.

"I'll hit you with the lube, too!" Elle answered, unable to hold back her laughter.

Abby went to her, probe in hand, and hugged her.

Elle relaxed into her cousin's embrace. "Thank you for doing this with me, Abs."

"I love you, Elle. I'm always here for you. Always."

The door to the exam room opened.

"I see you've met Juan Julio."

Elle and Abby pulled apart to find a woman in a white coat.

"I don't think we've met anyone named Juan Julio," Elle answered, sharing a look with her cousin.

The doctor pointed to the probe. "He's right there."

"This thing has a name?" Abby asked.

The doctor grinned. "A while back, I had a patient who needed to be monitored weekly. She named the probe, and it stuck with the staff."

Abby handed the doctor the device, and she put it back into its compartment.

"Sorry, we were just curious. It's awfully big," Abby said, blushing.

The doctor grinned. "I can tell you one thing for sure. That probe is nothing compared to what it's like to deliver a child."

Elle and Abby looked at each other, neither were laughing now.

"You don't need to worry," the doctor began. "Women's bodies were made to do this. And there's always the choice to administer medication to numb the pain."

"Can you tick that box for me right now?" Elle asked.

The doctor chuckled and opened her chart. "We'll cross that bridge when we come to it. How about I introduce myself first? I'm Dr. Andrews. I see here that you're new to our practice."

Elle nodded. "I've only been in Denver for about a year."

"Hmm," the doctor said, gaze trained on her file.

"Is there something wrong?" Elle asked.

The doctor closed the chart and set it on the counter. "No, your hCG levels are a bit elevated, but that number fluctuates quite a bit from woman to woman."

Elle caught Abby's gaze, and her cousin came to her side. The nurse had mentioned that, too. She did her best to remain calm. She'd research the hell out of this hCG business the minute the appointment ended.

The doctor asked her a few more questions, then turned down the lights and rolled the ultrasound machine next to the examination table.

"Are you ready to meet your baby?" Dr. Andrews asked.

Elle glanced at her purse. "Abs, could you hand me the bear?"

Abby nodded, unzipped her bag, and gently removed Dean Largecox.

"Here," she said, handing it over then taking her hand.

The doctor patted her leg. "All right, Elle. Just relax."

"Get ready for Juan Julio," Abby whispered.

Elle released a shaky breath. Abby was only trying to break the tension and ease her nerves, but too many emotions stirred within her.

Excitement and anger. Disappointment and elation. One minute, she felt like she could do this. The next, all she wanted was to be wrapped in Jasper's arms. She ran her thumb across the embroidered letters on Dean's paw and watched the screen on the ultrasound machine come to life in shades of white, black, and gray.

"I'm just going to check a few things then take some measurements. How are you doing with Juan Julio?"

Elle nodded then Abby passed her a tissue.

"What's this for?"

Abby smiled, eyes shining. "It's for you. You're crying."

Elle touched her cheeks. Jesus, she was—and she was not a crier.

"It's completely normal for your emotions to be all over the place. Knowing you're pregnant is one thing. Seeing your baby for the first time can really hit home that you're going to be a mother."

A mother.

She'd known this. But to hear the word, the actual word spoken aloud, sent a rush of heat through her body. This was real, and it was happening. She was going to be someone's mother.

"I've had women laugh, cry, one woman wanted to play the harmonica during the ultrasound," the doctor added.

"How'd that go?" Elle asked, blinking back tears.

"The entire office had Blues Traveler songs stuck in their heads for weeks," the doctor answered, then paused. "Well, look at that."

The breath caught in Elle's throat. "Is everything okay with the baby?"

Dr. Andrew's expression grew serious. "Give me just a second. I'd like to take a look from a different angle."

Elle squeezed Abby's hand.

The doctor nodded. "Now I see why your hCG levels were elevated. Do multiples run in your family, Miss Reynolds?"

Elle and Abby looked at each other and gasped.

CHAPTER 18

JASPER

asper ran into The Dalton. Elle still wasn't answering her phone, and he had to start looking somewhere.

"Harvey!" he gasped. "Is Elle Reynolds home?"

The cranky old doorman stared him down. "You young people! Never a hello! Never a 'How's your day, Harvey.'"

Shit! He didn't have time for this.

"I'll check for myself." He ran to the elevators.

"You'll have to take the steps," Harvey called. "They're doing some maintenance work on the elevator shaft."

Double shit!

He ran to the door leading to the stairwell, threw it open, and hurried up. Taking the steps three at a time, he threw off his restrictive tie and jacket and clutched her hat. This had to work. He'd spill his guts. He'd do it while salsa dancing—if that's what she wanted.

He'd watched the viral video. He wasn't half bad.

He shook his head and got himself back into the game. Finally, he'd made it to the eleventh floor. He ran down the hall to find the door to her apartment wide open.

He burst inside, holding up the hat like the Olympic torch.

"Eleanor! Elle! I love you! I want a life with you! I want to have this baby with you!"

He glanced around the apartment and found...

His brother—in the kitchen—eating peanut butter off a spoon.

Brennen put his hands up. "Don't tell Elle I raided her fridge. I just got her to start to like me."

Jasper looked around, waiting for Elle to materialize. "Bren, where's Elle, and why the hell are you here?"

"To get her bag," he said, pointing the spoon toward the suitcase next to the door.

"Is she leaving?" His heart rate kicked up. Was she not only done with him, but done with Denver?

"No, Abby texted me and asked me to get it. Elle's going to stay with us in the bungalow for a while."

"Why? Is she unwell? Is it something with the baby?"

Brennen twisted the lid back onto the jar of peanut butter. "I don't think there's anything wrong. Elle just got back into town last night."

Jasper ran his hand through his hair. "Do you know where she is now?"

A pang of agitation rippled through him. How could his brother be casually eating peanut butter at a time like this?

Brennen put the spoon into the dishwasher then joined him in the living room. "Abby's with her. Well, was with her."

"Where'd they go?"

Bren looked away. "Elle had an ultrasound appointment."

Jasper rolled up his sleeves, ready to spring into action. "Let's go! Call Abby. Find out which doctor."

Brennen shook his head. "I think it's over."

Dammit! He should have been there. "Where are they now?"

Brennen checked his watch. "Abby's back at Whitmore. She took the morning off to be with Elle, but her class has a poetry thing this afternoon, and she had to get back to school."

Jasper shifted his weight, trying to work out a plan. "Can you call her? Can you ask her where Elle is?"

Brennen's expression grew guarded. "She doesn't have her phone on when she's teaching and—"

He cut his brother off. "And I royally screwed up with Elle. I know, Bren. I know! And now, I've got to make it right."

"Jas, it's just…"

"Just what? Spit it out, Bren."

"I think you really hurt her. From what Abby's told me, it sounds like Elle is ready to raise the baby on her own."

Jasper swallowed hard. What hurt more—thinking of Elle raising a child by herself or knowing with her strength and drive, she'd probably be all right without him?

He paced the length of the apartment and stopped when he passed her bedroom and saw the teddy bears lined up in a neat row across her dresser. He went into her room and picked up the mother bear and the two cubs. He held them up for his brother to see.

"She still cares about me. If she didn't, she wouldn't have these."

"Stuffed animals?"

"Yes, stuffed animals. I sent them to her. This is the mother bear and her two cubs from our first night together in the cabin." He scanned all the bears. "Hold on! The Dean Largecox bear is missing."

"Dean, who?" Brennen shot back.

"Largecox. He's my bear alter ego," he answered, checking her bookcase.

"You have a stuffed animal alter ego named Dean Largecox?" His brother's mouth hung open.

It sounded a hell of a lot crazier discussing Dean Largecox with anyone but Elle.

He met his brother's gaze. "Bren! I don't have time to get into it. I need to find Elle."

But Brennen wasn't done. "Where did this alter ego come from, Jas?"

"Elle! She made it up because she's creative and inventive, and

I need to get her back. Can you get over Dean Largecox and help me out here? This is the mother of my child we're talking about."

"Okay, okay," Bren said, pacing the room. "Abby would know where she is."

"But she's teaching."

Excitement lit Brennen's face. "Yeah, but her students are doing a poetry reading for their parents this afternoon. We could go to her school, pretend like we're there for the reading, and slip in and ask her about Elle. Come on, let's head over there now. The reading starts soon."

"Wait!" Jasper said and ran into the kitchen.

His brother frowned. "What are you doing, Jas? Are you going to make a sandwich?"

"No, I need eggs."

Bren's frown grew into a look of complete astonishment. "You're going to fry a flipping egg? Now?"

"No! I just need them. Grandad and Allen Parker told me the story of when mom told dad she was pregnant with me."

"Why'd they do that?"

"Because Dad freaked out on Mom sort of like how I freaked out on Elle."

"No way!" Bren replied.

"Yeah, Mom threw eggs at him."

"Mom always had a good arm," Bren mused. "But, wait! Why are *you* getting eggs?"

"Just in case Elle wants to throw something at me."

Bren nodded. "Good call! I'll drive."

Jasper grabbed the carton of eggs, tucked Elle's hat under one arm and the plush bears under the other.

Brennen held the door open, and they ran to the elevator.

Still out of order.

They hit the stairs. It wasn't easy running with a carton of eggs, and soon, the carton grew damp. He wiped the leaking egg onto his shirt as they passed his discarded tie and jacket and kept going. Finally, they made it to Brennen's car and tore out of the garage—but not before another egg cracked.

Like a bat out of hell, Bren turned onto the boulevard that led to Abby's school and glanced over at him. "I'm proud of you. Stepping up. Doing the right thing."

Jesus Christ on a cracker! Was he really going to have to listen to his brother, the former manwhore of Denver, lecture him on being a good man? On stepping up?

Oh, if his father could see him now—covered in raw egg, listening to Bren spew relationship advice. But he couldn't help smiling, thinking of his dad—and believing there was a chance Elle could forgive him just like his mother had forgiven his father.

Then he caught a glimpse of himself in the side mirror.

Disheveled didn't even come close to describing what he looked like. Businessman versus garbage truck and garbage truck wins was more like it.

But he didn't care. Whatever it took, he'd prove himself.

"We're here," Bren said and parked the car in the Whitmore lot. He glanced over. "Holy flip, dude!"

Jasper shifted in his seat, careful not to get egg on the hat or the bears. "I know! I know! I'm a damn mess."

His brother grinned. "No, that's not what I meant. You look more like yourself than you have in years."

"Covered in egg yolks?"

Bren grinned. "No, like you're passionate about something—like how you used to look when you were on ski patrol."

Jasper shook his head. "Elle used to call me a hollow bunny."

"What's that?"

"Someone who's empty on the inside."

Bren chuckled. "That's spot-on. Elle doesn't mince words." His expression grew serious. "But don't think for a minute I don't know why you turned into a hollow bunny. We all changed—you, me, and Cam—because it just..."

It just hurt so damned much to lose their parents.

Jasper swallowed past the emotion in his throat. "I know, Bren. I know."

Brennen released a tight breath. "Even if we find Elle and she kicks your ass to the curb—which you probably deserve—don't go back to that place. Don't go back to living like a robot. It's not you."

Jasper blew out a shaky breath. "Let's hope she forgives me."

"Bergen brothers on three?" Bren said, putting out his hand like they were about to play in a Junior Varsity soccer tournament.

Jasper stared at his brother.

"Too much?" Bren asked.

"Yes, but…" Jasper put in his hand. "Screw it! If I'm all in, I'm all in. Bergen brothers on three."

They did the cheer then stared at each other.

Brennen cringed. "Let's never do that again."

Jasper opened the car door. "Agreed. Let's go!"

They jogged up to the school and joined the line of parents entering the building. Jasper recognized the school's principal, Mrs. Ramos, greeting the families and directing them into the auditorium.

"Hello, Brennen and…" The principal stared at him.

"You remember my brother, Jasper," Brennen replied smoothly.

The woman pasted on a smile, and her gaze darted to his egg covered shirt. "Yes, hello, Jasper."

Brennen stepped forward. "We wanted to wish Abby and her class good luck before the poetry reading began. Would you mind if we went to her room?"

The principal's cheery grin was gone. "But the reading starts in five minutes. We pride ourselves on running like a well-oiled machine here at Whitmore Country Day."

Crap! They could not get shut down by the punctuality patrol!

Jasper glanced at the wall and saw a poster with a graph of the money the school had raised for a new playground.

He pointed to it. "We'd also like to donate the rest of the funds needed to build the new playground," Jasper added. He was not above a little wink-wink nod-nod bribery to bust into this building.

The woman's eyes went wide. "That's quite generous of you!" She glanced at her watch. "Now we've only got four minutes before the children are expected in the auditorium." Her gaze flicked to the graph. "But I can't see the harm in saying a quick hello and wishing them good luck."

Bingo!

They bypassed the principal and started down the hall.

"Which classroom is Abby's?" he asked.

He and his brothers had attended Whitmore as kids, and he knew the place like the back of his hand.

"Room 104," Bren answered.

And he was off! He passed Brennen and threaded himself through a line of older children walking down the hall before hopping over an errant backpack lying on the ground and locating room 104. He swung open the door and burst into the room.

"Ahh!" came a loud shriek as something warm and gooey collided with his leg.

"Stranger danger!" came a child's voice, followed by a shot of liquid straight into his eye.

"Jasper, what are you doing here?"

He blinked and looked down to see Abby and her entire class staring at him. Directly in front of him stood a child with a cafeteria tray of what looked like tuna surprise—he still had nightmares about that Whitmore lunchtime staple—and a little girl holding a juice box like she wasn't afraid to blast him with another stream of the sticky liquid.

"The bad man got in my way, and I spilled on him!" said the child with what was left of the tuna surprise dangling off the tray.

"It's all right, Porter. He's not a bad man or a stranger. His name is Mr. Bergen," Abby said, reassuringly.

"Like Brennen Bergen?" the boy asked.

"Yes," Abby answered.

The girl with the juice box perked up. "Does this guy want to marry you, too?"

Jasper looked down at the little girl. "No, I want to marry your teacher's cousin."

Abby grinned. "You do?"

"More than anything, but I need to find her. I need to apologize," he said, then removed a chunk of tuna from his pants and set it on the boy's tray.

Brennen entered the room. "Jasper, what's wrong with you? You almost took out a kid racing down the hall!"

Abby turned to Brennen. "Jas says he wants to marry Elle."

"Yeah, we're trying to find her. Do you know where she is?"

Abby nodded. "Hold on! I need to have the children put away their lunches. We ate in the classroom today to get a little extra practice time before our poetry reading."

Jasper shifted his weight from foot to foot, nervous energy surging through him.

Another child tugged on his pant leg. "If you need to pee, the bathroom pass is next to Miss Quinn's desk."

He glanced at the kid. He didn't have time for bathroom questions or lunchtime cleanup. "Abby, we can't wait! I need to find Elle. I can't let any more time pass."

Abby nodded as she guided a child with a tray toward the garbage can. "Okay, she's skydiving at a place called Buddha Jump somewhere near Boulder, Colorado."

His jaw dropped. "She's what?"

"Hey, mister!" came a little voice. "Why do you smell so funny?"

He looked down to find a child staring at his food-stained clothing. "Because I'm covered in egg and tuna surprise."

Abby glanced at the clock on the wall. "I'm sorry, but it's time for me to bring the children to the auditorium. That's all I know. Elle should be there now." She narrowed her gaze. "Are you okay, Jasper? You look a little disheveled."

"Yeah, Jas! What happened?" Bren asked, looking at the remnants of tuna surprise flaking off his trousers.

He didn't have time to worry about being covered in egg and tuna—not to mention the red splotches of fruit punch now dotting his dress shirt from the pint-sized Capri Sun sharpshooter. He pulled his phone from his pocket and searched for Buddha Jump Skydiving.

"Got it! I found the place. Let's go!"

He whipped around and—bam—smacked into another tray.

"My goulash! My grandma made that for me!" a girl cried.

Jasper brushed the chunks of stew off his leg. "Sorry, kid! At least you didn't have to eat the tuna surprise."

Covered in egg, tuna, and now—fucking goulash—he ran down the hall and skirted past the parents trickling inside the building. He looked over his shoulder. Good, Brennen was only a few yards behind. He dialed up his pace, reached the Mercedes, and went to the driver's side.

"Throw me the keys, Bren."

"There's no flipping way I'm letting you drive! I don't even know if I want you in my car."

"Come on, Bren. I'm pulling rank. Big brother. CEO. I won the last thumb war we had twenty-five years ago. Hand the keys over."

"I was only five!" Brennen protested.

"Still counts," he said, extending his hand.

"Flip!" his brother groaned, then tossed him the keys.

Jasper threw him his phone. "You're the navigator. I've got the skydiving place entered in on the GPS."

In a stunt that would have put the *Fast and the Furious* drivers to shame, Jasper peeled out of the school's parking lot and headed toward the highway, his mind racing. Why the hell would she be skydiving? That couldn't be safe for a pregnant woman! It barely passed as safe for anyone *not* pregnant.

"Do you have a plan? You're awfully quiet over there," Bren asked.

Plan.

Shit!

The only plan he had was making Elle see that he was the only man for her and that she was the only woman for him. He glanced at her hat and the plush bears on the dash. That's what he had to work with. It had to be enough.

He glanced at Brennen. "No, I don't have a plan."

His brother set the eggs next to his feet and frowned. "You don't have a plan? The guy who follows a daily schedule like a Navy Seal doesn't have a plan when it's finally time to try and get the girl?"

Jasper chuckled and shook his head. "No, I think I've got to wing it."

Bren laughed.

"What?"

"I think wings are the only thing you don't have all over your pants."

Jasper turned on the blinker. "It's too late to worry about that. We're here."

CHAPTER 19

ELLE

E lle climbed into the back of the prop plane and secured her bag to a hook. "All right, Lloyd, tell me how you went from studying at a Buddhist monastery in the Himalayas to running your own skydiving business in Colorado."

She pulled her notebook and pen from her bag, careful not to let Dean Largecox fall out, and smiled at a man in a tie-dye shirt with gentle eyes who seemed more suited to be boarding a vintage Volkswagen bus covered in peace signs rather than jumping from an airplane.

But this was good. Work was good. She'd been given the okay to fly by her obstetrician, scheduled the rest of her prenatal appointments, and driven straight to Buddha Jump from the doctor's office. After the morning she'd had, she was happy to throw herself into the life of a gangly fifty-something ex-monk who enjoyed free falling from ten thousand feet up.

Lloyd set his gear on the floor and sat next to her on the bench. "I'm from Denver originally, and when I was younger, everything was a rat race. Everyone around me was focused on getting more. More money. More status. More things. But nobody seemed happy. That's when I found Buddhism and decided to give away all of my possessions. This world is so focused on material things.

I needed to leave it all behind and follow the path of mindfulness that didn't revolve around dollar signs."

"What brought you back?" she asked.

"A few years ago, I left the monastery to attend my niece's wedding, and I was on a plane that had engine failure."

"That had to be terrifying."

"It was. But I tried to stay calm. There was a guy in a suit next to me. We all thought these might be our last moments alive, and he was freaking out about the Wi-Fi going out and not getting a proposal submitted on time for a work deal."

She knew somebody like that. She swallowed hard and tried to ignore the ache of her broken heart.

"What happened?" she asked, taking notes.

"The plane started vibrating. It felt like it was about to come apart, like every nut and every bolt were separating. That's when the guy realized this might be it. He started freaking out and confessed everything he'd done wrong in his life. After he was done, I asked him what he'd do if we lived, and he had another chance."

"Wow! It sounds like you helped him find meaning in his life."

Lloyd shook his head. "No, he told me if we made it out alive, he'd upgrade his sixty-inch flat screen to an eighty-inch, and then he'd try to sleep with his best friend's wife. He indicated she was quite attractive."

Elle stopped writing. "I was not expecting that."

Lloyd raised his index finger. "But I was in the center seat, and the man to my other side was another story."

"How so?" Elle asked, trying to stay objective. Trying not to imagine Jasper on that plane as the businessman consumed with work.

"He shared, that if he made it out alive, he'd go back to his hometown and ask the girl he'd loved his whole life to marry him. It was a big risk. He'd never shared his feelings with her, but when everything was spiraling out of control, he was able to focus on what mattered."

Elle held the man's gaze. "And what would you say that was?"

The ex-monk grinned. "Love, what else?"

She loved her mother and Abby. They were her family.

But what about romantic love?

After enduring the fallout from her father's infidelity, living with the pain of Tate's deception, and now Jasper's rejection, could she ever trust in that kind of love?

"You think it's that simple?" she pressed.

"It can be—especially when you're falling from the sky," the man answered, patting the rig pack that contained the parachute.

"Is that how you got into skydiving? You're giving someone a chance to figure out what matters?"

A playful glint flashed in the man's eye. "That, or maybe just for the adrenaline kick. It's pretty awesome, too."

Elle chuckled and added a few notes.

"Ready to head up?" he asked.

She nodded, and Lloyd signaled for the pilot to start the plane.

"Are you sure you don't want to jump? I've got my tandem harness," Lloyd called over the buzz of the plane's propellers.

She jotted down a few more notes and shook her head. "No, I'm just a spectator today."

"That's weird," Lloyd said.

"What's weird about that?" Elle asked.

"No, not you. That is," Lloyd said and gestured out the plane's open door. "Are you expecting someone? We canceled all our jumps for this afternoon."

Elle glanced out the open hatch and saw three men running toward them. The second she recognized as Lloyd's partner and business manager, Bruce. She'd spoken with him when she'd arrived. Then she focused on the near-deranged looking man leading the pack, holding what looked to be a carton of eggs.

"Jasper?" she gasped.

Except it didn't look like Jasper—at least, not the perfectly coiffed, buttoned-up Jasper she was used to.

No jacket. No tie. His dark hair spiked out every which way as if he'd driven through the city with his head sticking out the car window—and he was filthy.

"What's going on?" the pilot asked from the cockpit.

"That's just my…" she began but stopped.

Her what? Her baby daddy. Her sort of ex-boyfriend?

The man she shouldn't love?

Jasper picked up his pace, sprinting the last ten yards then stopped outside the plane's open door, his chest heaving. "Elle," he panted. "You can't jump out of an airplane. You're pregnant."

"You're pregnant?" Lloyd echoed.

Men! She stifled the urge to smack them both.

"Yes, I'm pregnant. And no, I'm not skydiving. I'm working. I've been cleared by my doctor to fly. And guess what? Pregnant women work. They're actual human beings who just happen to be growing a person inside their uterus."

Jasper's gaze bounced between her to Lloyd. "But I thought…I mean, you're in the airplane."

"To interview the owner of Buddha Jump and watch him skydive. And it comes as no surprise that you'd expect me to be irresponsible and reckless," she shot back.

His expression grew pained. "Can you please get off the plane so we can have a conversation?"

She had to stay strong. She couldn't give an inch.

She shook her head. "No, I can't. This should be easy for you to understand. I'm working, and I have nothing to say to you. You made your feelings loud and clear in Miami."

She glanced over his shoulder as Bruce made it to the plane followed by Brennen.

Bruce pointed to Jasper. "Sorry, Lloyd! This dude is nuts! He came in with a carton of eggs and said I needed to stop you from going up with Miss Reynolds."

Lloyd frowned. "What do you think you're doing running toward an airplane about to take off?"

She stared at Jasper as he caught his breath.

"Can I get on the plane? I need to speak with Miss Reynolds."

Lloyd shook his head. "I'm sorry. You're not an employee, and you're not jumping. So, no."

Jasper met her gaze—and nothing in his eyes said hollow bunny or tin man. She saw passion and fire and determination. A look with such intensity she felt it in the tips of her toes.

Jasper nodded to himself as if he'd decided something, then looked from Bruce to Lloyd. "How would you like to join Bergen Enterprises?"

"What do you mean?" Lloyd asked.

What the hell was he doing?

"I'm Jasper Bergen, the CEO of Bergen Enterprises. My family owns Bergen Mountain Sports."

Bruce's jaw dropped. "I thought you looked familiar."

"I'll give you four times what your company is worth," Jasper continued. "You'll maintain your autonomy and continue to operate the business as you like. You'll just be under the umbrella of Bergen Enterprises."

"You're buying a skydiving company?" she asked, disbelief lacing her words.

"No," Lloyd said, sharing a wide grin with an equally elated-looking Bruce. "He just bought a skydiving company. You've got a deal," he added, leaning out of the plane and shaking Jasper's hand.

Her jaw dropped. "Lloyd, what was all that talk about giving up material things and finding a higher purpose? Wasn't that the whole reason you chose to become a Buddhist monk?"

Lloyd shrugged. "Higher purpose still needs to pay for airplane fuel and parachutes." He turned to Jasper. "Are we talking health insurance and 401(k)s?"

Jasper nodded as Bruce and Lloyd high fived.

Billionaire jackass!

She crossed her arms, furious. Jasper had no right intruding on her work. No right to buy the damn business to corner her into having a conversation.

Jasper turned to Brennen, and the two of them, along with Bruce, spoke briefly before Brennen and Bruce headed back toward the small Buddha Jump office.

"I was just starting to like you, Brennen Bergen," she yelled from the plane.

Bren turned and shrugged his shoulders with an unapologetic grin then continued back to the small office with Bruce.

"May I?" Jasper asked, gesturing inside the plane.

"Welcome aboard, boss!" Lloyd said, his wide grin still in place.

Elle rolled her eyes as Jasper climbed into the small space. Lloyd gave the pilot the thumbs-up then turned his attention to inspecting his gear as the plane bumped along the makeshift runway.

Elle glared at Jasper and scooted away from him, but she couldn't get far—trapped inside a single prop Cessna. She sighed and cradled her head in her hands.

"How did you even know I was here?" she asked without looking up.

"I went to your apartment and found Bren there."

That got her attention. "Why was Brennen in my apartment?"

"He was picking up your bag."

Shit! That's right.

Jasper leaned forward. "Bren said you had an ultrasound this morning."

She sucked her teeth. "Yeah, we irresponsible types sometimes practice actual responsibility from time to time."

"How'd it go?" he asked softly.

She looked away. "You don't get to ask how it went."

"I saw the bears on your dresser when I was at your apartment. I brought a few with me."

He set the mama bear and the two little cubs on the bench between them, and she stiffened.

He ran his finger along one of the cub's tiny plush paw. "I figured if you still had these, then I may still have a chance."

She held his gaze. "A chance at what?"

"A chance you still care about me. A chance you could forgive me."

She leaned back. "What did you think I'd do, Jasper? Cut off their cute little bear limbs or shove them down the garbage disposal?"

"Dean wasn't there."

Good! Let him think she'd chucked the lumberjack bear into the garbage! But her heart got the best of her, and she glanced at her bag where the stuffed animal sat nestled next to her wallet, house keys, and the fuzzy black and white ultrasound picture the doctor had printed off for her.

She could feel Jasper watching her, and she turned her attention to the plush bear cubs on the bench.

"What did Abby tell you?" She held her breath. Hopefully, not everything.

He looked down at his pants and scraped at something encrusted on his knee. "Not much. I tried to talk to her at Whitmore, but she was busy getting her class ready for a poetry thing. They were finishing up eating lunch in her classroom, and the kids mostly spilled food on me. One attacked me with a juice box," he added, pointing to the spattering of red dots on his wrinkled white Oxford shirt.

She almost smiled, but the shake and bump of the plane taking off jostled her. She bumped against Jasper and steadied herself by grasping his arm. Strong and solid, the image of his limbs wrapped around her flashed through her mind before she forced herself to pull away.

She released a tight breath then glanced over as a smiling Lloyd gave her the thumbs-up.

Yeah, thumbs-up for you, buddy boy!

If it weren't unprofessional to flip off the subject of an interview, she'd be rocking the bird at this Buddhist sellout.

She turned to Jasper. "You clearly made his day. But I can tell you one thing. You can't buy me."

"I know. I met with Allen today."

"Good, because I don't want a penny from you. I can take care of myself," she added.

He nodded. "That's why I've asked Allen to speak with your mom and have her help us choose a charity that supports people with Multiple Sclerosis, so that we can donate the money from your contract with Bergen Enterprises to them in her name."

She opened her mouth to speak but was at a loss.

Shit! That was thoughtful—the bastard!

"And this came today," he said and pulled the faded cap she'd had since she was a girl out of his pocket.

"That's my…"

"Your Fell's Peak hat. The one that blew over the guard rail," he finished.

She stared at it in disbelief. A gift from her mom. A memento of life before her mother's illness, before she learned of her father's cheating. "How did you find it? Where did you find it?"

"I asked a few of the Bergen Resort employees to look for it a while back. It came today."

Today. The day of her ultrasound. The day the word mother hit her like a one-two punch.

She turned the hat over and rubbed her fingertips over her name printed in her mom's handwriting and swallowed past the emotion in her throat.

The hat. The ultrasound. This man who looked like he'd escaped a prison mess hall food fight to get to her. She wanted to believe he was here because he cared for her, but he'd told her he'd wanted her before. Told her that she was his everything.

Until he learned she was pregnant.

She lifted her chin. "Why the hell do you have a carton of eggs?"

"I had them in case you wanted to throw them at me," he said, opening the lid and grimacing. "But they're all pretty cracked and gooey now. They're your eggs. I took them from your refrigerator."

"You stole a carton of eggs from my apartment so that I could throw them at you?" She glanced at his clothing. "It looks like somebody's already done that. And you smell like a fishmonger who rolled through a chicken coop."

He pointed to a brown stain on his pants. "There's some goulash, too."

She shook her head. "Where would you get the idea that I'd want to throw eggs at you?"

"My dad."

"Your father?"

His expression warmed. "Yeah, it turns out the Bergen men have a history of losing their shit when the women we love tell us they're pregnant."

Love.

She held his gaze. Unable to speak. Unable to move.

"After my mom told my dad she was pregnant with me, he told her he wasn't even sure he wanted kids."

She watched him closely for any sign of anguish or disappointment—but his smile widened.

"Apart from my grandad, my father is…was the best man I've ever known. He loved us. He adored my mother. He worked hard. He loved our company, but he always had time for family." Jasper ran his hand over the leaky carton of eggs. "I figured if my dad could turn things around and prove to my mom that he was ready to be a father, then there has to be hope for me. Hope for us."

"And the eggs?" she asked with a shake to her voice.

"My dad made the mistake of freaking out just as my mom was about to make breakfast. She was so mad, she started pelting him with the carton she'd taken out to make scrambled eggs."

Elle stared at the bear cubs. "I think I would have liked your mom."

"I know she would have loved you."

She looked up and met his gaze.

Jasper took her hand. "Both of my parents would have

because anything important to me was important to them. And you and our baby are what matters the most to me—over any spreadsheet or board meeting." He threaded their fingers together. "I want to fight with you. I want to salsa dance with you. I want to lose at every single staring war with you. I want to eat junk food off your body, and I don't want to spend another moment without you by my side. I want this baby, and I want you, Eleanor. I love you."

He brushed his thumb over her wrist, and a heated charge surged through her body.

He leaned in. "I'm ready, Elle. I'm ready for everything. I'm ready to take the plunge, and I'll do whatever it takes to prove that to you."

"Anything?" she asked.

He tightened his grip. "Anything."

She glanced past him to where Lloyd was doing the last check of the parachute's automatic activation device.

"Lloyd, what's your altimeter reading at?"

He looked down at the device strapped to his wrist. "Ten thousand feet. We're over the drop zone, and I'm good to go."

She squeezed Jasper's hand. "You say you're ready to take the plunge—that you love me and that you'll do anything?"

He nodded. "I'm ready. I'm all in."

"Would you jump out of an airplane for me?"

His brow creased. "Me, jump?"

This was it. He hated skydiving. He'd said as much the night they comforted Bodhi.

"Yes, you." She waved to Lloyd. "You've got all the equipment to do a tandem jump, right?"

Now it was Lloyd's turn to frown. "I can't jump with you, Elle. You're pregnant."

"But your new boss isn't," she said, excitement building in her chest.

Jasper looked out the opening in the plane. "You want me to skydive?"

"You said you're ready to take the plunge. Call it your *dramatic flair* and prove it."

Lloyd held up the harness. "You'll love it, boss!"

Jasper went as pale as the egg whites splattered all over him. "I don't know the first thing about jumping out of a plane."

Lloyd waved him off. "That's the easy part."

"It is?" Jasper said, the color returning to his cheeks.

Lloyd patted Jasper's shoulder. "Yeah, it's the landing that can kill you."

"What?" Jasper replied, back to his shade of egg white.

"Don't worry! As long as we don't bounce, we're golden," Lloyd said, handing him a helmet.

"Bounce?"

"On the ground," the ex-monk replied and pointed out the open hatch.

Jasper turned to her. "If I do this. If I jump out of this airplane —like a lunatic and embrace my *dramatic flair*—you'll forgive me? You'll give me another chance?"

She held his gaze. "Yes."

He took a breath. "I don't want to be apart from you. I want us to live together. I want to marry you."

She cupped his cheek in her hand. "Are we negotiating the terms of the man feast?"

The panic in Jasper's gaze receded, and he schooled his features. "I'd like to offer you a permanent man feast."

"An infinite extension to the extension to the extension?" she asked, biting back a grin.

Minus the slight curve to his lips, he kept his CEO mask in place. "Those are my terms, Miss Reynolds. What do you say? Could you spend the rest of your life with a hollow bunny?"

She stroked her thumb across his cheek. "Nobody who can salsa like you could be called a hollow bunny."

He smiled, his gaze growing glassy—or maybe it was her eyes welling with tears.

It didn't matter. This was it. This was the moment.

Tears trailed down her cheeks. "Yes. Yes, to all of it. Yes, to a permanent man feast."

His warm hands cradled her face. She closed her eyes, ready to have Jasper's lips pressed to hers when Lloyd clapped his hands.

"Sorry, folks! We've got to get the show on the road. Time to harness up, boss!"

Jasper held her gaze. "Am I going to be okay?"

She gave him a thumbs-up and watched as Lloyd helped him into the harness and gave him a quick crash course in tandem skydiving.

She unzipped her purse and pulled out Dean Largecox. "Here, Jas! Take Dean!"

"You still have him?"

She grinned. "I could never part with Dean Largecox."

He touched the bear's paw. "You want me to jump out of a plane with Dean Largecox?"

She nodded, handed him the bear, then watched as Lloyd guided Jasper toward the hatch. The skydiving ex-monk positioned their bodies, so his back hung out of the plane while Jasper remained partially inside, allowing him to hold her gaze. Lloyd started to count them down, but she stopped him.

"Wait!" she called out and dropped to her knees. She tugged the straps of Jasper's harness and pulled him in close, their lips millimeters apart. "Don't bounce," she said, then kissed him.

A weird kind of experience, kissing a man attached to another man. But she needed to do it.

He winked. "Got it."

She wiped another tear and went back to the bench. Lloyd got them into position, but she jumped up again.

"One more thing!" She touched his cheek. "I love you, Jasper Bergen."

He grinned—a smile so sweet and so full of happiness it sent her pulse racing.

"I love you, too, Jemima Sex Kitten."

She chuckled through her tears. "Oh, and it's not one baby," she added.

This seemed like a good time to drop the bomb.

His brow knit together. "Not one baby?"

"We've got to go!" Lloyd called, angling them out of the plane.

She shook her head. "It's two. We're having twins."

A look of pure joy lit Jasper's face just as Lloyd let go and the two of them tumbled backward toward the earth.

EPILOGUE

JASPER

"Here," Elle purred and ran her index finger between her breasts.

Jasper gazed down at his stunning fiancée, took the honey dipper from where it rested in a glass jar on the nightstand and trailed a thin line between Elle's breasts. He returned the dipper to the honeypot and licked the syrupy-sweetness from her chest.

She arched her back and hummed her delight. "Now, here," she purred, her fingertips gliding over her kiss-swollen lips.

He dipped his finger into the pot of golden honey and dabbed along the smooth surface.

She pressed her lips together, then ran her tongue across her top lip. "What are you waiting for? Don't you want a taste?"

"Not waiting, just admiring," he said, leaning in and devouring her honey-sweet mouth in a scorching kiss.

After he jumped out of the airplane and plummeted over ten thousand feet, he had Elle back up in the air seventy-two hours later—but not for skydiving. Nope, he'd had the jet take them down to the Bergen compound on Grand Cayman for a tropical getaway to jump-start their permanent man feast.

There were no bears on Grand Cayman, but they did have

bees. And bees meant honey—and that meant a sweet man feast with white sand beaches and clear blue water.

A seaside man feast.

A getaway man feast.

An everything man feast that started with the ring he'd slid on her finger.

He'd wanted to whisk her away the minute the skydiving plane landed and he had her on solid ground. But he knew he'd never hear the end of it from his gram and grandad if they didn't share the news that there wasn't just one Bergen baby on the way, but two.

They also paid another visit to Elle's doctor so he could see Bergen Baby number one and Bergen Baby number two for himself.

Oh, and he cried like a damn baby—his hollow bunny days firmly a thing of the past.

And the skydiving?

Let's just say, he was damned excited to welcome Buddha Jump to Bergen Enterprises and had a standing weekly jump scheduled on the books.

Never in his wildest dreams did he expect to catch the skydiving bug. He never imagined he'd be expecting twins. And he'd never thought he'd find the deep, soul connection he'd found with Eleanor Jayne Reynolds.

"Hello there, Mr. Largecox," Elle said, drawing her fingertips down the muscled plane of his abdomen and cupping his hard length in her hand.

She stroked him in a slow, steady rhythm that sent a rush of heat through his body.

Holy fuck, he could die a happy man as Dean Largecox! But it wasn't the roleplay or the fun they had with food that got his cock rock-hard and his pulse racing.

It was Elle.

With her, everything was brighter and more vibrant. He'd

lived the last ten years in black and white. She was the technicolor pop that changed everything.

Everything.

With her, that's what he had.

She sighed and worked his cock, driving him crazy.

"Where do you want me to put the honey next?" he bit out between clenched teeth.

She grinned against his lips. "Let's put the honey on hold. Jemima Sex Kitten is ready to ride her lumberjack."

Holy fuck! He said that a lot these days.

Elle pushed him onto his back, and he gazed up at her as she straddled him, dragging her nails along the length of his thighs and sending his desire into overdrive.

The fourposter bed they'd barely left since they'd arrived sat in the middle of the large master bedroom. He'd opened the doors to the terrace to allow the cool ocean breeze to wash over their naked bodies as the scent of the sweet honey and the salty sea hung in the warm tropical air.

Elle positioned his hard length at her entrance and sank down, taking him slowly, as the sheer white curtains covering the floor-to-ceiling windows billowed with each gentle gust of wind, casting Elle in a cascade of shimmery, sun-dappled light.

She was beautiful, radiant, and he was completely captivated.

Brujería. Witchcraft. She'd worked her magic on him, and there was no spell that could change that.

He gripped her hips, and she gasped as he found her sweet spot.

She rested her palms on his chest, and he met her lapis blue gaze.

"I will never get tired of this view," he vowed and caressed her sensitive bud.

"Me, in charge?" she said with a sexy smirk.

"I think you've always been in charge. It just took me a while to figure that out."

She leaned in. "Dean Largecox is helpless against Jemima Sex Kitten's power of persuasion."

"Oh yeah?" he asked, thrusting his hips.

She moaned and bit her lip as the throb of carnal victory pulsed through him.

Dean Largecox was no lightweight in the bedroom either.

She closed her eyes and rolled her hips, riding his cock, up and down, building speed. He set the pace and guided her body in a steady rhythm, but he needed more. He needed to take her in his arms.

"I have to kiss you," he growled and shifted into a seated position.

Elle's breasts pressed against his chest as he brought her to him, and her arms encircled his neck. He loved her pregnant body. He worshipped every curve and every inch of this strong, driven, loving, and forgiving woman who owned his heart.

He gripped her ass with his hand while the other slid up her back and tangled itself into her wild chestnut locks.

"I love you, Eleanor," he bit out, taking her earlobe between his teeth.

She dug her nails into his back. "I know. How could you not?"

Jesus! This woman!

He drove into her hard as her body contracted around him. Taking her higher and higher, they moved together as one. She gasped his name and met her release, and her sweet sighs and sultry moans sent a jolt of lust rocketing through his body.

Skydiving thrilled him—but it couldn't hold a candle to making Elle come in his arms.

He held her close and followed her over ecstasy's cliff. Pistoning his hips, he pumped into her with fierce intensity, losing himself to her warm embrace and those lapis blue eyes.

Their bodies slick with sweat, she rested her head on his shoulder, and he listened as her breathing slowed. He loved this part. He treasured everything about making love to Elle, but this, the gentle stretch of time where they were silent, bodies fused as they wound down from their release, felt like they were hidden away.

He glanced down at the floor to where her fuzzy slippers rested near the foot of the bed and smiled. The man who didn't take vacations was on vacation, celebrating the first of many lazy Sunday mornings in bed with the woman he loved. And, besides skydiving, he'd taken up another hobby: reading. When they weren't tangled together in bed, he'd settle himself in a beach chair and crack open one of Elle's books. He loved her words almost as much as he loved worshipping her body—almost.

She tilted her head and glanced at the nightstand. "We're getting low on honey."

He chuckled. "Don't worry. I've got another case out in the car."

"And pickles?"

"Plenty of those, too," he answered.

"It's still weird that I don't crave chocolate. It's been my go-to stress reliever since I was a kid."

He lowered their bodies to the bed and rested Elle's head onto the pillow. She stretched like a cat, and he caressed her belly then pressed a kiss below her navel.

"Your stomach occupants may have something to do with your cravings."

"You mean the girls?" she said, playing with the hair at the nape of his neck.

He laid down next to her. "Or the boys."

"Or one of each," she countered.

He cupped her cheek. "A little girl with dark hair and lapis blue eyes."

She grinned. "Or a little boy with a briefcase and a tiny little suit and tie."

He pulled her close and chuckled. "Whatever they are, they'll be ours and they'll be perfect."

He tucked a lock of hair behind her ear and stared down at his everything. His forever. He leaned in and trailed kisses down her jawline, and she ran her hand down his back.

Hello, round two, until Van Halen's "Hot for the Teacher" came blasting from Elle's phone.

"What's that?" he asked.

She grinned. "That's my ringtone for Abby."

He shook his head. "Do you want to get it?"

Elle slid her hand lower and gripped his ass. "She knows we're on our permanent man feast getaway. I'll call her later."

The rock anthem ringing stopped.

"See," Elle said but frowned as the *ping, ping, ping* of a new text message sliced through the room.

"I better look," she said.

He reached over and handed her the phone.

"Holy shit!" she exclaimed.

"Is everything all right?"

She stared at her phone. "Your brother's in Denver."

"Brennen? Did he go somewhere?"

Elle turned to him. "No, not Bren. Camden. Did you know he was coming back?"

He'd barely spoken to Cam over the last decade. After the accident, he'd left the country and had been holed up in Switzerland. He'd only talk to Gram—and even that only happened once in a blue moon.

Elle met his gaze. "What do you think brought him back?"

He shook his head, stunned. "I have no idea. But it has to be something important."

She pushed up onto her elbow. "Should we head home?"

He tucked a lock of hair behind her ear. "Is the travel goddess, Elle Reynolds, contemplating cutting short a vacation?"

"Don't you want to see your brother? I know it's been years." Elle watched him carefully.

"Camden's always been a bit of a loner. If he's back in Denver, the last thing he'd want is for us to make a fuss over him. He's got my contact information. When he wants to be found, he'll let me know how to find him."

She nodded, then ran her tongue across her top lip. "Well, then. What would you like to do for the rest of the day?"

The old Jasper would have been checking emails and making calls.

But not him. Not anymore.

He still planned on working hard. That was just who he was. Except now, he was equally devoted to the beautiful brunette lying in bed next to him.

He stared into her lapis blue eyes and gazed down at the ring on her finger. Marriage. Children. He couldn't wait for what life had in store for them.

He kissed the sensitive skin below her earlobe. "We do have one thing on the schedule for today."

"What's that?" she asked.

He reached for the honey then gave his fiancée a wolfish grin. "What else? The man feast."

ACKNOWLEDGMENTS

It's a joy to continue the Bergen Brother Series and share my love of Colorado with you. I knew the moment I created Elle and Jasper's characters in *Man Fast* (Bergen Brothers, #1) that these two needed a story.

And boy did they get one in *Man Feast*!

I have many talented people to thank for helping *Man Feast* sparkle and shine.

I don't know where I'd be without my beta readers and editor. They're an integral part of the process, finding mistakes and suggesting ways to tighten up the story. Shayne, Kendra, Tera, Courtney, and Marla, I treasure your friendship and value your judgment. Thank you for being my safe space to share my book babies.

Before I entered the world of romance, I would not have been able to tell you what an ARC team was. Now, I couldn't succeed at writing books and growing my business without one. Thank you to my Advanced Reader Team. These are the dedicated readers who receive an early copy of the book. Thank you for your beautiful reviews. Thank you for sharing my books. Thank you for your love and encouragement.

Now, you may be wondering if Fell's Peak is a real place. It's not, but my friend Sue Fell is. Sue is a former ski patroller who could give any of the Bergen brothers a run for their money on the slopes. She talked me through the ins and outs of being on ski patrol. Her input helped me craft Jasper and write the scenes where Elle and Jasper encounter the Parkers at the spa and the part when Jasper tries to help his mother. Thank you, Sue!

And OMG, the cover! Candy Castle Designs crafted an incredible, cohesive design for the Bergen Brothers Series. From the images to the fonts, she knocked it out of the park. Thank you!

And to my husband, David, who would agree that I'm married to a Jasper. My husband is smart, organized, and methodical. Lucky for him, he didn't have to jump out of a plane to get me to marry him. And just like Elle, I couldn't imagine a life without my not-so hollow bunny.

One of my favorite memories of my husband is the first time we went skiing. He's a Colorado native and an expert on the slopes. He'd be right there with Sue, keeping up with the Bergen brothers. I, however, wasn't sure how to buckle my ski boots.

After getting into our ski gear, we finally hit the slopes—after he fixed my boots—and we made our way down the run.

Slowly.

Very slowly.

We were moving along at a snail's speed when we came upon a family in trouble. The wife and daughter had collided, and the husband called out to my husband and asked him to alert ski patrol.

My husband asked if I'd be okay on my own. I told him that I'd be fine, and then my heart skipped a beat.

The man who'd skied beside me and matched my painfully slow pace, shot down the mountain at mach speed, weaving seamlessly between the other skiers.

My little heart went pitter-patter. If I were a cartoon, hearts would have popped from my eyes. Just thinking about that man —my husband—sailing down the run, still makes me smile more than fifteen years later.

It's a sight I will never forget. And in case you're wondering, the injured wife and daughter were okay—just a little shaken.

So, while skiing may not be in my blood, it's an activity I hold close to my heart. I also still love watching my husband tear it up on the slopes. And now, I get to watch him do it with our sons. I'm one lucky slow-as-hell skier.

And to you, dear reader, your kind words, reviews, and recommendations mean the world to me. It's an honor to share my stories with you. Thank you for your love and support!

Final Note: Want to hear the salsa song that Elle and Jasper danced to in the cabin? Search for *Brujería* by El Gran Combo de Puerto Rico.

ALSO BY KRISTA SANDOR

The Bergen Brothers Series

A sassy and sexy series about three brothers who are heirs to a billion-dollar mountain sports empire.

Book One: Man Fast

Book Two: Man Feast

Book Three: Man Find

Own the Eights Series

A delightfully sexy enemies to lovers series

Book One: Own the Eights

Book Two: Own the Eights Gets Married (June 2020)

Book Three: Coming Soon

The Langley Park Series

A steamy, suspenseful second-chance at love series set in the quaint town of Langley Park.

Book One: The Road Home

Book Two: The Sound of Home

Book Three: The Beginning of Home

Book Four: The Measure of Home

Book Five: The Story of Home

Sign up for my newsletter to stay in the loop.

www.KristaSandor.com

ABOUT KRISTA SANDOR

 If there's one thing Krista Sandor knows for sure, it's that romance saved her. After she was diagnosed with Multiple Sclerosis in 2015, her world turned upside down. During those difficult first days, her dear friend sent her a romance novel. That kind gesture provided the escape she needed and ignited her love of the genre. Inspired by strong heroines and happily ever afters, Krista decided to write her own romance series. Today, she's living life to the fullest. When she's not writing, you can find her running 5Ks with her husband or chasing after their growing boys in Denver, Colorado.

Never miss a release, contest, or author event! Visit www.KristaSandor.com to sign up for her romance newsletter.